A Just Man

Choosing Family
Book 4

Jennifer Raines

A Just Man
Copyright © 2025 Jennifer Raines
All rights reserved.

ISBN (ebook) 978-1-964636-35-1
(print) 978-1-964636-36-8

Inkspell Publishing
207 Moonglow Circle #101
Murrells Inlet, SC 29576

Edited By Yezanira Venecia
Cover art By Emily's World By Design

DEDICATION

To the teachers in my family and in my life—you
make a difference

JENNIFER RAINES

PROLOGUE

Kelly Steele—16 years old

Buttoning her thick flannel shirt, Kelly alighted from the inter-city express bus, a crowd of one. With shadows encroaching, and an orangey-pink sky fast fading to pewter, she'd need to get across the river and into Hay proper fast if she wanted to beat the dark. Hay, New South Wales, Australia, population just shy of three and a half thousand. An entire world away from big city Sydney.

"Got somewhere to stay?" The driver looked like a concerned grandfather, not that Kelly had one.

"Yes, thanks." She took her backpack from him and slung it over one shoulder.

"To new beginnings," she whispered to no one, the bus having made a quick getaway. "Thank you, Lahn Nguyen." The wind carried Kelly's words away.

She'd found the social worker—or Lahn had found her—just when Kelly had hit the point past desperate. Her mother's latest boyfriend had complained loudly and often about the cost of keeping Kelly, about the hassle of having her around, about her watching him. Her mother had said she'd deal with it. Apparently, her mother had taken too long, because one night Kelly woke to the guy in her bed. Her mother blamed Kelly, claimed she'd invited him.

Gross, disgusting, just yuck.

Kelly ran from the far south western suburbs to Sydney's centre.

A few months seesawing between living on the street, couch surfing and dodging cops had cured her of any romantic imaginings about life being easier away from a home where she wasn't welcome.

Her new friends' stories spooked her. One pressed into domestic labour in return for a bed, a second who'd had her drink spiked and woken to find her few meagre possessions stolen, and a third who'd found a naked man on top of her in the middle of the night. "*You knew fucking was the price,*" he'd grunted before rolling off her.

Being fast on her feet was essential, being on permanent guard exhausting, and trying to make herself invisible a constant slap at her desire to learn.

One night she hadn't been fast enough. Picked up by the police, paraded in court, she'd had her first stroke of luck in years. The judge had referred her to social services and Lahn Nguyen.

"*You're smarter than this, Kelly,*" Lahn had said. "*This is a chance to make something of yourself.*"

I want the chance.

The icy whip of the wind whistling viciously to sneak under her shirt made the regional town on the other side of the Murrumbidgee River seem more forsaken than it was. Wanting to push back against the cold and the anxiety crowding her, she started counting blessings, like the fact that Lahn had filled Kelly's backpack with clean second-hand clothes and arranged accommodation for her in a decent, if plain, boarding house. While Kelly's government allowance was meagre, rather than generous, it was regular and would cover essential costs. The greatest gift was enrolment at the local high school.

A few people glanced her way when she hit midtown.

Kelly didn't meet their stares, instead choosing to follow the map she had in her head. She double-checked the number on the two-storey red brick building before pushing through the front door. The woman on the boarding house desk was efficiently friendly, echoing the manner of overworked front-office staff everywhere.

One flight of stairs, a dimly lit hallway, the place was reminiscent of black-and-white movies on late-night TV, and Kelly giggled. Her smile died when she opened her door; a dingy room she guessed hadn't seen new paint since its initial whitewash fifty years ago. Antiseptic clean, and the acrid disinfectant smell burned her nostrils. She fought the window to get a few inches of fresh air. Clean sheets on the single bed, a wardrobe and a desk with a battered work lamp—fifth-hand or salvaged from a dumpster. The circle of light it cast on the pock-marked wood was small and faint. Decent and spartan rather than plain. Placing her bag beside the bed, Kelly decided she could make something of it. Just not now.

Unable to settle in the sterile space, she went with the nervous-itchy feeling inching up her spine. It didn't pay to get soft. You never knew when you'd be back on the streets. New place. It'd be better to check out the school before presenting herself there in the morning. Just to track the exits, get a sense of the layout. Education was the promise she'd come for.

Ignoring the creeping cold, she navigated the few blocks to the school. First, she walked the perimeter, then circled the main building, irresistibly drawn to a partly lit room at the back. Like a magnet, the library pulled her in. Pastel colours on the walls, rows of books, and banks of computer desks. She smiled, the tension she carried easing when she imagined herself in that room. Quiet, secure—a place to dream in as well as study. Knowledge was the fire in her belly. The lure of it kept her strong. With a law degree, she'd screw all those cop bastards who thought a badge gave them the right to do what they pleased.

"Hey you." An overweight security guard was plodding her way. "What're you doing?"

The voice out of nowhere kickstarted her heart. Her flight response was tempered knowing she had youth and a fast, out-of-the-blocks sprint on her side. Plus the benefit of her earlier reconnoitre. She'd run, because being caught in the wrong place at the wrong time was no way to start a new life.

"Stop." He lumbered after her.

Zipping out the nearest gate, she bolted for a block. She turned right, jogged another few blocks before taking a sharp left into a narrow laneway. Leaning against a wall, she sucked in air. Hell—a month off the streets, and she was out of practice.

"Hey, babe." A kid, half his face obscured by a hoodie, stepped in front of her. "You looking for me?" The first flicker of fear trickled through her.

"Nah, dude. It's me she wants." His friend sounded meaner.

A wave of alcohol and stale sweat threatened to gag her. Heart pumping, she scanned the area. A third boy joined them. The hoodie and jeans made them indistinguishable from each other. Lean, which might make them fast, depending on what they'd consumed. Her odds weren't good. If a single backhander connected she'd be on her knees. And the lecherous smirks twisting their lips told her what was in store if they caught her.

No way in hell will you catch me.

"You lot smell too pissed to keep it up."

They'd pay Kelly back for the taunt, but it gave her a split-second's advantage. She grabbed the handle of a nearby garbage bin, flinging it into their legs. Spinning on her heel, she picked up speed, her gaze sweeping her surroundings for a hiding place.

Damn! Stupid to explore any new place after dark.

But she'd wanted to see the school, to see what hope looked like.

A three-story apartment block loomed on her left. She turned a corner searching for an entrance, the laboured breathing of the hoodies following her. She spotted a row of garages lining the back fence. Squeezing around a broken roller door, she flattened herself against the corrugations of the metal wall. Ragged breaths dragged at her lungs; she sucked them in, listening with her whole body. The teens ran a few metres past, then their steps slowed, their boots dancing on the cement yard, far enough away to hear them yelling, although she couldn't make out the words. Then the words became a string of obscenities—they'd turned back.

Sweat poured down Kelly's back. A few stars shone through the missing sheet metal in the roof. The space was large, open, able to house at least four cars. She clambered onto a high bench at the back, curled her fingers around a wooden roof strut, and swung her legs up to lock around the beam.

"You can do it." Adrenalin pumped fire through her system. With a final burst, she hauled herself into a sitting position, inched her way along the post until she reached a crossbeam. She pressed herself into the wood, trying to become invisible.

"I've called the cops." A guy yelled from the direction of the apartments. "I've had it with you trashing the place and stealing my gear."

Shit!

Furious with herself, Kelly assessed the situation. The guy was probably yelling at the hoodies. Had he seen her? Could she sit it out?

The boys scrambled out of the yard, the smash of upturned bins and broken bottles marking their escape. A siren sounded nearby, brakes squealed, then car doors slammed.

Don't open the door.

Kelly tightened her hold on the post.

The guy who'd called the cops yelled out, "I reckon someone's in the garage."

Damn!

Her skin iced. Someone dragged a door open, the sound scraping against her nerves. A large torch flicked on, flooding the front of the garage with light. The holder used high beam to scan the four corners, then slowly played the light up the walls, along the roof joists. The beam skated over her, then backtracked to spotlight her. She froze, her muscles stretched painfully tight. Her mind played out the scene to come.

"Come on down, girlie." Impossible to make out the face behind the voice, but the tone and the emphasis on "girlie" were familiar tells. Tried, judged and found guilty. This burly cop was keen on punishment.

His offsider hoisted a ladder she'd missed against the side wall, slapping it against the beam next to her. It bounced, the echo shuddering through her.

"You're under arrest," top cop roared. "Come down by yourself, or I might have to tell my boy to come up and get you."

"What's the charge?" Kelly's mouth went dry.

She knew her rights. She also knew they were worth zilch in a small town where rogue police could make their own rules. Lack of official oversight was explicit permission for some tin-pot dictators. Her caramel skin tones, dark hair and eyes complicated the equation.

"Trespassing on private property. Vandalism and intent to injure."

She started down the ladder, the unsteadiness in her legs pissing her off. She faced him, head high. "Can I ask you your name, Officer?"

"Senior Sergeant George Hogan." He loomed over her. "What's yours?"

Welcome to bumfuck, as they say in the classics.

"Kelly Manners."

"Don't think I've come across that name before?" he mused, keeping the flashlight on her.

"I'm new in town." Kelly pulled her shoulders back.

She'd done nothing wrong, and despite living independently, in New South Wales at sixteen, she was entitled to the presence of a non-partisan adult at any interview.

He tut-tutted, and something nasty slithered down her spine. "And already in with a bad crowd."

"I haven't done anything wrong. Those boys chased me. They're the ones you want." She pretended a calm she didn't feel.

"Looks like your mama named you wrongly. Maybe we should teach you a few manners." Hogan looked her up and down, his gaze lingering on her breasts.

Junior officer's body twitched, drawing Kelly's attention. Younger, his tight-lipped expression made her mouth go dry.

"Those boys threatened me. *They* chased me. I came in here to hide from them."

I've done nothing wrong.

"We only have your word for that."

"I'd like to speak to the Legal Aid Youth Hotline, please, Senior Sergeant." Kelly was proud her voice didn't crack, despite the nausea swirling in her belly.

"We'll get to that. You young vandals are getting a bit too cocky—carrying knives and other weapons." Hogan turned to the younger cop. "Search her."

The junior officer stepped closer. He hadn't said a word, his face grim in the light that spilled from the security lights outside the open door. "At the station?"

"Shift's almost done. Why bother with the paperwork when we can do it here and now?" Hogan smirked.

The younger cop turned his back on Kelly, his head tilted at a slight angle. "We don't have a good enough reason." He'd dropped his voice. Still, Kelly caught his words.

"You'll follow orders." Hogan drawled his answer before returning to slam the garage door shut.

Fear closed her throat, but she'd be damned if she let them see it.

Hogan trained the torch on Kelly. "Better be thorough. Who knows what she's carrying?"

Kelly held out her arms at shoulder height. "You can see I'm carrying nothing."

"Strip her."

"That's ... against the law." To her shame, she stuttered. *This is Australia, Kelly, not the U S of A.*

But she'd heard the stories of illegal strip-searching, mostly at music festivals, hands that wandered—nothing more reported.

You're trying to scare me. And it's working.

"Go on, boy. I'm waiting." Hogan waved the torch around, then steadied his arm.

Kelly wrapped her arms around herself, a primal terror rooting her to the spot. She stared at the younger cop's face, all shadows and angles in the outer circle of light cast by the torch. His steady gaze held hers.

Kelly swallowed her scream.

CHAPTER ONE

17 years later

Kelly stood, waiting for her two friends to finish weaving their way through packed tables to the one she'd reserved. A celebration called for their favourite bistro.

"I've ordered champagne. Bella's sprung for it." Bella was Arabella Steele, adoptive parent and fairy godmother to Kelly Steele, previously Kelly Manners.

Although Kelly was also prepared to award sainthood to Lahn Nguyen, the social worker who hadn't turned her back when Kelly had slunk back into Sydney after her nightmare in Hay almost two decades ago. Lahn had taken her to a care home and a bedroom, which she'd shared with two other "unattached" kids. Lucy—Liùsaidh—McTavish and Clem—Clementine—Delgado had become her closest friends.

"You got the job." Lucy tightened her hold before stepping back. Lucy's mother had died, and the ten-year-old had been parked at the home while authorities searched for any family who might take her. Her grandparents had stepped in. "Congratulations."

"I've been 'acting' in the job a few months." Kelly

9

smiled. "But, yeah, it's been confirmed."

"Move aside, Lucy." Clem nudged Lucy out of the way with her hip and took her place, dancing a little on the spot. Clem had landed foster parents who'd stuck. "Go, girl. I knew you'd get it."

"You're both way more confident than I was." Kelly sank into her seat.

"But you're pleased?" Lucy dropped beside her.

"Over the moon." Kelly grinned. "I love the idea of combining school and community libraries. They make sense in small country towns. Plus, they're a better use of public resources."

"But the job's based in Sydney. You're the NSW Education Department's state-wide coordinator for school community libraries. You advise, you suggest, you research models to improve school library services across NSW, right? You just visit sites occasionally?" An edge of concern entered Clem's voice.

"Mostly."

A waiter appeared at Kelly's elbow, champagne bottle in hand, momentarily pausing their conversation. The cork popped, and he filled three glass flutes. Kelly saw Lucy signal Clem to zip it while the waiter hovered and prepared herself for the cross-examination. They loved her, so were entitled.

"Don't you just love champagne?" Kelly searched for the right words in her glass. "The pop of the cork, the bubbles tumbling into the crystal flute, the scent of the effervescence."

"You can smell the effervescence?" Clem drawled.

"Can't you?" Kelly offered a question for a question, a time-honoured way of avoiding difficult subjects. "Thank you." She smiled, and the waiter retreated.

"What does 'mostly' mean?" Lucy barely waited until he was out of earshot.

"Here's to new opportunities." Kelly raised her glass. Her friends did the same.

"New opportunities." Lucy clinked her glass against Kelly's.

"Add 'new' to 'mostly,' and I want to know what this opportunity is." Clem wouldn't be distracted.

"The department supervises a few school community libraries, but it's a growing trend. One of our most ambitious ventures is in Tullamore."

"Tullamore. Brand new building. Ayesha Patel. Your equivalent of a guru." Lucy rolled her eyes. "You were present for the handover of the completed but empty building to the school just before Christmas. Ayesha is deputy principal and has carriage of the project."

"You're a broken record on the subject," Clem agreed.

"Am not."

"Are too," Lucy shot back.

"Ayesha has taken emergency leave. Someone else will take over the deputy principal role, but the library isn't fully stocked or set up, and it needs someone who understands the way school community libraries work. The summer school holidays end in late January. That's two weeks. I've been asked to go to Tullamore to make sure it opens for the new school year. Get hands-on experience of doing this from scratch," Kelly blurted it out in one go, and hoped they didn't ask for details on Ayesha's emergency. Kelly didn't know but had a gut feeling something at the school, not something in Ayesha's private life, had precipitated the deputy principal's sudden departure.

"Are you sure, Kel?" Lucy exchanged a worried glance with Clem.

"Stop with the loaded looks. I'm right here. It's a short-term placement."

"School starts the week after next. When did Ayesha disappear?"

"She didn't disappear," Kelly insisted, crossing her fingers under the table. "She's taken leave. She hasn't resigned."

"When's she due back?" Clem held up a hand. "Where

will you stay? Will you take Boo? You don't have a car. Define short term. You hate the country."

Kelly answered the last accusation. "I had one bad experience—"

"Bad!" Her two friends cried in unison.

"Okay—shitty, sexist, demeaning—"

"Try criminal," Clem said drily.

"But I'm over it." A mantra Kelly still repeated to herself at regular intervals. "And I can't blame every small town in the state for one with a twisted cop shop."

"You were violated," Lucy said.

"I can say the words aloud now without going to pieces." Kelly closed her eyes briefly. "I was illegally strip-searched."

"Based on current reports, sexist, misogynistic cops litter the state, despite various attempts to re-educate them." As a social worker, Clem had first-hand experience. "Some cops still carry out illegal strip searches of young women and girls."

"Cops break the law because they can get away with it, but I'll be working between the high school and the community library."

"I remember seeing you the day you came back." Anger was the backbeat to Lucy's quiet words. "You couldn't settle, couldn't sleep, and when you did, you had nightmares."

"And now I'm okay," Kelly insisted, because her friends were worrywarts. "Hell, it's been seventeen years."

"I bet you can still smell that hell hole they held you in when you close your eyes. You can see the smirks on their faces. Hear the fear buzzing within you. Feel the sweat slithering down your back. Taste the helplessness." Clem's voice throbbed with remembered pain, and Kelly reached across the table to take her hand. All three of them had childhood memories they'd fought to forget, and Clem's description roiled in Kelly's belly.

"Geez, are you this sensitive with your clients?" Kelly squeezed her friend's fingers.

"You're my friend. I love you."

"I love you both, which is why I'm telling you first. After Bella. She said you'd need the champagne."

As if on cue, the waiter reappeared. "Your usual order?"

"Please," Lucy replied for them.

The eggplant parmigiana was authentically Italian, the salad with its secret dressing the perfect accompaniment. Crisp bread rolls completed the dish.

"Although we won't need the wine tonight," Kelly added.

"What did Bella say?" Lucy respected Bella's opinion. That didn't mean she always agreed. Kelly wasn't fooled.

"That it was my decision. That I had her support. It was Bella who renamed Hay Abbadon Central, the place of lost souls. Part of our exorcism."

After Kelly's flight back to Sydney, Lahn had cared enough to find her a foster placement. One of the worst experiences of her life had delivered the best experience of her life. Fate had handed her Arabella Steele.

Kelly continued, "I won't need a car in Tullamore. I'm taking the bicycle. I'm also taking Boo."

"You'd better be taking that dog."

"I just said I was. Remember, you met Star?" Kelly didn't wait for agreement. "Her brother Dean's driving me up in his van on Monday. Ten weeks, one term tops. I'll be staying in a government house—"

"This Monday?" Clem set her flute on the table with a snap. "Three days from now."

"Once upon a time I dreamed of living in a small country town. Maybe it's time I tested that dream."

"I could have driven you up in the McTavish van." Lucy glanced at Clem before she made the offer, but Kelly recognised the signs. Her friends were making a silent pact to protect Kelly from herself.

"That's a generous offer I couldn't accept," said Kelly. Especially since the van was in constant use these days, not just with Lucy's family antiques centre, but her new husband, Niall Quinn, used it for his bespoke woodworking business—*Quinn, by design.*

"If you want out at any time, Lucy and I can be there before you finish packing." Clem made her words a vow.

"You're the best." Kelly smiled, blinking back tears. "I've been asked to help, and it'll deepen my experience. I need to do this. To be blunt, it's time I check whether demons still lurk beyond the city limits. Think of this as a controlled experiment—time-limited, part of a team, with Boo at my side."

"Boo's the only reason I'm not shouting like a banshee," Clem muttered. "Daily updates. That's non-negotiable."

"Deal. Although you're worse than Bella."

"What did she ask for?" Lucy leaned back to allow the waiter to slide her meal onto the table.

"*Regular* updates." Kelly grinned. "And we checked the Tullamore cop shop before I agreed. Senior Sergeant George Hogan didn't transfer there."

"Just as well." Clem nodded her thanks to the waiter. "Did you ever find out the name of the second cop?"

"I didn't ask." Kelly had never been fully able to answer why she'd never searched, although psychologists had offered reasons. "He was an automaton following orders."

"That wasn't what you said at the time." Clem was gently tenacious. "I learned a few new cusses that night."

"I shouted every obscenity I knew. Maybe that was enough," Kelly lied. Her friends didn't challenge her lie, instead opening their eyes wide to let her know they didn't believe her.

Kelly saw the junior cop in her nightmares. Panic blurred the edges of the image, so she couldn't recall each detail just the overwhelming sense that she was stranded and powerless. When he'd dropped her back at the boarding house, she'd run.

* * *

"We agreed Condobolin would be my last troubleshooting assignment." Mick Jamieson settled more comfortably into the deep leather armchair in front of the fireplace, currently filled with iconic Australian red waratahs in a vintage jug.

"I'm only the regional director of schools." Roslyn Morales toasted him over a glass of fine Riverland merlot. She occupied a second armchair, part mentor, part friend, and all boss.

Mick snorted.

She continued, "I've been overruled. You'll keep your Head of Maths position at Appin, but right now, the department needs someone discreet and trustworthy at Tullamore. We've identified some odd patterns involving appointments to senior school positions, an unusually large turnover of young, inexperienced female staff, and a nosedive in science and maths performance of female students."

"I've done a few of these troubleshooting jobs now." Mick held his glass up to the light, the rich plum colour of the wine reflecting its red fruit flavours and a fraction of his frustration. Did it always have to be men refusing to treat women as equals? What planet were they on? "Are you sure no one's worked out what I'm doing?"

I'm tired of fixing up other people's messes. I want more.

"Pretty confident. You're a late starter to teaching, late-twenties before you took your degree, and you're greedy for promotion. You're prepared to do short stints at different schools to build experience. This school's large enough for both a principal and a deputy principal. You split responsibilities, although the principal is the final decision maker. He also had no teaching responsibilities. You'll be expected to take a few maths classes on top of your administrative load."

"I like teaching."

"Deputy is a good move for you. The old days when time served was a stepping stone to becoming a principal are long gone."

His boss had been delighted to discover Mick was an ex-cop.

"Coppers or teachers, makes no difference. My whistleblowing at the last two schools I was assigned to got people sacked. People hold grudges."

"Your name hasn't been used in any official or unofficial documents."

"What about text messages, messaging apps or other sites?"

"Last time, Mick. I promise. Then you can apply for whatever promotion position you want."

Mick sighed inwardly. He'd done enough penance for his sin as a rookie cop. He'd taken on these informal investigative roles in schools because the abuse of power by public officials shot him back to a poorly lit garage and a vulnerable young woman.

"Can I refuse?"

It was time to move on with his life. To follow his dream of running his own school, helping kids to be their best selves, and proving that treating both staff and students with respect paid dividends.

"I want you to accept." She held his gaze.

"What aren't you telling me?" He liked Roslyn, and she'd never made a job personal before.

"Ayesha's request is sudden. Plausible"—Roslyn placed her drink carefully on the coffee table—"but I have a bad feeling about it. I approved her request and told her I'll hold her job open until she's ready to return. I also said I was available for a chat at any time. I haven't heard another word."

"Compassionate leave is to cope with sudden changes in fortune."

"I've known Ayesha for years"—Roslyn paused—"there's something off about this."

"Schools open in less than two weeks. Executive staff have already been assigned. Long-term staff at Tullamore might be pissed off not to be offered the opportunity. I'll need enough information to know what I'm looking for and to cover my back." Mick let a little of his frustration show. "What's the deal?"

"Ayesha's request gives us an opportunity to move someone into the school and get an objective assessment of what's happening."

"Did Ayesha give you anything?"

"The library might be the key. Ayesha's the brains and drive behind a new school-community library. I'm worried about progress."

"Could Ayesha be the problem and have decided to do a runner?" The cop in Mick was already considering angles.

"That's part of what I want you to find out. Although Ayesha was being white-anted—deliberately undermined—by the school's principal. And Ayesha didn't share that."

"Who did?"

"There was an official handover at the end of last year, a walk-through of the empty building to take possession." Roslyn sat back in her chair. "I invited the new state-wide coordinator of community school libraries to represent the department—a flying visit."

"She's your informant?"

"At this stage, I don't have an informant, just a gut feeling, and some disconnected pieces of information. Kelly reported the white-anting on her return. It apparently formed part of the principal's short speech at the handover."

"Who's the principal?"

"Dom Ellis. Been there a few years." Roslyn winced. "Another thing. Kelly didn't take kindly to having her butt fondled at the celebratory party afterwards."

"Did she lodge a complaint against anyone?"

"Apparently it was a bit of a scrum. It was also at the local pub, ostensibly not school business. Hard to identify an individual, but she provided a list of names." Roslyn handed him a slip of paper. "Burn that after you memorise it."

"Part of my plan, then I bury the ashes at midnight under a new moon in a dense forest."

Ros giggled, a most un-Ros action. "Kelly considered a police complaint. That would have involved CCTV. Kelly said no woman got much joy from making a complaint in a situation like that."

"Ouch. Am I in charge of the library too?"

"You're job-sharing. I spoke to my boss, who spoke to Kelly's boss. I rang Kelly after I got Ayesha's application. Kelly's agreed to return for first term to ensure the successful opening. She's got no history, no connections to the place, no pre-conceptions."

"Apart from thinking someone on the executive is a sleazebag." Mick raised an eyebrow. "Why did she agree?"

"She's an admirer of Ayesha and wants the library to succeed."

"What's my role?"

"As deputy principal, you'll replace Ayesha as the school representative on the Library Board of Management. Kelly reports to you. You'll need to be hands-on enough to take over from Kelly when she leaves, although by that time you should have clarified whether a teacher librarian or a council librarian will take the senior role."

"What's Kelly's last name?" Mick didn't know many of the state office staff. He'd never forget the one Kelly he'd met in his life.

"Kelly Steele."

"Don't know the name. What's Kelly Steele been told about why Ayesha needs to be replaced?"

"Compassionate leave, same story you got." Roslyn reached for the bowl of cashews.

"Bet she'll have lots of questions."

"You'll like her. She's a straight shooter, smart, loves her job."

"That's it?"

"You're single, able to go anywhere at short notice. More

logical than uprooting a family. You jumped at the chance of being a deputy principal—your first job at that level." She held up the bottle of wine.

"No more for me. I'm driving." He stood.

"To be honest I'm hoping Kelly asks questions."

"If she's as smart as you say, she might not take kindly to being used as a Trojan horse."

"I'll keep in touch"—Roslyn rose and led the way to the door—"pass on anything else I learn."

You've given me stuff all, Mick reflected, unlocking his car ten minutes later. Less than usual.

CHAPTER TWO

Kelly didn't regret a cent of the van rental to Tullamore. Bella, adoptive parent—grandparent–inspiration—had supervised loading and waved her off. A sparkling summer Monday morning in Sydney had soared into scorching temperatures this far from the sea.

"Boo." She opened the van door.

"Woof." The dog's response showed deep offense. Six hours in the back of a locked van with only one short break was enough to disturb anyone's equilibrium.

"I'm sorry, darling." Kelly unclipped the safety harness from the seat belt restraint. The chocolate Labrador placed her paws on Kelly's shoulders to nuzzle her throat, then stepped onto the ground beside her.

"All good?" Dean, the driver, and brother of a colleague, came up alongside her. He glanced toward the house and whistled. "Fancy digs."

Kelly tried to imagine what he saw. A well-kept yard, a rambling old house painted a crisp white with a dark green trim and verandas on three sides. The front veranda sported a cane table and chair setting. Solidly middle-class. That definition probably fit Kelly these days. Kelly had stayed overnight on her whirlwind visit for the official handover in

December. For this stay, she'd claimed the bedroom with double doors opening to the secure yard, knowing she could keep Boo and any housemate apart if needed.

"Looks comfortable," Dean added.

"It's government-owned," she said. "Available for government employees in town for short work appointments."

"How long did you say you were staying?"

"One term, maximum. That takes us to Easter. I'm hoping you'll come back to get us." She patted his arm. "In the meantime, I've got tea in my hamper before you head back."

"Let's unload first." He hauled out Boo's mattress, then reached for her bicycle. "Where do you want these?"

"Side veranda near the double full-length windows. Room one's mine."

"How do you know? Have they scratched your name on it?"

"Is that what you did?" Kelly registered his guilty look. "Bedrooms are allocated in strict order of arrival, but I got first dibs because I was appointed before any other transfers were processed."

"Keys?"

"Should be under the mat. I texted the neighbour at our last pit stop. Front door, front and back security doors, and the key to bedroom number one."

"You open up. I'll start unloading." Dean headed for the side veranda with the dog mattress and bicycle.

Kelly found the keys where promised and unlocked the front door. Dean came up behind her with two more boxes.

"In here."

She nudged the bedroom door open with her hip, then spotted a deep red rose through the window. She pushed the window high. Bella loved roses, especially heavily scented heritage roses like these. The scent grounded Kelly. For a moment, when she'd opened the door, fear had washed through her. A frisson of a memory from Abbadon, but this bedroom was nothing like the one she'd fled seventeen years before. She shook her head to free herself of unwanted memories.

Her world was different now. Boo at her heels was testimony to that.

"Boo," she called him to her side. "Home. This is home for now." She planted a kiss on his head. "Let's get this show on the road."

Boo trotted backward and forward with her while Dean shifted the heavier gear until the van was unloaded.

"Time for a cup of tea?" she asked.

"Just. I've got an early start tomorrow, so won't hang about."

"Kitchen's this way." Kelly headed down the hall, then halted. "Looks like I might already have a housemate."

Dean opened the fridge. "I'm guessing male from the six pack of beer."

"That's sexist. Women drink beer." She peered around him. "And that's a bottle of white wine."

Dean lifted the lid of a large casserole on the top shelf. "Whoever it is, cooks. And likes Tim Tams." He grinned and reached for the packet. "A couple?"

"Men cook."

"Not this one." He puffed up his chest.

"That's not something to boast about." She filled the kettle. "And I don't believe you. Your sister is an equal-opportunity kind of gal, and she'd have kicked you out of her apartment if you didn't pull your weight."

"I'm a whiz at laundry and cleaning. She cooks. We call it fair." Dean shrugged. "So, do we snoop around the laundry here for clues to gender?"

"We do not. I wait until my new housemate gets home and I politely introduce myself."

"And Boo?" He raised an eyebrow.

"Boo's the reason I chose that bedroom. If I have a housemate who doesn't like dogs, Boo can use the veranda to enter and exit and stay out of the rest of the house." But she'd leave all the doors ajar when she was home, so Boo could reach her if needed.

Dean drained his cup in a final swallow and pushed to his feet. "I'd best make a move."

Kelly followed Dean up the hall and was still at the front door when his van disappeared around the corner.

"I know, I know." Kelly bent to stroke Boo's ears. "Unpacking can wait. But first things first." She opened the chat she'd set up for Bella, Lucy and Clem, speaking as she typed.

"Arrived safely. Housemate already in residence. Not yet sighted. Early evidence suggests housetrained."

Then she surrendered to her need to explore. The compulsion to know the lay of the land, the exits from every building and cul-de-sac hadn't left her. Although it was more muted now Boo walked at her side. The centre of town was a simple grid pattern. The main shopping street was two blocks over from the house, the school a block beyond that. A park sat diagonally opposite the school, stretching through to the main street. The library was perched on the edge of a park. Two stories of high energy efficiency design—functional, elegant, and in command of the government-owned land. The perfect location for both the school and community to access.

Kelly's current plan was to check out the shops, replace the packet of Tim Tams she'd tucked in Dean's bag, and get access to the library. She didn't spot any workers in a library scheduled to open with the start of the new term seven days from now. More ominously, piles of unopened boxes and empty shelves were clearly visible. The timeline Ayesha had outlined during Kelly's visit to Tullamore last year meant the books should all be shelved by now.

Holy hell. What's going on?

A prickle of unease skated across her shoulders. She wasn't afraid of hard work, but she also hadn't expected to start from scratch. With few options, she rang Ayesha's old office landline.

* * *

Mick scrubbed his hands across his face. Still locked out of the school IT system, despite Dom Ellis's promises. An oversight or a pattern? Patterns fascinated Mick; one reason he'd found himself enrolled in a teaching degree majoring in maths after his exit from the police force and a year spent wandering Australia trying to get his head straight.

When the landline rang, he automatically reached for it. "Tullamore High School."

"Who are you?" Low-pitched and husky, her voice was better suited to a smoky bar, bluegrass and heads tilted toward each other to catch every word.

"Mick Jamieson. Can I help you?"

"Maybe."

Before she could hang up, Mick interrupted. "I'm replacing Ayesha Patel."

"Not possible." Her tart response suggested he lacked the skills.

"I'll rephrase that. I'm acting deputy principal, while Ms. Patel is on leave."

"I know she's on leave." With a hint of concern added, her low-pitched voice gained a gravelly vibrato. "Is she okay?"

"As far as I know. At this stage, she's asked for indefinite leave."

"That makes no sense." She had the sexiest voice Mick had heard since Grace Cumming's debut album.

"Can I help you?"

"I'm Kelly Steele, the librarian."

"I know. I mean, I know Kelly Steele is the librarian." He'd be living with that glorious voice, a hint of sex and soul over morning cereal. Did she eat cereal?

Get a grip, Jamieson.

"We're housemates."

"You're room 2?" She paused. "I took your Tim Tams."

"I'm sure we can negotiate a repayment plan."

"I replaced them. The removalist needed a sugar hit for the ride home." Her crisp confession got past his guard faster than a police records check.

"Better than the alternative stimulants. I've cooked an Indian curry for dinner. You're welcome to share."

"That's"—she seemed to be searching for a word—"kind."

"But you don't eat Indian?" He didn't need to eat; he could survive on her voice.

"Indian's a favourite, if you don't count Italian, Thai, Turkish or French or anything that's barbequed."

"It's a while since I've been in share housing. You'll have to explain the protocols."

"What makes you think I know the protocols?"

"Then we make our own." Mick wasn't looking to share confidences, but sharing a house with a straight-talking woman with an incredible voice couldn't be all bad. Although her questions confirmed she *was* curious. She'd spent time with Ayesha, knew the woman was being white-anted, and had suddenly disappeared.

Ros hadn't given Kelly his name. An oversight or deliberate? Or did it just mean Mick was a cleanskin to Kelly, as she was to him? Two flatmates might share their impressions of a new school and new town. Potential allies? You never said no to an ally, especially when it was notoriously difficult to pin deliberate bias on an offender if no one made a formal complaint.

"I was planning to do a quick walk-through of the library later this afternoon. See where we're up to," she said. "I'll need to check a few things first."

"I'd like to join you, have a look around. I arrived Saturday. Still finding my feet."

"A sudden decision?" What was she asking him?

"I'm on the unattached list. And sudden decisions are part of the nature of compassionate requests. If you meet me here at four, we can walk across together."

"Works for me."

The music of her voice lingered after she'd ended the call. Sight unseen, he had a good feeling about Kelly Steele.

Mick trawled through the emails Ros had forwarded from Ayesha Patel. He followed his usual routine—delete, deal with immediately, save for review, forward to someone else to action. A routine he'd learned too late to help him as a whistleblowing cop. He'd pinned the staff chart to the notice board in his office and was trying to put faces to names before classes started. He wasn't the only one spending time at school, the heads of English and Science had both dropped in to chat. Both had been in the school longer than the headmaster. Neither was interested in taking on the top job. Both were curiously non-committal about the sudden departure of Ayesha.

The knock on his door had him lifting his head.

Kelly Steele—it could only be her—was searching his face, disgust chasing disbelief and confusion in horrified succession.

"You!" She spat the words. Her body trembled, and Mick would bet his promotion she hated showing the slightest sign of weakness.

Shit. Kelly Steele was Kelly Manners. He'd looked for her, dreamed of her and fretted about her for years. Now, she was here.

He closed his eyes. Briefly.

She'd been terrified. By him. Of him. So, Mick had ended his search for her. Realisation of other implications followed more slowly. She could also blow his cover as an ex-cop. Maybe he should worry about that?

Except Kelly's peace of mind was more important. *Sorry, Ros.*

"Hello, Kelly." He stayed in his seat, barely breathing. Sudden moves might spook her more.

"You knew I'd be here." She was poised in the doorway,

ready to flee, like the girl Mick had wronged all those years ago.

"I knew Kelly Steele would be here. I had no idea you were Kelly Steele." He gentled his voice. "No one told me you'd married." He remembered her eyes, a rich dark chocolate, almost black, giving away emotions she'd wanted to hide.

"I changed my name," she said reluctantly.

"I looked for you." Mick had waited years for this chance. Ironic it should happen now when revealing his history could potentially allow another misogynistic arsehole to go free.

"To charge me." Rage was replacing shock, and that was a good sign.

"To ask you to testify against Senior Sergeant George Hogan."

"Bullshit." She sounded like the Kelly he remembered.

"I changed my mind." Mick paused. "Circumstances changed my mind. I decided it would be unfair to subject you to further interrogation and potential cross-examination." He'd decided police prosecutors would rip her to shreds. By then he knew she'd gone to Hay for a fresh start. George Hogan and he had cost her that chance.

"So you let Senior Sergeant George Hogan continue business as usual." She crossed her arms defensively.

"I made a complaint to the Police Standards Unit." He raised his hands, palm up, before placing them flat on the desk in a conciliatory gesture. "Ultimately he was demoted and took early retirement." Not before George had called in every debt he was owed and blackened Mick's name. Even Mick's father, a long-standing and honest cop—or so Mick had believed—had asked Mick to drop the complaint.

"How do I know that's true?" She hadn't run screaming from the building, which had to count for something.

"I've been told you're good at your job. You'll find public records of the case."

The same records held the accusations against him. He'd

been vindicated, although dirt stuck. He could live with that. He hadn't been able to live with the knowledge he'd taken part in an illegal strip search of a vulnerable teenager, Kelly, and hadn't tried to right the wrong.

"I'll check. Does the Education Department know about your past?"

"Yes."

"I'll check that too." She was sounding more confident.

"Roslyn Morales appointed me. Feel free to ask her anything you like."

"Does she know about your past with me?" Her gaze narrowed.

"I don't have a past with Kelly Steele."

But Roslyn, and her senior managers, knew about Mick's time in the police force. He hadn't lied on his application or in the recruitment meeting when more detailed questions were asked.

"You took part in an illegal strip search of a sixteen-year-old girl, and *you're* the acting deputy principal in a school full of adolescent girls." She had the right to accuse him and to refuse to work with him.

"I apologise for that day and for the anguish you've had to live with because of my actions."

I sound like a pompous dickhead.

His search for her all those years ago had been driven by his need to apologise to her. Until he'd realised an apology wasn't justice. His best apology would be stopping George.

Seconds stretched while she studied him in silence, and Mick waited for her judgement. His muscles were tight cords, although he remained motionless. He was still taller than her, heavier than her, and the best way to reassure her was to allow her to control the space around them.

"I'll check the records and speak to Roslyn. Then we'll talk again."

"Thank you." He eased back in his chair. *"We."* She was keeping it between them for now. "Do you want the keys to the library? To check it yourself?"

"Why is Mick Jamieson replacing Ayesha?" She took a few steps forward, joining dots she wasn't supposed to join.

"I'm on the short-term placements list. A late starter to teaching, prepared to move around to get experience." Mick used Roslyn's excuse and gestured to the chair in front of his desk.

"And the reason for her leave?" She remained standing.

"I can't answer that. An invasion of Ayesha's privacy for one thing, and I genuinely don't know."

She seemed to come to a decision. "I said I wanted to check a few things before I came in. The council library employed two librarians. I met them briefly at the official handover last year."

"I haven't read all the files on the library yet."

"I called them to see how far they've got in stocking shelves, etc." She crossed her arms. "They were told they wouldn't be needed."

"I know nothing about that."

"Are you replacing Ayesha on the Library Board?"

"Yes."

"Why did you say she left?" She was persistent, but that tallied with the teenager fighting for a fresh chance. "The new library's her baby."

"Can't help you." He took a chance and flashed his best innocent smile, the one showing his dimples—the one his eldest sister resented the hell out of because the dimple gene had bypassed Mel—although his fantasy about getting to know Kelly and her smoky-blues-bar voice was shot to pieces.

Never gonna happen.

"When did she decide to go?" she demanded.

"I was offered the job less than a week ago, arrived Saturday."

"Kelly, Mick. Good, you've met." The man in the doorway arrived silently and offered a genial smile.

How much had he heard?

"I'm about to press 'send' on an all-staff memo letting

everyone know Ayesha had pressing family business, which necessitated her leave."

Mick stood. He'd seen photos, read the file, and spoken to the principal exactly twice on the phone. Once, shortly after his appointment, once yesterday afternoon to organise access to the school grounds. Dominic Ellis, "Dom" to his colleagues and friends, standing in profile provided additional information. He was carrying a slight paunch and the skin tone of a guy who didn't spend much time outdoors. Not even over the summer holidays. His colourful button-up short-sleeved shirt and jeans were at odds with his hyper-alert manner. Late forties, handsome once, he had a knock-about charm, which he was working for all he was worth.

"Why did she go?" Kelly pushed. She'd been collecting information and cross-referencing since she'd entered the room.

"You know I can't answer that." Dom held his palms open.

Mick's second sister would have started plotting Dom's downfall at the first sighting of his smug smirk.

It's okay, Em. I've got this one covered.

"Where did she go?" Kelly was persistent. *Worried?*

"She didn't confide in me." Dom mustered a disappointed sigh.

"The council librarians said you'd called to say their services weren't needed."

"They must have misunderstood." Dom smiled straight at Kelly—a dead giveaway that he was lying and didn't expect to be caught. "Why would I say that? The library won't work without the council-school collaboration."

"They were very clear." Kelly had backed herself into a corner—physically—and Mick moved from behind his desk to stand between the principal and Kelly.

"They've been in the jobs a long time." Dom shook his head regretfully. "I've worried they've been getting a bit forgetful. I might need to bring that up with the new library board."

"I'll be chairing the board," Mick inserted smoothly and was surprised to see the relief on Kelly's face.

"Of course. Ayesha did rather fancy herself as an expert." Dom chortled gently, mocking the absent woman.

"Roslyn said that's her biggest regret with Ayesha's sudden departure. Ayesha's a bit of a legend apparently. Roslyn told me if I stuff up on this library, I'm cactus." Mick waited for the principal to back down.

"I'm sure between you and Kelly, you can sort it out." Dom waved a dismissive hand.

"Kelly's here to collect the keys for the library." Mick handed Kelly the keys, and she slid around Dom to escape.

Dom's head swivelled to watch Kelly's departure—*flight?* The expression in Dom's eyes when he swung back toward Mick struck him as off—part sexual assessment, part cold calculation—before the principal sauntered into the room. "How are you settling in?" A belated question. The security guard had let Mick in this morning—Dom had been delayed.

"Fine." Mick returned to his chair. "My login details haven't come through yet."

"Haven't they?" Dom scratched his jaw. "It can sometimes take a few days. I'll follow up."

"Thanks." Mick would follow up himself if he wasn't online in the morning.

"We have a good team here," Dom added. "My head teachers are experienced, know the school, and can probably run the place without me."

Having competent staff was a blessing. Having staff blind to unethical practices suggested they weren't competent. Although, if Dom had been harassing women for years and hadn't been caught, he was a particularly skilled predator.

"We'll have a few new teachers this year, but your major role is getting the library sorted. I dropped by to suggest a drink, maybe a meal tonight, an informal introduction and planning session."

"Sounds good." Being paraded as one of the principal's people at the local pub wouldn't give Mick much independence. "Unfortunately, I've got a prior commitment."

"Already?" Dom laughed. "You're a quick mover. Who is it? I know most of the talent in town." His smirk implied he'd also sampled the talent. *Jerk*.

"I've invited my new housemate to share an Indian curry." Mick shrugged. "Seemed like the sociable thing to do."

"Indian? You cook?" Dom sounded like an unreconstructed chauvinist.

"A necessity if I wanted to live in the family home."

"Maybe next Friday?" Dom said.

"Hell." Mick shrugged. "Who can even think that far ahead?"

Mick spent a long time staring into space after Dom left. Keeping his cop background quiet was essential for the job he'd been sent to do. Kelly's agreement was core to that. At the moment, he didn't like his chances.

This time she held all the power. There was a certain justice in that. He rose and crossed to the filing cabinet. With no access to the system, he'd have to hope Ayesha kept some paper records.

Based on the correspondence, Ayesha Patel and this Kelly Steele were a match made in heaven. Roslyn's insistence he take the job made more sense. Ayesha's passion and commitment deserved a better reward than what? Undue pressure? Constant white-anting? Did Dom Ellis find it hard to deal with successful women? Young women? Misogyny was Mick's working hypothesis. Not a criminal offense, but unacceptable in a modern education system.

Evidence, Jamieson.

Without evidence all you've got is rage and a burning sense of injustice.

He rubbed his hands over his face. Time to make a move. He hoped like hell Kelly hadn't done a runner, and not just because Ros would kill him if he'd scared off their only librarian.

CHAPTER THREE

Kelly was still shaking when she unlocked the library. Resting her back against the solid wood structure, she used its stability to steady herself. Her instinct had been to run. She was older now, had other strategies for protecting herself.

His name is Mick Jamieson.

His name hadn't come up *that* night.

He'd topped her list of cop targets back then—after George Hogan—formed part of her fantasy of a court case where he and others like him were exposed for the pathetic creeps they were. Her #MeToo moment.

A few months with Bella, and Kelly had needed all her wits to keep up with the older woman's intellectual challenges. Reaction had also hit like a mother fucker, and Kelly had stopped searching for his name.

Mick Jamieson is a teacher. Not newly minted, if he's deputy principal material. So there's a chance his story of leaving the police is true.

Kelly had worked hard to bring calm and control to her life. Boo's predecessor, Charlie, had made a difference. Never being in a closed space with a big man was a key tactic. Today she'd found herself with two. Bizarrely, she'd been grateful Mick was in the room when Dom arrived. She'd think about that later.

She hadn't recognised Mick's voice on the phone. There was a time when she'd thought she'd never forget it.

That was crazy. He'd actually said little during the entire degrading performance. George Hogan couldn't stop talking.

Seventeen years, Kelly.

How many voices could she remember from seventeen years ago? He hadn't recognised hers, but, like her, he'd recognised her face. It had taken a split second for her to scan his face. His nose was still unremarkable, straight, not too wide; his short hair revealed the shape of his head, but he still tilted it slightly to the right when weighing options, and his gaze was dark and steady.

Mick Jamieson had held her stare through the entire shameful, illegal strip search. She'd never forgotten that. His hands had been steady too, his fingers cool. Today he'd placed them in plain sight—*See, I'm no threat.* In that half-lit garage, she'd been simultaneously humiliated and enraged, silently vowing vengeance as her only defence against shattering into a million pieces.

I'm no longer defenceless or alone.

Seventeen years, Kel.

She wasn't going to turn tail and scamper back to Sydney, nor would she tell Bella or Lucy or Clem … yet. But she'd use the forcefield they'd help build around her. Lucy was married to Niall Quinn, who was the brother of Liam Quinn—a lawyer, technically an environmental specialist. Liam was known to make a few inquiries on behalf of family. By association, Kelly was family.

Liam picked up immediately. "Hello, Kel. I heard you'd gone bush. How can I help?"

"How do you know I need help?" Some of the tightness in her chest eased.

"Because the family grapevine doesn't lie. You're in some small town in the middle of a working afternoon, and you're calling me direct." He was part of her tribe, but their group gatherings were usually organised by Lucy or Liam's wife, Kate. Liam knew the bare bones of her history but had never questioned her.

Kelly gave him names, dates, a location, and a summary of what Mick had told her. "Can you find out if he's telling the truth?"

"In the matter of George Hogan, I can." Liam was telling her to be careful. "I should be able to get back to you in a few days."

"Thanks, Liam. Can we keep this between ourselves until then?"

"If you promise to protect me when the girlfriends go ballistic." He was only half-joking.

"It won't come to that." Kelly was backing her judgement that she could handle this, needed to handle this.

"Call—at any time"—he paused—"if you *want* to be rescued."

After she disconnected, Kelly did her tour of the library. And her focus shifted. She'd need a miracle or a squad of helpers to have the library ready to open with the school year next week. Boxes were stacked everywhere with few shelves stocked. New computers sat in yet more unopened boxes on desks. Needing the connection, she messaged her girl pack, choosing her words with care:

Met housemate. He's the acting deputy principal. Library prep in worse state than expected. I'm hoping he has ideas.

Kelly neared the house, her pace slowing. Her unknown housemate had invited her to dinner. A bizarre concept, now that she'd identified him. But she'd shifted closer to Mick when Dom had arrived, had learned enough from Clem to register Mick's body language was non-aggressive, whereas Dom made her feel uncomfortable on some primal level. She'd come to Tullamore to confront some demons and had found the devil.

She did a quick scan of her mood—pulse steady, breathing normal, flight response not triggered.

You've got this, Kel.

Boo wasn't in the side garden when she arrived. Instead, she was greeted by the aroma of subtly blended Indian spices and music coming from the back of the house, low, a touch of country. The gate between the front and back yards was open. Had Mick let Boo out?

She rounded the back of the house. "Boo."

The dog bounded in her direction, but he'd been sitting alongside Mick-Ex-Cop-Jamieson with his chin on the man's knee. Both of them imitating some town and country poster of man and dog, beer in hand—at least Mick had a beer—staring off into the distance in perfect harmony.

"Traitor," she whispered to Boo, while fondling him.

"Can I get you a beer?" Mick held up his own but didn't move from the back veranda. His movements were slow and deliberate, designed not to rattle anyone. Was that standard cop training? If so, it was training a lot of cops failed to absorb. She didn't want to remember, but Mick had signalled every move in that half-dark garage.

"I might start with a water." Kelly waved a hand, indicating Mick should stay where he was. "I'll get it." Boo followed her into the kitchen, waited while she filled a glass, then followed her back outside. She took the other end of the wide steps. "You don't mind a dog in the kitchen?"

"Not when they're as well-behaved as Boo." He matched her stare. "His name's on the tag."

"He let you close enough to read his tag?" Kelly watched Boo settle between them. Closer to her, but comfortable with the acting deputy principal. She rested her hand on Boo's back. "He did bad things, boy," she said silently. The dog blinked at her, his message, *You must be wrong.*

"I like dogs."

"Boo's usually more discerning." She took a sip of water, but she'd told Boo this house was home, and it carried Mick's scent. She'd as good as told him Mick was safe. "The library's weeks off opening."

"Why?"

The situation at the library was a disaster. And with Ayesha absent, it would be so easy to blame her. Stuff that. Kelly was here for her expertise so, she'd go in guns blazing.

* * *

What had Kelly done, and who had she called, in the few hours since Mick had seen her? After her outburst in his office, he hadn't figured she'd settle a few feet from him on the porch steps. Then again, the dog was between them. A big dog, well-trained.

"You want my honest opinion?"

"I imagine you pride yourself on giving honest opinions. And Roslyn described Ayesha as extremely competent and conscientious, making it unlikely she left us a problem."

"A big part of the problem is the council librarians being told their services were no longer needed." She was testing him.

Her voice rolling over him in seductive waves was a different kind of test.

"Dom said that was a misunderstanding." Dom's claim of a misunderstanding left him with plausible deniability and Mick without concrete evidence.

"I think Dom's prone to being misunderstood." She leaned forward and kissed her dog on the nose.

Mick would settle for a friendly pat.

"Ayesha also said she had some senior student volunteers."

"That explains the list of names I found in the file." Mick had made exonerating Ayesha his starting point in this conversation because his searches confirmed Kelly's "honest opinion." He pulled a piece of paper from his back pocket and handed it over. "I made a copy for you. It's got names and contact numbers. I did a quick ring around this afternoon and half a dozen can be on site at nine tomorrow morning."

"Thank you."

But she looked deliciously baffled. She'd clearly been expecting a fight. This close, he caught a whiff of woman, some soft scent mixed with the day's exertions blended with a dash of dog. Comforting. And comfort and Kelly Steele, previously Kelly Manners, weren't concepts he'd paired before now.

"I also called the council librarians, explained the misunderstanding and asked if they were available from tomorrow. If you need extras, we could probably check if the local market has any shelf-stackers who'd like extra work."

"That's quick action."

He shrugged. "I'm currently responsible for the library."

"And it wouldn't do your reputation or your ambition any favours for it to go pear-shaped?"

"Exactly." He drained his beer. "Would you like some curry?"

"I'd like you to tell me why you followed orders that night when you were ordered to commit a crime."

"Because I was young—twenty-three—stupid and thought the situation might escalate if I didn't manage it carefully." Mick stared at the empty bottle he was nursing, set it down, and turned to face her. "I'd only been at the station a few weeks. It was a posting I hoped would see me on my way to promotion."

"Escalate how?"

"I'd been there long enough to learn no one questioned George Hogan. Some of the other cops agreed with his approach. I don't know if you remember—"

She hunched in on herself, and Boo edged closer to her side.

"George said he'd call for reinforcements."

"I remember." Her voice was threadbare.

"I decided it was better to make it quick and not include anyone else." Mick had planned to say these words when he asked for her help in prosecuting George. Years ago, and he'd abandoned that plan. "That probably sounds heartless."

"Self-serving." Her dead-flat voice was a gut punch when he'd exulted in its rich power earlier today.

Mick's actions had cost him his job, his reputation in some people's eyes, and his girlfriend. Even his cop father still wasn't keen to be seen with him. "Doing it my way meant I didn't see your body and minimised what George could see."

"You're claiming good cop because you looked me in the eye when you told me to drop my pants, when you ran your hands up my thighs and around my buttocks?" Her voice was back at full strength. Rage was better than defeat. Rage had helped him survive. "When you ran your hands up my flanks, over my breasts?"

"I didn't look at you, Kelly. My hands didn't linger or molest. I did a by-the-book pat down. And I made sure George saw almost nothing."

"By blocking his view?"

"By *goddam* blocking his view. By dancing around so my body was between yours and his all the time." George had backhanded him for that at the station. Turned and coldcocked him in front of witnesses who conveniently forgot.

"I hated you. I looked into your eyes and hated you with every fibre of my being." She was hugging Boo by now, the dog draped over her lap. "I'm still furious."

"I'm guessing that saved you." Because she was alive, had a decent job and was prepared to call him on it. Mick pushed to his feet. "I'm also guessing you'd rather not eat with me tonight. I'll take a plate to my room. See you tomorrow."

She looked surprised.

"If you have more questions, ask. You're entitled."

Once in his room, Mick heard her moving in the kitchen. She ate his food, so she didn't think he was planning to poison her and bury the evidence. He heard her feeding the dog, crooning to the dog, and envied her for being able to bring a loyal companion on a short-notice posting.

Loneliness was the other lasting legacy from that disastrous night.

* * *

Young and stupid. Twenty-three.

Kelly calculated he must have started training as soon as he'd turned eighteen. Definitely junior, out-weighed, and out-manoeuvred by the older man. Now, spooling the scene out in her head, she could admit he hadn't once lowered his gaze below her collar, hadn't lingered, hadn't touched her in any sexual way, but the shame had been too great for her to see that then.

"Hold on, Boo. I'll find a mat to put your dish on." The bottom shelf in the pantry held some plastic mats, and she set one on the floor. "Here you go."

She served herself a small bowl of curry and rice, refilled her water glass and sat at the table. Her appetite had deserted her. She should be the one eating, or not eating, in her room. She covered the bowl and put it in the fridge.

Mick had vacated the kitchen for her.

He'd organised help with the library.

He'd defended Ayesha.

Boo liked him. Although, by claiming the place as home, she'd unwittingly given Mick a head-start. Boo had never been wrong before.

It was hard to go back to Abbadon Central—Bella's very accurate term. Bella refused to be squeamish. Harder still to admit there might have been victims other than herself. If what he'd told Kelly at the school earlier was correct, and he had prosecuted George Hogan, then Mick Jamieson stood against the entire police force, oaths of loyalty, brothers above all else, forget right and wrong.

He'd taken responsibility, when the instigator had been

his bigger, beefer, senior officer.

Young and stupid. Kelly had been young and stupid too and had known it at the time. Exploring a strange town after dark. And she'd been bolshie, not meek like some others on the street when confronted by cops.

Boo pushed his nose under her hand.

"Want a run, boy?" His tail wagged. "Just around the block, then bed."

She stopped a block away and tapped out another message to her chat group:

> *Housemate can cook. He's summoned help for the library starting tomorrow. Boo likes him.*

It was early when Kelly knocked on Mick's door the next morning. Not impossibly early. After all, she'd heard the front door, spotted him through the window in well-worn jogging gear, and followed his warm-up routine. He was a regular runner then, and a hunk, as Liam's romance-writing wife, Kate, would say. While Kelly never rated men on the triple-6 dating rule, she'd heard the chitchat about it, and Mick's tank top and running shorts scored him a definite two out of three: six foot and super fit.

Forty minutes later, she'd heard him return, heard the thump of old plumbing coming alive when he stepped into the shower, and now, silence. A strange intimacy to know what a man was doing and to not know. Imagination was a curse when you had long bare limbs, compact muscles, and rugged good looks to work with.

With her hand raised to knock again, his door opened.

"Good morning," she said. He looked mature, fit, and a bit too hunky for a deputy principal in his worn jeans and short-sleeved tee, the antithesis of seventeen-years-ago cop in a sharply ironed new uniform. "I've got hot coffee, and I've made scrambled eggs. It's something I do well, if you'd like some."

"Sounds great." He tagged after her to the kitchen.

43

"How do you like your coffee?" Bella had instilled basic manners into her.

"Strong and black in the morning—wow, you didn't have to go to this trouble." He gestured at the table. She'd laid out a small fruit platter, a choice of cereals, while the eggs were simmering and the toast perched in the toaster.

"You didn't emerge from your room last night." She pointed at the half-full plate of food he'd carried out with him. "And you didn't eat any more than I did last night. I thought you'd be hungry."

"Thanks." He emptied his dinner plate, rinsed it and stacked it in the dishwasher, confirming her assessment of housetrained. "Thanks for cleaning up last night too."

"What do we do now?" Kelly hadn't planned past the invitation in her head in case he'd refused.

"Share a meal like civilised people and negotiate a truce." His expression matched Boo's when her dog was pretending he hadn't pinched Bella's favourite slipper.

"Civilised? Not sure I do that."

"You just have. Join me?"

She slid into the seat opposite. Dining with the devil. She bumped his knee accidentally. "Sorry."

He'd said sorry the previous day. *It's not the same, Kelly.*

"Can I offer you anything?"

"I'm just having fruit and cereal this morning," she said, reaching for the cereal packet and shaking some into her bowl, before pouring milk over it. She looked up when he made no move to help himself.

"Then extra thanks are in order, and I'll make the toast."

"No dinner last night and you've been running," she explained. "I thought you'd be hungry."

The moment seemed momentous in some indefinable way, but they finished breakfast in a surprisingly comfortable silence.

Inviting him to accompany Kelly on her walk to the

library was another exercise in mutual good behaviour. He matched Kelly's stride and kept a polite physical distance. Kelly was aware of him anyway. No fear—she probed the corners of her mind and tested her emotions. She was a different person to garage girl. Hard to deny Mick the same right, especially given the years of study and scrutiny by senior managers he'd endured to get to his current position.

"I'll just have a look around. I drove past on Saturday. It looks good from the outside. There are some design images in Ayesha's office, so I've got a sense of the internal layout." He disappeared, returning ten minutes later. "Why are you assembling the computers?"

"Because it needs to be done." She straightened, glancing around the alcove designed for computers. Last night she'd unpacked them. "Last time I looked I was the only one here."

"It's a good space. A computer room with a wall of trees and green on the outside."

"A bit of focusing on the horizon, to offset the screen time."

"You're assuming they'll look up." He grinned.

"I set an alarm that goes off every hour—'Look up here, Bob,' it mutters. There might not be a Bob in the place, but the unexpectedness produces results."

"How long does that work?"

"A day if I'm lucky. I play it randomly. It goes with the screen saver signs advising a break in activities. Although it's more how you engage with content than actual screen time that's the issue. So, I expect teacher supervision during school visits. Ideally we'd have a librarian available to chat and keep an eye on things for other groups."

"I can give you an hour until the crew arrives at nine." He glanced at his watch. "It'll give me a chance to meet them." Perfectly plausible, but he was expanding the locations where they shared space. Companionable space? "Where do you want me to start?"

Breakfast had worked out. He'd raised the topic of a kitty

for food; Kelly had pointed out she was feeding two, and Boo was a big boy. He'd started a list, she'd added to it. They'd agreed to cook on alternate nights, but either one might be out for a night, or they could opt for takeaway. Normalising their relationship, yet bizarre in a way she struggled to define.

"If you're staying, I'll leave the door open for our helpers."

He studied her, understanding without being told that she didn't leave doors unlocked when she was alone.

He'd been an enemy since that night. Now Kelly had no category for him. Boo had greeted him like a friend this morning. Despite being more companion than service dog, Boo was trained, although not to Charlie's level. Charlie had been her bodyguard for twelve years. And despite declaring the place was now home, Boo didn't usually make friends so quickly.

"The removalists dumped all the boxes in the main area, but from my quick look last night they've stacked like with like. Books from the old school library at one end, and books from the council library at the other. We'll find some overlap, but it's about prioritising at this stage."

"And the computers are your first priority?"

"A lot of people with limited resources rely on the library for internet access these days. The world's moved online, and not everyone has had a chance to catch up. I'm guessing there'll be a backlog of requests when we open our doors."

"Makes sense. What else?"

"It's all important, but pre-schoolers. The deal includes weekly reading sessions for bubs and mums." She'd made her way to the boxes she'd found yesterday. She pointed. "There's a trolley there; the reading room's there"—she stopped—"the boxes marked with yellow tags should all be in there."

He didn't hesitate, just started loading the trolley and ferrying boxes into the reading room. He hefted boxes as if they weighed no more than the wheat bran cereal box she'd found in the cupboard this morning. Stack, repeat, stack, repeat—until he had a full load. His T-shirt was starting to cling. The air-conditioning wasn't activated yet, so the longer he worked, the more his T-shirt clung to powerful muscles. When he bent and stretched, his jeans revealed what she should have known without staring. The man was a runner, for goodness' sake, his glutes got a regular workout. And it showed. Okay, the guy looked good.

More than good.

About forty-five minutes later, their rhythm was broken by the sound of voices arriving. Mick stood upright, stretching his arms above his head. A line of bare skin was visible, and the sight of a man's midriff shouldn't confuse her, but it did. He's … *ridiculously* attractive.

I'm aware of him as a person, as a man, not only as an ex-copper. And for a long time, he's sat in the back of my head under the label perpetrator.

And what the hell do I do with that insight?

He wandered toward her. He smelled healthy, and despite his labours, clean.

Now you're being fanciful, Kelly.

The way a man smells has nothing to do with his personality. Some of the biggest sleazes in creation have smelled delectable.

"Showtime," Mick murmured.

"We're in here," Kelly called out, and heads appeared in the doorway. Although anyone walking up the path to the library would have known where to find Mick and herself: the front, main wall was largely glass.

"Hi, I'm Mick Jamieson, temporary deputy principal, taking Ayesha's place. Thanks for agreeing to help out." He was relaxed, welcoming to the women and teenagers.

Kelly noted Mick had said "taking over from Ayesha temporarily." Did he know more than he was telling her about Ayesha's reasons for leaving?

"And I'm Kelly Steele, Ayesha's other replacement. I'll be helping get the library up and running."

"I'll leave them in your capable hands, Kelly, and check in later. I'll also see about sending the school's storeman across for a few hours today." He wandered toward the front entrance. Her eyes on his retreating butt were just to make sure he closed the door when he left. *Right.*

Kelly sent another chat message.

Met some of the library staff. And some kids. Trying not to rush to judgement. Boo likes housemate. Housemate's proving helpful with the library.

CHAPTER FOUR

Mick wasn't sure when he'd decided to check in later, but he'd already formulated a plan. He could walk her to the library in the mornings and collect her in the afternoons. Ostensibly to check progress, build a relationship with the other librarians and chat to the kids. But his brain was assembling facts and impressions. No patterns yet, just fragments.

Ayesha Patel's decision to leave her pet project, a project years in the making, had been sudden and inexplicable. Was the library and its success the key to the problem? Dom was non-committal about Ayesha's departure and claimed to be misunderstood by the council librarians, gently implying they were at fault. Kelly's report to Ros of the library handover implied Dom side-lined Ayesha. Was Dom still prepared to see the library fail? Would he transfer that animosity to Kelly?

Not a risk Mick was prepared to take. Nothing personal. He just wasn't prepared to see her mistreated on his watch a second time.

Now that they were on speaking terms, he'd find a time to ask why she didn't like the amiable, popular principal. If her assessment was solely based on his presence in the scrum around her at the party after the handover? That would be enough given Kelly's past. A misuse of authority. She had no more patience for corrupt officials than Mick had.

Once at his desk, Mick tried to log in to the departmental system. He had his old password, but that didn't grant him access to Tullamore's records. "Access denied."

Shit.

He flopped back against his seat and spotted the mid-thirties woman in designer jeans, wedge-heeled ankle boots, and a starched business shirt leaning against the doorjamb.

"Who are you?" she asked.

"Mick Jamieson." He rose to his feet. "And you are?"

The woman sank into a chair, pushing a sweep of lush dark hair over her shoulder. "Stephanie Bryant, Steph. Head of Art and Music. Where's Ayesha?" She scanned the room, taking in the empty spaces on shelves. A frown formed between her eyes. "Are you replacing her?"

"Short-term, while she deals with whatever crisis came up."

"Her kids?" Steph's half-hopeful question raised the hairs on the back of Mick's neck.

"Don't know. Dom said he'd send out an internal email yesterday, letting staff know about the changes."

"He's forgetful. Or, at least, that's his story. Think of him as a tall, graceful giraffe—impressive but memory span of a few seconds." Her fingers tangled in a multi-coloured bead necklace.

"A bit of a drawback for a principal."

"During term time he has many minions to handle menial tasks." She was acerbic.

"Do you have minions?"

"Art and music aren't a big part of our curriculum. There's me and some peripatetic instrumental teachers."

"Is something holding you back?"

"Sport." She grimaced. "Don't get me wrong, I've got nothing against sport."

"You're an advocate for balance?" Mick grinned.

"Yeah." Stephanie pushed to her feet. "Speaking of which, I've got to line up those instrumental teachers."

"Maybe later in the week we can talk about what you'd like to see happen."

Her eyes widened in disbelief. "Good luck with that."

"Before you go, who handles system access here?"

"Ralph Ventino. He should be on site or not far. He's usually available for new staff, to fix any glitches before term starts." She pulled out a phone and pressed a few buttons. "Ralph, it's Steph. You're needed in Ayesha's office. Mmm. Ten minutes?" She glanced at Mick, and he nodded. "Great." She rang off. "I'll leave you to explain yourself. BTW, my office is further down this hall."

Mick mentally began drafting his own email to all staff. He'd send it to Dom to forward. Someone clearing their throat brought his head up.

"Who are you?" A lanky, ponytailed man appeared in his doorway.

Hi, I'm X, welcome would make a change from the startled "Who are you?' Mick had received from Stephanie and now Ralph.

"Ayesha's temporary replacement"—Mick held up a hand—"and if you can log me into the system, I'll see about organising an email for all staff to explain what's going on."

"Fair enough." The guy pointed at the machine. "Can I?"

"Be my guest." Mick vacated his chair, crossing to stand at the window. The playgrounds were empty today. The students would start coming in next week, staggered over a few days. Year Seven, first year of high school, would arrive first. Mick had discovered he loved teaching, so he'd chosen a few junior maths classes alongside his administrative duties.

"You should be right, now," said Ralph.

"I'll get your number in case I need more help."

"Sure. Have you got Ayesha's work mobile?"

Mick hadn't been told about a work phone. "Got my own." He recited his number and heard the ping announcing Ralph's contact details. "Did Dom give you a list of new staff needing connections?"

"Two new teachers. I've fixed them up."

"What about Kelly Steele?"

"Nope, not on my list." Ralph shook his head.

"Please add her. She's working on getting the library open. Her main office is at the library, but I also want a desk for her here. I'll send you her number so you can check what she needs here and at the library."

"Sure thing."

"I'd like that sorted today. Maybe you could pop down to the new library now. She's got a pile of new computers she's trying to set up."

"No problem."

Forgetful, slightly absent-minded, distracted by the weight of the job—all plausible, but inconsistent with the Dom that Mick had met and read about. The dossier Roslyn had given him detailed a slow start to Dom's teaching career, a faster upward trajectory after his marriage. Mick scrolled through the files in his head. Dom had married his first wife, daughter of the town mayor, within a year of arriving at his first school, first child born six months later. Marriage would encourage anyone to seek promotion. Children cost money; college-age children living with his first wife still required support. No record of a reason for the divorce that Mick could find, but Dom had transferred as a head of department five years after entering a classroom.

Country placements were often a war of attrition. If you stayed longer than most, you moved up the food chain. A bit like the police. After more than a decade in his second school, also regional, Dom had left for a deputy principalship in a new location with a new wife, daughter of the local bank manager. Dom had been in Tullamore three years, time enough to manage recruitment for senior positions, time enough to have an all-male executive with the exception of Ayesha Patel and Stephanie Bryant.

And then there was one.

Mick could understand a bit of male jockeying for power in Dom's "forgetfulness" about Mick's security access. The missing email had the potential to create resentment amongst staff who had no warning or reason for his arrival. Leaving Kelly and the library off Ralph Ventino's list of new staff was a little too personal.

It was after five when Mick texted Kelly.

I'm outside, if you can let me in.

"Didn't you bring your keys?" she said, opening the locked door, her head cocked to one side.

He held them up. "I thought you'd prefer a warning."

"Thank you." She continued to study him.

"How long have you been here on your own?"

"The kids left around three. They were hot, sweaty, and the pool has enormous appeal."

"Did they say that?"

"There was a bit of chat. 'What are you going to do later?' 'Wanna go to the pool?' Call me a fast learner. They tumbled and danced across the park like Boo did when he was a puppy. The council crew, Ellen and Maeve, left about four. Ralph also stayed here until then. Thanks for sending me Ralph."

"No problem." Had Ralph told Kelly she wasn't on his list?

"Want to see what we did?"

"I might check in the morning. You look like you could do with a cool drink, and I bet Boo's missing you."

"Probably better if we do the shopping before he sees me. He'll want to come."

"I called at the market while getting lunch today. Picked up everything on our list and dropped it at the house." Mick deliberately didn't use the word home.

"What's going on, Mr. Jamieson?"

"I'd like to ask you a few questions, but they can wait until later."

She didn't talk on the way home, which suited Mick fine, although she probably had heaps about why the library was so far behind. He didn't have any answers. Yet.

The second he raised the latch on the front gate, Boo appeared around the side of the house.

"He's worked out the sound already." She opened the gate between the side yard and the front. Immediately, Boo pressed himself against her side. "Hello, darling," she crooned in her sultry night-dark voice.

Lucky dog.

"Hi, Boo." Mick said when the dog gave him a nudge. "I'm assuming you have some sort of routine with him?"

"A walk, or a run, depending how I'm feeling."

"Why don't you do that, and I'll start dinner."

"At the risk of repeating myself, what's going on, Mr. Jamieson?"

"Name's Mick, or Michael, if you insist. Mum calls me Michael Barrymore when she's seriously pissed. Calling me Mr. Jamieson makes me feel like I'm in some prissy private school where the male staff are trying to make a man of me."

"Did you go to one?" She sounded interested.

"Nope." He opened a cupboard, placed two glasses on the benchtop, pulled a bottle of cold water from the fridge and poured them each a glass. "Local high school. You made breakfast today, so I'm happy to call this day one in our meal routine."

"Thanks again." She turned and headed toward her bedroom, Boo hard on her heels.

He saluted her retreating back with his water. So far today, neither of them had put a foot wrong. Could they manage this peace pact until bedtime?

"How was the run?" Mick slid the last of the halved

cherry tomatoes into a bowl.

She was damp from the shower and more relaxed than when he'd met her at the library. A light floral scent teased his nostrils when she stopped beside him to fill her glass with tap water. He inhaled deeply, tormenting himself with the discovery that his housemate's perfume was as alluring as her smoky voice.

Having seen her take off in gym shorts and sneakers, he knew her legs stretched forever. Now, her Capri pants hid them from view. Too late. The image of honed quads and calf muscles was already lodged in his head. She had the curves of a woman who rated good health above being a fashion stick figure. He approved, not that he'd be asked to venture an opinion.

"Longer than I was up for this afternoon," she admitted, pulling out a chair. "I did more physical labour today than I have in the last twelve months."

"Boo looks happy." Mick glanced at the dog. "I took the liberty of buying him a 'Welcome to Tullamore' T-R-E-A-T." Even though he spelled out the last word, Boo started thumping his tail.

"Boo can spell," she deadpanned.

"I don't believe you. I do believe he has a finely developed sense of smell. Is it okay if I give him his, you know what?"

"Yes," she answered. "Boo, present."

"'Present?' That's the instruction?" Mick put a dish down on the mat where he'd seen Kelly put it at breakfast. Boo sat patiently beside it, his tail gently sweeping the floor.

"Yep."

"Does he take a bite out of anything you call a present?"

"That'd be telling." Her smile was pure mischief. "Relax, Boo." The docile dog nibbled at his treat.

Mick was unaccountably pleased with himself. "Would you like a drink with dinner?"

"What's for dinner?"

"A tomato and caper pasta."

"Sounds wonderful. Maybe a small glass of red wine. Otherwise I might fall flat on my face on the table."

He served the meals, then poured them both a glass of wine.

"That's delicious." She lifted another spoonful to her mouth.

Mick had been ensnared by her voice before he met her, then distracted by a history he hoped they'd deal with tonight, and told himself he shouldn't be noticing her as a woman. Except … she was a woman. An attractive woman, sure, with a voice that lured a man to sin, but also a nice woman tackling a difficult job without complaint. Unsurprising that she stirred yearnings he'd suppressed long ago.

She continued, "You're setting an impossible standard for me to meet."

"I'm happy with a barbeque and salad." Mick leaned back in his chair.

"Noted. Where did you learn to cook?"

"Two older sisters and a mother who insisted I take my turn, all three of whom were unstinting in their suggestions for improvements."

"A father in any of this?"

"Divorced when I was twelve."

Mick shared because in his search for Kelly he'd learned things about her background. Things that had made him back off and not subject Kelly to a court case that was bound to get ugly. There were no records of her father, her mother had skated close to prostitution, and had seemingly spent more time with any current partner than Kelly. No wonder Kelly had run.

"You said you started to follow me. Why did you stop?"

"I'd had time to think." How much of the truth should Mick give her?

"Think about what? George Hogan's instruction was illegal." Anger rippled through her voice; she hadn't lost any of her fierceness.

"By the time I'd got that far, I was starting to get pushback."

She fondled Boo's ears, and the gentleness and affection in her gesture gave him pause. She was tough because she had to be. Wary because for too many years she couldn't afford to turn her back. But she hadn't lost the capacity to love.

Thank Dog, as his sister Mel would say. The relief was enormous. During his blackest days, his mum's love had been the beacon pulling him through the dark. Love mattered. His mum loved him. So did his sisters.

"Cops in all shapes and sizes tried to talk me out of the complaint." He didn't often share this story. People were either of the "all cops are corrupt brigade" or "it's a tough job and you have to cut some corners."

"You were forced out." She wasn't asking a question.

"We made a mutual decision to part company." Eight words to summarise false accusations against him, an estrangement from his father, which might never be mended, and an ex-girlfriend who'd called him a traitor to his tribe.

"Thank you." She huffed out air he guessed had been trapped in her lungs for years.

"You're welcome. But I did it as much for me as for you." And Mick didn't regret the decision.

"Why did you become a cop in the first place?"

"Dad's a cop."

And even after everything that had happened, Mick's feelings were a mix of pride and disappointment. His father had received commendations for bravery. He'd saved lives, but he wouldn't give evidence against another cop for "*the odd mistake in policing.*"

"Overnight we became an all-female household—Mum and two sisters—so I kind of glorified the police as a kid."

His dad's words still rang in Mick's ears. "*It's not about doing things by the book. It's about looking after our mates.*" Mates, right or wrong, wasn't a code Mick could live with.

"There was never any question about what I'd be."

Mick considered his and Kelly's joint past, their present, and decided he was prepared to sacrifice more of his privacy. He wasn't happy with Dom's little games, and Mick had been here only a few days. Shithouse timing, but he wanted Kelly to believe he was a different man, even while he might be forced to exhibit some of the old male bonding behaviours.

"They divorced because Dad lost the capacity to see the other point of view. That's Mum's version, although I didn't hear it until after I lodged my official complaint against George Hogan."

"I'm sorry." She was smart enough to understand the politics and the dirty tricks involved in his separation from the police force.

"Mum also told me that she still loved my dad, just hated the institution that changed the man." He reached a hand to stroke Boo. He'd never told another soul about the heart-to-heart he and his mum had shared after Mick's resignation. "Guess I inherited more from her than I thought."

"Did your father ask you to drop the complaint?" She had a jaundiced opinion of the police, and who was he to blame her?

"Dad had to wait in line."

"What about your mother?" Her voice was liquid hot chocolate, luring him into confessions he'd kept to himself.

"Mum supported me throughout." At one point, when things were looking desperate, his mother had called a family meeting. She and his sisters had voted to mortgage the family home to bankroll him for whatever he needed. His maternal grandpa had stepped in then. "After telling me in minute and graphic detail how they'd feel if I did to them what I did to you, and spelling out the revenge they'd plot, my sisters also supported me."

"Do they still talk to you?"

"All the time. There's a chance you'll meet one or both

if you stay for the full term."

"Are you planning to sack me?"

"I don't employ you."

"Then, as current librarian in charge, you should know that Ayesha talked to me about the library. It was a standing item at staff meetings. She made a series of formal requests. Should be in the meeting minutes." Kelly clearly had her own suspicions about Ayesha's sudden departure and the library and was giving him what she had.

Mick and she were finding their balance. "I'll have a look."

CHAPTER FIVE

Kelly pushed back from the dinner table, still trying to process what Mick had just said. *He'd told his mum and sisters what he'd done. And they'd told him he was a bad man.* Of all the things he'd said and done since she'd met him yesterday, she believed this story absolutely.

Kelly had told Clem and Lucy immediately. On her first night back in Sydney, she'd shared her disgust with the two younger girls. Shock, fear—in those initial moments when her survival was on the line, Kelly had chosen rage. She'd had to let it out or explode. Clem and Lucy had agreed with her every curse—a shared bitterness against the world it had taken them years to shake. Kelly had reserved her most obscene cusses for the young cop. She'd been wrong about him.

"What did you want to ask me?" she asked, tracing the figure eight with the end of her knife on the table.

"I've forgotten."

Or maybe, he'd decided not to ask her. This adult version of Mick Jamieson was cautious with his words, thinking about impacts and consequences.

Despite George Hogan's presence, Mick had handled the strip search. A shared experience bound Kelly and Mick.

The half dark, the decaying odour of spilled garbage, a star though the broken roof, her gaze captive to his, the sound of her heartbeat, or had it been his—fast, loud, panicked?

Only Mick could answer her questions about that night.

He might have questions of his own.

Kelly had said she'd check the records about Mick's departure from the police force. He must know she'd wait for answers before sharing more. Even if he didn't know exactly what or whom she'd asked. Maybe he was waiting for Kelly to raise the details of what had happened that night?

He continued, "It's cooler on the veranda. Want a goodnight tea or coffee?"

"I should clear up," Kelly said. Although he was one of those clean-as-you-go cooks. Pushing to her feet, she started stacking dishes. Boo stood with her.

"You can do both. Tea, coffee, water or nothing?"

"Tea would be good." And surprise, surprise, talking to him a bit longer held appeal.

Mick's sharing of domestic tasks was unforced and, having learned about his upbringing, probably ingrained. The few minutes at the sink gave her time to guess at the question he'd had for her. If not the garage in Hay, then Dom Ellis. The principal was a potential point of conflict between them. In the end, it was easy. Kelly took one outdoor chair, Mick took the other, Boo lay half under the side table between them.

"I attended the official handover of the library late last year. Dom claimed all the credit for Ayesha's work. And not a single one of those other men on his executive contradicted him," she began.

"Do you have a theory why?"

"Yes. He's a sexist deadshit who thinks women are on this planet to serve men."

"Met many like that?"

"Hard to avoid. Exhibit A—George Hogan."

"Touché."

"Exhibit B—my mother's boyfriend insisting I was uncontrollable and a financial burden, and either he went or I did." Not a fact Kelly shared often.

"You're saying your mum chose him." There was enough incredulity in his voice to comfort Kelly.

"Didn't you know?"

"I didn't." An emphatic no. So he'd only snooped enough to be able to find her to testify. "She abandoned you."

"I left them." Kelly had run. Running had represented liberation and a giddying power in that first moment.

"She abandoned you. Don't play semantic games," he growled. "If pushed, I say the cops cut me loose after Hay. But it's the same. Abandonment. You feel you're worthless."

"Who else abandoned you?" Kelly knew about his father, his colleagues, but this sounded closer.

He was silent for a long time. "My girlfriend was with me in Hay."

"I see," Kelly said.

And he was right. Being abandoned scarred you in big and small ways, especially being abandoned by someone you thought would love you forever. Ambush, the conviction you truly were worthless, waited around every corner.

"What about you?"

Answering his question was a leap into the unknown. A secret horror few people knew. Mentally, she poked at the edges of the dark.

"My mother left me in a bus shelter when I was five. She told me to wait while she went across the road. It got darker and darker. A lady stopped and asked me where my mummy was. I wasn't supposed to talk to strangers, but I was scared. I pointed to the building. The lady took me there. Mum was in a booth with a guy. She was furious with me for cutting in." Kelly glanced at her hands. They were trembling, and she pressed them flat against her thighs. "I don't know if she planned to come back for me."

"Where were you before Hay?" His voice was impossibly gentle, robbing the ancient memory of some of its horror. He'd have seen cases like hers while working as a cop. They hadn't hardened him.

"Seesawed between couch-surfing and the streets." She'd been terrified every moment of those four months. "Then I got lucky with a social worker."

"You were enrolled at Hay High School for the final years of school, you had a long-term booking at a boarding house. George Hogan and I took that from you. I'm sorry."

"You changed my trajectory." She hadn't expected to discover that if someone asked her today if finding a home with Bella was worth an hour with bent cops, a return trip to Sydney where she'd expected the bus to be pulled over any second and hauled back to a cell, and years of nightmares, she'd say yes.

He nursed his tea. "Why's your dog called Boo?"

"Because he wouldn't say boo to a goose."

"Right. Until the goose starts sniffing at your ankles."

"The goose wouldn't get that close." Kelly gave him her sweetest smile.

"Had him long?"

"Since he was a puppy. He was a gift."

"Birthday?"

"Why so curious?" She sent him a sideways glance.

"Interested. That you let someone close enough they knew you'd welcome a guard dog."

"Arabella Steele." Bella was the lifeline Kelly hadn't fully realised she was looking for. "My first dog was Charlie. He really was a service dog. Bella worked out that I'd stopped running. I love to run. She said with Charlie I could go out alone."

"Steele? You've got her name."

She shrugged. "She was the one good thing to come out of my visit to bumfuck."

"Hay is actually a nice town. Some nice people. None of whom deserved the cop sent to keep charge."

"Bella named it Abbadon Central. She agreed with you. Didn't think Hay deserved the flak."

"What does Abbadon mean?"

"It's a sixteenth century word meaning an underworld of lost souls. Name your demon, she said, then defeat it."

"Have you?"

"I thought so."

"Take Boo with you to the library," he said.

"He's not an official service animal," Kelly said.

And you're not just a pretty face and body, are you?

Mick had recognised her self-drawn boundaries and was treating them with respect.

"The kids'll love him. It's a huge space, and you're spending time there alone." He seemed to be warming to the task. "He's probably lonely here by himself. Doesn't he have Arabella in Sydney when you're at work?"

"Sometimes." She drew out the word, disarmed by his insistence. "Bella dropped to part-time work when she turned sixty."

A few times, after everyone had left the library this afternoon, Kelly had thought she'd heard noises, someone else moving around. She'd called out but got no answer. Imagination, she'd decided.

"New buildings can echo and creak as much as old ones. Don't tell me you wouldn't feel more relaxed if Boo was around?"

There's no way he can read my mind.

"What about school rules? Not to mention council rules on animals in the library?"

"It's not open to the public or the school until next week. In fact, maybe I should order you to take Boo." He bent, caught the dog's chin and turned the animal to him. Boo's big eyes looked at him solemnly. "See, he agrees with me."

"Thank you." She didn't add the words, that makes me feel safer, but he'd know. "Boo and I might call it a night."

Once in her room, Kelly updated the sisterhood:

Library prep still behind. Working all hours of day and then some. Deputy principal housemate ordered me to take Boo to work.

* * *

Thursday—two week days left until the official start of the school year—and Mick's unanswered questions were mounting up. While Monday was technically the start of the academic year, it was a pupil-free day. A staff meeting to start the day, followed by some professional development. Mick was keen to see how the Head of English handled the state-nominated topic of literacy across the curriculum.

Mick made the secretaries' office his first stop, on the off-chance one or other of the women had decided to get a head start on the year, and found the two women were already there.

"Hi." He adopted the non-threatening manner he'd cultivated in his first year off the force. His conscious beta male persona. "I'm Mick Jamieson, replacing Ayesha Patel while she's on leave."

"Has she left permanently?" An odd question from someone who must have known Ayesha professionally and personally for years.

"I don't know enough to be able to answer that." He waited for the woman to introduce herself.

"I'm Bev Wallace, the senior secretary."

"Nice to meet you." He flashed his best smile at the second woman."

"Maria Callos. How can we help you?"

"I've got a problem accessing some files. Not technical." He held up one hand. "Ralph Ventino has set me up, so all systems are go. I just want to understand something about the general files all staff can access."

The two women exchanged a glance. Bev spoke. "I can help."

"Great. Just give me five to open up."

Mick returned to his office, fired up his computer and

pulled up the general admin files. A few minutes later, he lifted his head at the knock on his open door. "Perfect timing. Come in, Bev. Are you comfortable taking a seat with me beside you?"

She sent him a considering look before settling into the chair he offered. "Fine."

"As you can see, I've got files up." Mick had run a search last night for records of staff meetings.

Formal minutes, or any written records of the staff meetings, taken by one or other of the secretaries, had dried up in the second half of last year. For a few more months, the minutes consisted of lists of actions, including half a dozen related to the library, signed off by Dom, but no record of whether or not actions were completed.

"What specifically are you looking for?"

"Minutes of staff meetings for the last six months. I want to get a sense of the recent top issues. Monday's meeting is special, a chance for new staff to be introduced and to timetable professional development before we have students everywhere. Dom said you have weekly staff meetings on Friday afternoons." Dom had added that a few people gathered for drinks after that.

"The executive decided action lists were more efficient." Bev's jaw set.

"So, Dom lists the actions, which frees you and Bev up to participate?" Mick feigned casual interest.

"About October, Dom suggested Bev and I had a big load approaching the end of the year, processing reports, setting up parent-teacher meetings, prize nights."

"The end of the year comes with a rush, doesn't it?" Mick kept his gaze on the screen. The lists of actions dried up in November. "It's a new year. I'd like you and Maria to come back to staff meetings, commencing next Monday. I'd also like one of you to take the minutes. I've got a few items I want formally minuted."

"Has Dom okay'd our attendance?" Bev's hands twisted in her lap.

"As deputy principal, I have the authority to invite you and Maria to the meeting." Mick observed her agitation and offered a smile. "I'll let Dom know."

"Do you need anything else?" she asked.

"Not at the moment. Although I appreciate your help."

Mick did a further search of the files when she excused herself. "What in blazes are you playing at, Dom?"

Easy to challenge Dom on minor malfeasance. But it was unlikely to go anywhere. Dom would trot out the same excuse—end-of-year workload, not enough staff, staff run ragged. Easy to argue this year would be different, but from Bev's reaction, she and her colleague hadn't been invited to Monday's staff meeting until Mick brought it up.

The familiar ringtone brought a smile to Mick's face. "Hi, Mel. How's things?"

"I can hear you smiling. Are you still using 'Sisters Are Doin' It for Themselves' as my ringtone?"

"I remember you dancing around the loungeroom and singing at the top of your lungs when we were kids. It's an anthem."

"I wanted to be a singer."

"Pity about your voice then." He chuckled.

"Smartarse. Why is a lawyer asking questions about you?"

It took him a few seconds to process. *Kelly?* Had Kelly hired a lawyer? "What lawyer, and what sorts of questions?"

"You're sounding like a cop."

"Careful, Mel." Telling Mel what had happened in Hay had been one of the toughest days of Mick's life.

"Sorry." His sister hated when her mouth moved faster than her brain, usually only happened with family these days. "Liam Quinn. He's actually a contact from law school days. But he was inquiring on behalf of family—extended family."

"What did he want to know?" Mick's mind raced.

"I got the impression he had what he wanted and was touching base to see if I was estranged from my ex-cop brother. I said no. That was it. It felt like I was giving a character reference."

"Kelly Manners, now Kelly Steele, is here in Tullamore."

"Define here."

"One of my direct reports. We're working together on a major project, and"—he paused—"I don't want this to go further." He waited.

"Not fair to ask for promises when I don't know what's happening."

"You'll have to trust me."

"Low blow, Mick." Her turn to hesitate. "You have my word."

"We're sharing a house." And memories and meals and inching toward—what? He didn't know. But a low throb of desire had snuck into the mix.

"How long have you been sharing a house?" She sounded curious.

"Since Monday."

"No fatalities?"

"She's got a guard dog." Boo liked Mick.

"Did she arrive with a guard dog or decide she needed one?"

"Ha ha! Kelly's had Boo for years. She took the name of her foster parent, an Arabella Steele." He pictured Mel at her desk in Sydney, swallowing the million questions she had. "We recognised each other, and we're talking."

"With a guard dog between you?" She snorted. "Be careful. If you need me, call."

She'd be here in a New York minute. Drop everything. "Love you too."

He'd known Kelly hadn't been joking when she'd said she'd check, but a top-flight lawyer? He'd hoped for a gentler interrogation, that they'd somehow find their own way. Now another stranger was ransacking his past, circling him, making judgements. Would it never end?

* * *

Kelly's phone vibrated mid-afternoon. She slipped it from her pocket. Liam.

Liam's text read: *I've got news. Are you free for a call?*

"Excuse me—" she held the handset so her motley library team could see—"I've got to take this." She closed her office door behind Boo to prevent being overheard, her heart thumping like a kettle drum. Was she ready for what Liam had to say?

After three days, she and Mick had found a routine— shared platonic living. She was starting to like him.

Admit it, Kel.

This morning, you watched the way his big, sleek body moved during his warm-up ritual, watched him jogging away, and you weren't just impressed by his fitness. Heat rose up her throat at the memory of where else her gaze had lingered—he's tall enough and broad enough for our bodies to fit—

Sinking into her chair, she pressed *Call.*

With some of her barriers down, Kelly could admit Mick was attractive. Very attractive. His voice held authority, rather than command, a hard balance to achieve. He was at the library often enough to win the confidence of the kids and Maeve and Ellen. His requests didn't incite resentment or pushback. Maeve, in particular, studied him when she thought he wasn't looking—assessing the nature of the man. Maeve was of the "handsome is as handsome does" brigade. *Who could fault her?*

"Liam. That was quick." She rested her hand on Boo's head. She trusted Liam absolutely. A surprise to discover she wanted to trust Mick a bit too.

"I'll be brief. Mick lodged a complaint. The pushback from other members in the force was brutal. A lot of mud was thrown. He persisted but lost his job. Did he ever try to get you to give evidence?"

"He said he changed his mind, said"—Kelly fondled Boo's ear, recalling Mick's exact words—"said circumstances changed his mind. He decided it would be unfair to subject me to further interrogation and potential cross-examination."

"Probably decided police prosecutors would rip you to shreds," Liam said dryly. "That was remarkably self-aware of him, given the threats against his life. A lot of cops would have shifted the responsibility to you, made it look like he was forced to give evidence. Might have saved his job. His father's also a cop."

Kelly heard respect in Liam's summary of Mick's actions. "He said his mum and sisters supported him, after they essentially called him a dick for doing what he did."

"That explains a lot. I've met his older sister."

"He has two."

"Lucky boy. This one's a lawyer and activist. Why on earth did he become a cop in the first place?"

"He said young and stupid." Kelly sighed. "No, that's wrong. His parents' divorce hit him hard. He wanted a connection with his dad, to be like his dad."

"Tough place to be in. And now he's a teacher. Interesting background for a teacher." Liam was asking a question.

"Mick said the education department is fully aware of his background." Kelly found herself defending him.

"Want me to check that out?" Liam waited while Kelly searched her heart and mind for how much prying into Mick's life she wanted to do. "Kelly?"

"So far, everything he's told me is true. I know the regional director who appointed him. I can call her if I have any questions."

"Back your judgement, Kel. You're stronger than you think."

"Give my love to Kate and Lily."

"After I tell her you rang about an obscure matter relating to the Magna Carta. Lily is going to be a big sister. Excellent training for boys, I've heard. To have a big sister."

"I'm an only child."

"You can change that for your children." He was a sweetheart.

"Thanks, Liam." Motherhood had been off the table for years. "You can't be what you can't see." Except people broke that rule every day. And life had changed for the sisterhood in recent years. Clem and Lucy were fast revising their shared vow on no babies.

"Any time. When are you going to share with the sisterhood?"

"Soon."

Kelly scrolled through her phone to Mick's number, then paused before pressing call.

How do I explain what I've done?

I told him I'd check, but that was before I got to know him better. If he asks Liam's name, I'll tell him. Hell, Liam knows Mick's sister. She's probably already rung Mick.

She tucked her phone in her back pocket. This was the kind of conversation that needed to be face-to-face. Or maybe face forward walking home. Neutral space. That worked. She'd leave Boo's leash long. No one to overhear them, the hazy heat that marked late January afternoons, Boo dancing around them doggy-delighted to be out of doors, making new friends, sniffing every pole and verge on the few blocks back to the house.

A few hours later, her phone buzzed with a new text:

I'm outside.

"Hi." She smiled then turned her back to lock the dog. When she turned back, he was on his haunches, saying hello to Boo, and her stomach flipped over. "Ready?"

"Yep." He fell into step beside her.

"There's no easy way to start this conversation." She touched his arm, a compulsion to reassure and part apology for needing third-party verification of his story.

Four days ago I was right to doubt him.

"That sounds ominous." He stared down at her fingers on his bare forearm.

"I said I'd verify your story from Hay," she whispered.

"My friend verified your story."

"I hear an 'and.'" He sent her a sideways glance.

"Liam said it might have been easier for you if you'd asked me to testify."

"I'd stirred the beast, Kelly," he replied sombrely. "It was never going to get easier, unless I backed down. Even then, I would have had to watch my back. I was a traitor."

"They're the ones who shouldn't be on the force."

"Thanks for the vote of confidence, I think. But there are plenty of good cops out there. The bad ones get the most press. What?"

"I, and the fringe-dwellers I mixed with, confronted ten mean and gratuitously cruel cops for every good one." It had to be said. "Liam's never had that problem. In Australia, being white, male, and having a solid background gives you a pass most days."

"Liam's your source?"

"Liam Quinn's a lawyer, but he's also family." Kelly shared her informant's name because she and Mick were negotiating a lasting peace, an advance on their existing truce.

"Is he from Arabella's family?"

"Bella loves Liam, but no. Indirectly, it was Lahn, the social worker who set me up in Hay, who created this connection."

The name was easier to say if you kept saying it. And to be honest, Kelly hadn't been in Hay long enough to discover more than the town had its share of aggro teenagers, residents unhappy with soft-on-crime approaches, and a cop who should never have been given a badge much less a promotion.

"I called Lahn when I got back to Sydney."

"Guessed that's where you went."

"I needed somewhere to stay while Lahn checked options. I shared a room with two girls, Lucy and Clem. Liam is Lucy's brother-in-law. We're family."

"So, do Lucy and Clem know I'm here?"

"Not yet." Kelly was still mulling when and what to tell them, and she hadn't kept a secret from them since that night.

"Why?"

"Apart from the fact they'd be here almost before I hung up?" Kelly didn't want that, so she started at the other end of the story. "Lahn offered a few options. Another small town where I'd know no one, or Arabella Steele—a woman of mature years who was prepared to offer me room and board as long as I studied."

"Interesting condition."

"Study is what I wanted. I was going to be a lawyer and see every bent cop I'd ever met prosecuted." Kelly deliberately provoked him. He didn't take the bait.

"Life isn't that long, and I'm guessing Arabella had other ideas?"

"She's a force of nature."

"I've got three women like that in my family." He unlocked the front door of the house and let her and Boo precede him.

"I thought education was power, but Bella taught me it was also fun and maybe a better way to insulate the world against hate and fear, than the use of force and punishment."

"You're losing me here. What's the connection with you not telling your friends about me?" He left his briefcase by his bedroom door.

Boo padded down the hall to the kitchen and curled up on his mat.

"I'm not sure." Kelly turned to stare at him when they reached the kitchen, searching for words to explain her bewilderment. "Bella upended her life to make me strong. Some weird trick of the universe has dumped us here together. I should be able to deal with this alone. We should be able to deal with this."

"I'm glad you're giving us that chance." Stepping closer, he linked his fingers with hers, slowly, giving her the chance to accept or reject his touch. Then he lifted their joined hands to his chest. His strong, steady heart beat against the back of her palm.

It was a chance. Kelly wasn't sure how it would turn out. "I'll take Boo for a run, then fix dinner. Seven-thirty suit you?"

"That works." He pointed back up the hall to where his briefcase sat. "No rest for the wicked. I brought work home."

CHAPTER SIX

Kelly sent her last chat message of the day:

Still working all hours of day. Boo likes the library. Housemate and I have started a kitty and cook alternate nights. He's more adventurous than me.

George Hogan and Hay had smashed Mick Jamieson's dream to follow in his father's footsteps, changing Mick's future in that instant as much as hers. Even before Liam's report, she'd been ninety-nine-point-nine percent sure his report would vindicate ex-cop Mick Jamieson.

Mick had reinvented himself. Now, she and Mick shared an odd intimacy. Not because of the job and the house, but built upon their cascading series of conversations. Each one peeling back another layer.

Restoring trust?

She had people she trusted, so did Mick.

Could they trust each other?

She fell asleep with Boo's soft snores in her ears and Mick Jamieson in her head. She had no reservations about sharing a house with him. In some way she couldn't quite define, she knew she was safe. And not only because Boo was present.

Kelly tumbled into darkness and the terror of being

helpless.

Kelly stood in the dusty, half-empty garage in Hay. It carried the musty, stale scents of damp, old urine, spilt petrol, and new menace. Fear threatened to paralyse her, and she held tightly to her defiance.

"She's armed. Search her," George Hogan issued the sharp order to the younger cop.

"I'm not armed."

"Strip her." Hogan smirked. "I think we should know what she's hiding. Protect the citizenry."

Kelly lifted her chin, but rage and fear clogged her nostrils. "You need a female cop present for that."

"None on duty. Now ain't that a pity. Do it, punk." Hogan jerked his chin at the young cop.

"I'll use the corner." The younger cop's gaze was blank. Nausea swirled in her stomach.

"Nothing wrong with right here." Hogan reached a hand to his crotch, and Kelly slapped a hand over her mouth to stop herself from gagging.

The young cop moved in front of her. "Unbutton your shirt." He kept his eyes on hers, his body partially shielding her from Hogan while she slipped the buttons from the thigh-length work shirt. She wore no bra. His hands ran quickly, neutrally over her breasts and torso. "Do it up." He waited while she rebuttoned the blouse. "Now the pants."

She slid the zipper down, the noise loud in the near-silent space.

Hogan moved nearer. "Come on, boy, move aside and let's all see what she's hiding."

"I do this," the younger cop gritted. "I do it my way."

"Won't share." Hogan guffawed. "I'll be noting that on your record."

A trickle of perspiration ran down Kelly's spine. Her breathing hitched. She pushed the jeans down her hips.

"Panties and jeans together." His eyes stayed on hers.

The shirt covered some of her nakedness. Had that been deliberate? She was too terrified to care. She'd run from situations like this. Instead, she'd run to. Cops couldn't be trusted. Not in the alleys of the city she'd come from.

Not in this town.

She wouldn't beg. She was itching to fight, to kick, to scream, to claw him, to leave a permanent mark on him.

His hands roamed impersonally up her thighs, over her buttocks, down her inner legs. "Get dressed." He turned his back on her. "She's clean."

A half sob escaped her. The younger cop's back stiffened. She'd never feel clean again.

"I'll drop you off, then take her back to wherever she's staying."

Kelly couldn't see the younger cop's face, but Hogan stepped back.

The younger cop pulled up at the boarding house. "You're safer staying in at night until you learn the town better."

"I'll never forgive you for this . . ."

"Kelly, wake up." A hand gently rested on Kelly's upper arm.

A wet nose nudged her shoulder. "Boo?" Her throat was dry, but the hand was urging her to wakefulness.

"Kelly. You're having a nightmare. I'm turning on the bedside light." The voice was low, calm, grounding her.

"What? Who?" Fear threatened to pull her back under. Mick's face was cast into shadow by the reading light. "Shit!"

"You're having a nightmare." He was motionless, but Kelly's heart pumped at triple time. "Want to talk about it?" He perched on the edge of the bed, level with her hips, his hands pressed flat on his thighs.

Boo whined and nudged her again. "It's okay, Boo. I'm okay." Kelly lifted her hand to Boo's head, and he sank back on his haunches. Boo held his position between Kelly and Mick, ready to protect, but not alerted by Mick's gestures or tone.

"Do you have nightmares often?"

Kelly pushed herself up in the bed and dragged her damp hair off her face. The nightmare was gone. In its place was clammy discomfort. She was disoriented, her chest still heaving, and the residue of fear thick in her throat. But she knew the contours of this nightmare, its hills and slopes and depressions. She'd never woken to find herself face-to-face with the person who triggered it.

"Not since before Charlie died. It's Boo's first." She smiled to reassure her dog. "Good dog, Boo."

"Our conversation set it off." Mick made a neutral statement.

"Yeah." But a fragment remained. Mick hadn't looked at her body, had shielded her. She covered his hand with her own. He looked like he needed reassurance more than Boo.

He looked down at her hand, and a shudder ran through him. "I'm sorry."

Kelly squeezed his fingers. "You're the one without a shirt this time."

Propped against the bedhead, Kelly was at eye level with his broad bare chest, lightly dusted with dark hair, muscled and narrowing to a flat belly—she'd seen him run, so no surprises there. The shadows from the bedside lamp danced lovingly across taut skin. She'd told herself Mick was eye candy and watching his warm-up was the normal reaction of any person with a pulse. Not true. While he had the requisite body parts, arranged in an impressive design, he had a maturity honed through making difficult choices and probably losing more friends than he'd gained. The combination lured her past wary to seriously intrigued.

"Are you okay?" He turned his hand up to link fingers. He'd taken her hand last night too.

"Getting there." Holding hands helped.

I'm not brave enough to tell him that.

"I'll get you some water." He left the room, flicking the overhead light on before he left.

Kelly blinked and checked her surroundings. The lightweight cover she'd drawn over herself before falling asleep lay tangled around her feet. Her pyjama pants were twisted halfway up her thighs, but the buttons on her sleeveless pyjama top had miraculously stayed done up. She righted herself.

"Here." He'd donned a T-shirt while collecting the water, and part of her was sorry. He'd exuded some of Boo's sense of comfort, with his slow movements, sleep-tousled hair and protective strength.

"Thanks."

What's wrong with you, Kelly?

He's a man who should be off-limits for a gazillion reasons, and that was before she asked Lucy and Clem their opinions. Except he'd walked away from his boyhood dream of being a cop, turned his back on his father, given evidence against his peers. All for a girl he'd spent less than an hour with. Integrity like that earned her respect.

"I'm sorry for all the years of nightmares." He'd stepped back after handing her the water.

Something in his tone made Kelly return the question. "Did you have nightmares?"

"Yeah." He released a breath, making an admission she guessed he rarely shared. "Still do. Maybe I should get a Boo." Boo still sat beside the bed, ready for action. "Will you be okay, now?"

"What time is it?"

"About five in the morning."

"I might go for an early run. Clear my head." Kelly swung her feet onto the floor. "It's not always easy to get back to sleep."

"Tell me about it." His lips quirked in a half smile, his first one hundred carat smile for her. "Want company? Apart from Boo, I mean."

"Meet you out front in ten." She stretched out her hand, inviting him to pull her to her feet.

Maybe this is what making peace looks like. An admission of shared nightmares and an early morning run.

* * *

Damn! Mick stripped off the drawstring pants he wore to bed. He still wasn't sure what had woken him, Kelly's whimpers graduating to cries, or Boo's distress trying to wake his mistress. He'd reached the hall when Boo barked. Boo had tracked every move he'd made in her room, ready to defend.

Thank Christ!

Copper Mick's actions had left a trail of pain. Last night she'd talked about dealing with the past. But she'd rehashed the details for her family lawyer, talked to Mick, and fuck that, woken with a nightmare she hadn't had in years.

Could they get past that?

Last night Mick had been hopeful.

Mel's call had warned Mick that Kelly's friend was on his trail. He'd been braced for some slick city lawyer's findings, to have his and Kelly's relationship torpedoed before it had begun. Did Kelly know she'd touched him before blurting out the findings?

"My friend verified your story."

"He said it might have been *easier for you if you'd asked me to testify."*

Direct, honest, but her simple touch had already drained most of the tension out of him. A voluntary touch. With it, the poisonous cocktail of guilt and shame he'd swallowed in Hay lost a lot of its power.

A human connection that off-balanced him enough to make a move himself. He'd held her hand, and she hadn't pulled away.

He'd have followed her, if she'd said no to his joining her on the run.

Right, Jamieson. Now you're a stalker.

But even with Boo, he didn't like the idea of her running alone in a strange town. Shit, that was how their relationship had started. With February around the corner, it was getting darker in the mornings, and she was still rattled.

I'm rattled.

He donned shorts and runners.

She'd been groggy when he'd arrived, unsure of her bearings, her prim pyjamas twisted—prim, if you didn't consider the book pattern with romance titles up the spines. The nightmare had roughened her smoky voice. Its gritty fierceness had buried itself deep in his psyche. When he'd been a kid and had nightmares, his mother had held him. With his adult nightmares, he'd been alone. They'd been harder to shift, waking sweaty and disoriented.

Damn it, he'd wanted to hold her—offer to hold her, to slide into the bed behind her and wrap himself around her and scare the demons away. Impossible when he was the demon in chief. He'd hesitated to touch her but had needed to bring her back to the room. She hadn't shaken him off or shown any fear. His relief had been enormous. She'd been soft, all silky skin and sleep-drugged, beautiful in a way he hadn't let himself see until that moment.

He scrubbed his face, exhaled deeply and remembered.

She'd touched him, held his hand, then let him help her to her feet. She was strong and brave and probably both of those things before she'd met Arabella Steele. A better name for her than Manners. She had a backbone of steel. He'd made a friendly gesture in the kitchen last night. Hey, let's see what happens next. Her touch, while still shadowed by a nightmare, was different by an order of magnitude he could barely compute.

"Meet me out front in ten."

Better than a truce. Trust?

He ached to touch her again.

Joining her for the run was a good decision for them both. No need for conversation. Boo keeping pace. Mick dropped his speed a notch, but Kelly kept up, the loping stride of a regular runner. He was content to breathe in fresh air and to watch the sun rise with a woman he admired and her faithful dog. Might go shopping for another T-R-E-A-T for Boo.

Dom cornered Mick in his office at four-thirty that afternoon. "Come for a drink, Mick? A few of the town's movers and shakers usually gather on a Friday. With school not yet officially open, it's a chance for me to introduce you. From next week a lot of staff will likely gather, and they'll want your time."

I want to pick up Kelly and Boo and go home.

Not an excuse he could use. Calling at the pub, making friendly, had ranked high on his to-do list before Kelly's arrival.

"Or are you planning another Indian curry with Kelly?" Dom watched him closely.

Mick was trying not to imagine knocking on her door and begging to hold her hand again. Offering to share her bed, in a purely platonic sense, to keep her nightmares at bay.

"I've got no idea what Kelly's doing. We're ships that pass in the night. She's almost living at the library at the moment. A drink sounds good."

"Career women." Dom shook his head. "They're in a class of their own. She's got that aloof, prissy, superior attitude perfected. Not a good fit for Tullamore."

Cocky bastard, if Dom had the confidence to spew sexist crap to a relative stranger.

Fuckwit. Not an answer Mick could give. Dom disgusted him. The job disgusted him. Knowing Kelly would support what Mick was doing if she knew was the only thing keeping him from doing a George Hogan and coldcocking the older man.

"Don't talk about Kelly that way." Mick couldn't let it pass. Stuff the ambitious-but-harmless persona he was trying to cultivate.

"Fancy her, do you?"

"She's smart, capable, and from what I've seen, a hard-working professional who's put herself out to help the school. She doesn't deserve criticism for doing her job."

Dom's attitude would wear any woman down, especially if Dom dripped his poison in private conversations. My word against your word. Ayesha's kids were in Sydney at university. Maybe the white-anting over the library was the last straw.

"Didn't take you for a closet feminist." Was Dom testing him? A test Mick was happy to fail.

"Call it what you will. Gender is irrelevant in the classroom, everyone deserves respect."

"We're a bit removed from city woke culture—a happy school, happy staff. Hope you're able to fit in." A threat? Interesting that Dom would be so blatant. Out of character for a successful manipulator, if that's what Dom was, to be so obvious.

"If Ayesha sorts out whatever sent her on compassionate leave, I'll be gone."

"It'll be great if she can come back. Brilliant at her job."
What the fuck? Dom is playing mind games with me.

"I was just testing you out on Kelly"—Dom grinned—"and you fell for it. A good principal needs to know his staff's attitudes on lots of things, including whether they treat their female colleagues fairly."

"Got me." Mick forced himself to grin in return. "I should know better."

"See you at the pub." Dom waved a hand on his way out.

His word against mine. Dom could—would—argue that he was testing Mick rather than stating his own opinion. Roslyn was right to be suspicious. Last night and this morning with Kelly had shot Mick's objectivity about Kelly, if he'd ever had any, to pieces. Now he'd dropped his guard, and Dom had slipped past. A mistake Mick would be careful not to repeat.

Dom's boyish charm coupled with his authority as principal would lead a lot of people to misinterpret the principal's remarks, to question themselves. The cunning bastard was hiding secrets. With Kelly in the firing line, Mick's determination to uncover them had shifted from professional to very personal.

CHAPTER SEVEN

Kelly was doing basic stretches when Mick joined her on the back veranda on Saturday morning. "Good morning."

"If you say so," he grunted, more Mr. Grumpy than the even-tempered man she'd seen until now.

Grumpy intrigued her. "Didn't sleep well?"

"No." Mr. Grumpy moved into his own warm-up routine.

A nightmare? He'd confessed to his own bad dreams earlier in the week. Although there was a second possibility.

"Heavy drinking plays hell with an athlete's body," Kelly commiserated.

"I'm new in town. I'll be here for an indefinite period. I have to work with these people. I had one beer at the pub to see who attends Dom's little gatherings." Grumpy and long-suffering.

"Reconnaissance." She grinned. "Makes perfect sense to identify your enemies."

He scowled. Grumpy, long-suffering, and taciturn. He hadn't enjoyed his sortie in the pub.

"Ready?" she asked.

"You said I'm an athlete. We're born ready."

Kelly took the lead with Boo at her side. Mick fell in

beside her. That had become their pattern in the last few days. A circuit around town of roughly three kilometres. He beat her to the kitchen after his shower, had a coffee waiting for her, had set cereal packets and a bowl of fruit salad on the table.

"By the way, Maeve and Ellen are taking the weekend off."

His grunt was a little mellower.

"Remember, I told you that yesterday, but the kids are coming in," she said. "You don't need to come with me this morning."

"I remember. Is that your way of saying 'piss off'?"

"If I was going to say 'piss off,' I'd say it. I don't do euphemisms."

"So what are you saying?" He upended wheat flakes into a bowl.

"If you have other work to do, if you need a break from me, if you need more sleep?" Kelly held up her hands in surrender. "It's my job. You've got a lot of others on your list."

"Any more nightmares?"

"Have you heard any?"

He cocked his head to one side.

"They're usually loud. What about yours?" Kelly pushed the milk toward him.

"Haven't had one in a while. Cold, clammy. I've always been alone, so can't comment on the noise. Feels like I wake up screaming."

So, a bad dream wasn't his problem.

"Wednesday night was probably my brain trying to deal with too many shocks at once. Meeting you. Hearing your version. Having Liam confirm your version. Spending time with you?"

"Done psych, have you?"

"A semester in my degree, but Clem's the psychologist in our girl pack." Kelly picked up her spoon.

"And you still haven't told your friends." He said the

words with a kind of wonder, which was better than him thinking she'd break her word.

"It's not easy, but we're dealing with it." She hesitated, but dealing with it meant complete honesty. "Wednesday's nightmare was different."

"Different how?"

"It's usually a tsunami of emotions, no place to hide, and believe me, I've searched. I have to ride the tiger until the end. Or until Charlie or Bella pulled me off it." She waved her spoon in the air. "Don't get me wrong, the fear and rage were just as real this time, but the sequence of actions was clearer. More a slow-motion video than a kaleidoscope of fractured images. You didn't grope me, Mick, didn't look anywhere but my face. You actively shielded me from Hogan. I'm not going anywhere."

"You said you'd never forgive me."

"It was true at the time."

"I want you to keep taking Boo to the library when it opens." He tossed out the non-sequitur, then splashed milk over his cereal.

Immediate relief. Kelly hadn't been aware of carrying tension until she released it. The library would be busy, with school kids, community sightseers, more strangers. Having Boo present gave her eyes in the back of her head.

"How do we explain that?"

"We don't need to. If asked, you're starting early and finishing late. It's a precaution."

"Against what?"

"Do you ever just accept a suggestion?" He grinned, mood seemingly miraculously improved.

"Yes."

"Yes, what?"

"Your suggestion sounded more like an instruction. Habit of command?"

"Didn't hold a senior command in the force." He spooned some fruit salad into his bowl.

"It's innate. Thank you. I accept your suggestion. Until

we have an established routine, I'll feel more comfortable knowing Boo's around." She was beginning to feel more comfortable knowing Mick was around.

"Can I eat now?" He picked up his spoon. "By the way, I've ordered takeaway for the library today. Lunch for the kids as a thank you. Chicken, lots of salads for any vegetarians and, because—hey—balanced diet, bread rolls, juice and water."

"That's a lovely way to thank the kids. You can eat now."

The day was filled with backbreaking work and the delighted laughter of the teens when they scored a free lunch. Many hours later, Kelly crawled into bed, then remembered her promise to the sisterhood.

Housemate organised thank-you lunch for the kids who helped out with the library. He knows how to blend healthy food with teenage decadent delights. Kids euphoric. Library not quite up and running. First full staff meeting Monday morning. Housemate insists Boo keeps coming to library.

* * *

Mick made sure he was first to the staff meeting on Monday, setting up a table at the front with three chairs, then standing at the door greeting staff members he'd met, introducing himself to others. The room was almost full when the principal arrived.

"Hi, Dom. I've invited the secretaries to today's meeting. A good chance to meet the new staff. I've also asked Bev to take the minutes."

Which I'll check.

"Not necessary. These are often informal chats," Dom dismissed the suggestion. "If it's something worth noting, I diarise it."

Bev stood at the back of the increasingly short queue. Had she heard Dom's remark?

Mick smiled at her and beckoned her forward. Abandoning his place at the door, he escorted her to the front table. "Please come and sit here. Dom, I've got a few things I'd like minuted. This saves you having to worry."

Dom looked about to protest.

Mick continued, "I've got my DP training wheels on. Don't want to miss anything in the rule book. I thought I'd take over checking minutes and keeping track of actions, if that's okay with you? It'll give me a faster grasp of what's happening."

"You *are* serious about a promotion." Dom's fixed smile almost robbed the words of insult.

Mick's neck prickled with cop awareness. Dom's ego meant he'd have to hit back.

Teachers and support staff were trickling into the large meeting space in ones and twos, helping themselves to tea or coffee or juice from the side table set up for the purpose before taking seats. Almost time. Kelly was last in and headed straight to the side table. She'd told Mick she'd go by the library, leave Boo there.

"Hey, Kelly. Be a pal and get me a coffee, please?" Dom called, loudly enough for heads to swivel in Kelly's direction.

Mick was on his feet before she had time to answer. "I'll get it, Dom. How'd you like it?"

"White, two sugars." Dom didn't hesitate, didn't push the point. Maybe he thought having the deputy principal making his coffee was as good a statement of power as having the most senior woman on staff act as his waiter.

"I know." Mick came up behind Kelly. Close enough to feel her tension, to provide some protection from the curious glances of other staff. "He's a sexist deadshit into petty power plays."

"Say that when you dump his coffee in his lap," Kelly snapped.

"I have a better idea."

Mick made a coffee, doctored it to Dom's liking and carried it back across the room. He made a huge show of serving Dom, executing a deep bow, inviting everyone in the room to share in the fun. "Anyone else need lessons in making their own coffee, you've just seen how it's done," he said, making sure his voice carried.

Dom rose to his feet, ostensibly to start the meeting, but probably to cut Mick off.

"Good morning, all. Great to see the regulars here, and we have a few newbies. Looks like being another terrific year. First off, I'd like to introduce the exec team."

New teachers would have already met their departmental heads, so this was to let the room at large know where the authority rested. Dom introduced Mick. He didn't introduce Kelly, or the two secretaries in the room, although there was a good chance not all new staff had met them yet—an oversight, or a calculated snub?

Somehow between Ayesha's departure and Mick's arrival, the standing item on the library had gone missing from the agenda. When they reached the general business item, Mick took the floor.

"It's good to be here, even though a few weeks ago, I thought I'd be teaching maths in the Southern Highlands. Please feel free to drop in and chat any time. I've only been here a few days, but I've made it my business to meet our hardworking secretaries—the backbone of any school. In case anyone hasn't yet had the chance, could you please stand up Bev"—the woman rose to her feet—"and Maria." A second woman stood. "Thank you both.

"I'd also like to formally introduce Kelly Steele, one of my direct reports. Some of you have met her, and Dom's welcome email gave a bit more information. Kelly's State Coordinator Community School Libraries. We're incredibly lucky to have her."

He let that sink in, registered the shift of dynamics in the room. Kelly's pay grade placed her higher in the pecking order than any other woman present and most of the men. Asking her to make his coffee had been a less-than-subtle putdown by Dom. A few women shifted uncomfortably in their seats. Stephanie refused to meet Mick's gaze. Bev, who he'd seen having coffee with Maeve, wore a tight smile he couldn't read.

"Roslyn Morales, regional director, asked for the minutes to note that Ayesha Patel has made an astonishing contribution to the school and the community and has the department's thanks. We wish her well at this difficult time." Mick stopped to look around before giving an oh-shucks shrug. "Effectively, head office decided you need two people to replace Ayesha Patel, at least in the short term. Unfortunately, when Ayesha took leave, work stopped on the library—"

"*Unfortunately,* due to Ayesha's personal problems, she dropped the ball on a few matters. But I've called in a few favours, and we'll get it sorted." Dom's self-serving poison—clothed as concerned, over-worked manager— ricocheted around the room.

"Family crises can mess with your day job." Mick kept his response mild, when Dom's sabotage was the key constraint on getting the library open.

"We've had a team of senior students helping out in the library. Kelly is suggesting we use them as guides to show Year 7 students around; then when they've practised a bit, they can show the rest of the senior students around. Any thoughts?"

"Can I join the Year 7s?" One of the new teachers, Josie, stuck up her hand. "I'm new too."

"Great idea," Mick said.

"Hard to operate without a functioning library. When will you be fully operational?" the Head of English, who'd offered zero assistance despite a personal request from Mick, was happy to play killjoy.

"We've got some issues to sort. With the council library staff getting clearance to come on board in the last week, we'll do better. Although, we're unlikely to open this week, we're doing our damnedest to get students and the community in by next week."

"Thanks, Mick." Dom rose to his feet. "We appreciate

the update. Given the failures, I think the conversation is more suited for an executive discussion rather than this meeting."

"Not sure I agree." Playing Ms. Congeniality, Mick pretended Dom's comment was an invitation to debate the topic, when Dom had intended to silence him. "For now, I think it should be a standing item on the general staff agenda. Can you organise that please, Bev?"

The secretary nodded.

"We'll have a lot of information to impart in the coming weeks, and that way everyone can ask questions and hear the answers. But extra executive support would be appreciated. When's the next meeting?" Not a question Mick should have to ask. Dom should have just said—
"Executive meetings are every Tuesday, or Thursday at ten in the morning or three in the afternoon or bloody midnight."

Even if Dom wasn't guilty of corruption, he was unfit to be a principal. He should be asking for volunteers to get the library open sooner. Instead, he seemed content to let Kelly take the flak for any failures. Mick hated himself for the mindless smile he plastered on his face.

* * *

Sitting in the air-conditioned hall, Kelly could add a few other qualities to Mick's quiet authority. He'd told her his side of the Hay story, what that cold, windy night in a deserted garage had cost them both, then had borne witness to its lingering tail by bringing her out of her nightmare. He listened to the council librarians, talked to the kids who were helping out, and provided practical help to her, despite grappling with his own workload.

He'd also recognised she'd be a whole lot more comfortable alone in a large library with Boo nearby. No fuss, no self-congratulation. *"Take Boo."*

Mick's performance with Dom's coffee had shifted the vibe in the room. The pleasant, softly-spoken new deputy had roared like a lion, and the secretary—Maria—had hidden a smile behind her hand. Kelly guessed she usually drew the short straw for Dom's maid's duty.

Now Mick was making it crystal clear that Ayesha Patel had done an outstanding job, and she—Kelly Steele—was a senior departmental official who'd volunteered to help the school out. From the confused looks on some faces, praise for the sisterhood was an alien beastie. Kelly appreciated the gesture.

"Hasn't he worked out that regional office won't hear his brown-nosing? We run our own ship," muttered a male voice—the Head of Maths—behind her, eliciting a few snorts.

Kelly remained silent. Almost everyone in this room was new to her. For the time being, she'd file impressions, put faces to names and departments. An all-male executive. She remembered the cluster of males at the official handover, hadn't considered that Ayesha was the only ranking female on staff. Technically, she and Stephanie should have been in the executive introductions. Stephanie's exclusion could be due to the small size of the music department.

Kelly glanced in Dom's direction to find his gaze on her, benign, but she sensed calculation, and wished she'd brought Boo along, if only to sort out the goodies from the baddies.

Dom's attention shifted to Mick, and he laughingly interrupted him "… more suited to an executive discussion." *Failures, unfortunately*—Dom was still muttering sanctimonious claptrap when Ayesha had left weeks ago, and he hadn't lifted a finger to get work on the library underway. Dom Ellis was the cause of the library's failure, and he was running an executive committee he'd excluded Kelly from.

Kelly whipped off a quick message:

Staff meeting confirming first impressions from last year.

Cryptic if a stranger picked up her phone, but clear to the sisterhood. Dom Ellis was not on the side of the angels.

*Housemate demonstrating an iron will in a velvet glove. Wish I
hadn't left Boo in the library.*

Kelly was still fuming when the library closed. Dom's high-handed behaviour had seriously pissed her off. Although, Dom was generous with his animosity, almost any woman was a worthy recipient. Dom exercised contempt with the kind of subtlety that had you questioning your judgement.

"Dom's behaviour this morning was inexcusable—" Mick said, backing away from the front door when Kelly barrelled through, Boo at her heels.

"To me, to you, to Stephanie, and I suspect all those present who'd like to know when executive meetings are scheduled so they can feed items for discussion up the food chain."

"Agreed, and at the risk of raising a touchy subject, you didn't seem really comfortable with Dom on that first afternoon in my office. Why?"

He'd noticed, but had saved his question until now.

"Is that the question you were going to ask me the other night?" Kelly started for the house.

"Maybe."

She shot him a sideways glance.

"Yeah.

"There was a party after the official handover of the library last year. It was a room at the back of the pub. Pretty crowded, got pretty rowdy after a while. Some of it was usual end-of-year letting off steam, but later in the evening it got uncomfortable." She picked up speed.

"Slow down." He rested a hand on her arm—a brief, powerful connection, and she dropped back to her usual walking pace. He might look relaxed, but he was paying close attention. "In what way?"

"As the guest of honour, I felt I had to hang around until the end. A lot of married teachers had left, most of the executive were still there. A few of the remaining women looked a bit too sloshed for what I'd seen them drink, a few of the men looked to me like they were wandering as a pack. Someone—I couldn't identify who—groped me."

"Did you call them out?" Interesting first question.

A trained investigator's first question?

"'Get your fuc … ing hands off me' is pretty direct." Kelly lifted her hair off her neck and let it drop. "No embarrassment, no apology, nothing. I left immediately."

"Did you think of pressing charges?"

"What do you think?" She let Boo through the front gate. When Mick remained silent, she sighed. "For about five seconds. We'd moved from official to unofficial function, the drinks were flowing freely, there was a crush, I'd have needed CCTV to support my claim."

"And a cop who'd listen," Mick said.

"Yes." She followed him down the hall. "And that's unfair to whoever's in charge here. As bad as calling Hay, bumfuck or Abbadon."

"Abbadon works on lots of levels. Water?" He opened the fridge.

"Please." She dropped into a chair.

"Ice?"

"Not for me."

He passed her a glass, added ice to his own. "So Dom's behaviour this morning didn't surprise you?"

"It disgusted me." She made no effort to censor her remarks, confident that in this Mick agreed with her. "He reminds me of why I was going to be a lawyer."

"I thought that was to screw every bent cop in Sydney, NSW, Australia, maybe the World."

"How did you guess I had my sights set on the UN?" Kelly glanced at him again. He met her gaze. "You're smiling. And you'd probably be happy if every bent copper in the universe turned purple overnight—easily identifiable."

"Purple's a good colour."

"My interests expanded. I decided that misuse of public office to oppress and exploit is what I hate."

"And you think Dom fits that description?" He trailed a finger through the condensation on his glass.

"Are you collecting evidence?"

"I'm having a conversation with my housemate."

"Then I'm reserving my opinion about Dom, but leaning that way."

"What changed your mind about law?" Now, he sounded curious.

"It was a who."

"Arabella?"

"The day I arrived Bella told me she had one rule. 'You do not, under any circumstances, desecrate a book.' I asked if she was for real. She was gimlet-eyed. So I asked if she expected me to understand the word 'desecrate.'"

"Bet she had an answer." He was laughing at her, and at Bella's parenting skills, in a way that said he appreciated Arabella Steele. Bella was worthy of appreciation.

"'I'm sure you do,' Bella said, 'If not, I expect you to learn.'" Kelly smiled at the memory.

"Doesn't seem like too bad a rule."

"Day two, she said she had another rule. I said what happened to one. Rule two stated that Sunday afternoons were exclusively for reading. The only interruption allowed—to this day—is the delivery of a Devonshire tea from The Tea Cosy."

"What did you have to read?"

"Anything I liked. I said I'd like two scones and preferred raspberry jam. Bella said fine."

"Mum and my sisters are big readers. They never bribed me with scones and jam and cream. Unfortunately. My oldest sister would sit on me to keep me quiet. I'm guessing that wasn't the end of Arabella's rules."

"One a day." Talking about her adoptive parent brought Bella into the room.

"Did they all relate to books and reading?"

"Pretty much."

"I reckon I'd like Arabella."

"A lot of people think she's eccentric."

"Give me another rule. Maybe we could try them with the kids on detention here."

"Bella gave me an iPad for my birthday the year they released iBooks and insisted we set up share family purchases so I could access all the books she bought. I was twenty-three, barely earning, so it was an incredibly generous gift. *Another* incredibly generous gift. Charlie was the first. By then a smart comeback had become our routine. I asked if she'd test me on her books over dinner. Only if I wanted to discuss them." Kelly paused. "My turn, I have a question for you."

"Ask." In the chair opposite her, he was a relaxed companion.

"Does Dom Ellis know you're an ex-cop?"

"Planning to tell him?" His switch to wary was instantaneous.

"Haven't you been listening to me?" Kelly regretted that suspicion had joined them at the table, when they'd negotiated a peace deal after her nightmare. "Answer the question."

"No."

"Roslyn appointed you, Roslyn knows you're an ex-cop, and you have that permanently alert air. Why send an ex-cop here"—Kelly held up a hand, when he opened his mouth—"and keep that information from the principal?"

"People don't like ex-cops around, almost as much as serving cops. Roslyn might have been allowing me the chance to be judged for myself?"

"True. I checked the names at the local cop shop before agreeing to come here."

"A healthy self-protective action if you didn't know George had left the force."

"No one will learn you're an ex-cop from me. And I for one wouldn't object to you applying some of your investigative skills to Mr. Ellis and his mates."

* * *

She was a total honey. Mick was enormously grateful she'd made it to adulthood, not only without self-destructing, but strong and independent and able to forgive. And she had his back, a strange sensation, when he was the one trained to protect. He welcomed her confidences, not sure if it was her nightmare, their shared runs, their successful partnership on the library, or just sharing a domestic space, but they'd moved beyond their truce. Her report from a trusted friend in Sydney had helped that. Independent vindication of what he'd told her, but he reckoned they'd have got here on their own.

She was the first woman Mick had no secrets from, apart from family. *Almost* no secrets. His pursuit of Dom wasn't his secret to share.

"So, if anyone asks, you and I met for the first time here in Tullamore?"

"Because it apparently needs two people to replace Ayesha Patel, who without warning abandoned a project she's spent years developing." Kelly was also smart and inching closer to working out his role in Tullamore.

Kelly's story about being groped was consistent with what she'd told Roslyn and the other details in the dossier. Dom allowed, or encouraged, a culture of toxic masculinity exercised by a small group with immediate impact on individual female staff and a corrosive impact on long-term staff morale.

Hard to pin down. Mick had finally gained access to recruitment records, ostensibly to look at the new staff, but he'd checked the records for the recent executive arrivals. Dom had supervised recruitment, apparently with an independent panel, but Dom had controlled the short list. Mick had fed that information back to Roslyn. Someone in Roslyn's office was checking hiring decisions in Dom's previous schools.

Too slow. It was taking too long. Mick had an itchy feeling on the back of his neck that he was being watched, rather than the other way around.

CHAPTER EIGHT

On Wednesday morning, Mick dropped into the library and ran Kelly to earth in her office. She was finishing up a call. "Any luck?" He sat opposite her.

"We're supposed to be leading this, not the council. Currently they're offering two full-time staff, while we have me. We need a full-time school librarian to replace me. More than one, for the school to meet its share of the workload." She leaned back in the chair, stretching her hands over her head. Her waist-length short-sleeved button-up shirt stretched with her.

Okay, she had curves. Excellent curves. Curves Mick now followed on his morning runs and saw in his dreams.

"Ayesha mentioned that she started requesting additional library staff around June last year." She lowered her arms.

"Haven't found any record of that. But I've only looked at recruitment requests for last term last year and first term this year." He'd have to check back further. "It makes sense she'd start earlier."

"We'll be lucky to get anyone if we advertise now." She scrubbed her face with her hands, her fatigue evident in the strain in her eyes.

"We might find some retired teachers, even English or History teachers would probably work short-term. I haven't had time to study the timetable in detail yet, but we might find some slack. What about on the community side? I'm meeting the council CEO tomorrow."

"Three full-time is a fairly basic load in a community library. That's if we open from say ten a.m. to five p.m. Monday to Wednesday, ten until seven on Thursday and Friday, plus noon to five p.m. on Saturday, and ten until one on Sunday. We could probably have a day off while we're starting, but we'd want to build up to seven days reasonably soon."

"So, we're competing with the council for the same available staff?"

"I don't see any competition." She scowled.

"Shared costs, staff and responsibilities are on the agenda for my meeting with the CEO."

"Rather you than me."

"I could take you with me." He grinned. "No? Any other ideas?"

"I'll check the local child care centres for part-timers looking for more work. Although they're usually scrabbling for staff too. We could audition for a storyteller. Mums are always with their bubs for story time. We could pay for the mandatory working with children police check for the right person. That lets us expand story time and take pressure off our librarians."

"Our biggest problem is still team leader." If Mick gave Roslyn the answers she needed, he could be gone by the end of term one. Same as Kelly. Although that didn't guarantee Ayesha's return. "Your work hours aren't sustainable."

"I'll talk to my boss. Maybe there was someone who applied for my Sydney job, who'd be interested in taking this on for a year to build their CV."

"Sounds like a long shot." Mick stretched his arms above his head, and noticed that her gaze followed the action. Was she interested in him? As a man, as a lover? The thought made his body tighten. "Let's leave it for tomorrow night"—after he'd checked whether Ayesha had followed through on recruitment—"after I've spoken to the CEO. Have you spoken to Ellen or Maeve?"

"I wanted to check with you first, but I've scheduled a mini library staff meeting for Friday morning. Do you think you can make it?" She rose to her feet.

"I'll be there. Maeve or Ellen will have a better idea than either of us about the talent in town." Mick followed her to the door. "I'll see you after school."

"What about Dom?" Her soft question was innocent but loaded. "I'm still trying to convince myself that cockup not conspiracy is the reason we're so far behind."

Her expression was more challenging. *Correct me if I'm wrong.*

"Not to take the current snafus with staff, shelf-stocking, and internet connection personally," she muttered.

"They started before you arrived." It was getting harder not to simply confess Mick agreed with her, and that he was investigating anomalies.

"That's why I'm working on not taking it personally. Plus, I know, like me, you're working your butt off to make this work."

If Dom was intent on proving the library was beyond Ayesha's or Kelly's ability to manage, it might not matter how hard they worked.

* * *

"Does thinly sliced steak on stir fried vegetables and rice work for you tonight?" Mick swallowed his mouthful of beer.

"Do you have a recipe memory bank?" she asked. "You trot out different meals without ever consulting a recipe book. And they're all better than I can produce. Remind me to send your mother and sisters a thank you note."

Kelly couldn't drag her stare from his throat.

Get a grip, Kel.

Adam's apples are not that interesting, but her gaze strayed to his body when he wasn't looking. When he played tag with Boo in the yard, when he moved through the library stopping to talk to Ellen and Maeve, when he ran beside her in the mornings. Strayed, and lingered more and more.

"You're still working." He gestured to the computer she'd placed on the end of the kitchen table. "Is that your agenda for tomorrow's library meeting?"

"Yes." Kelly twisted the computer to share her screen. "My aim is to finalise details with Ellen and Maeve before briefing everyone at the full school staff tomorrow afternoon."

With classes back, staff meetings had returned to their regular Friday afternoon timeslot; staff meetings that gravitated to social gatherings at the pub.

Not your problem, Kelly.

He scanned it quickly. "Looks good. Maeve mentioned Susie Morgan this morning. What do you think?"

"That we're very lucky Susie had a craving to move to the country to retire but is struggling to meet new people. Except for Maeve, who goes out of her way to be friendly, and who has a sharper eye for talent than our illustrious principal."

"I'm not sure Maeve's made up her mind about me," he murmured. "By the way, I've invited Rob Chan, the local copper, to meet the team and approve the security."

Kelly rolled her eyes. "Is he going to approve Boo?"

"Not his job. I've had Ralph check the IT connections via video linkup with the company that installed the system. Make sure we have no glitches. Boo's Plan B." He fondled Boo's ears, and Kelly's damn dog looked adoringly at him. "Tell me the plan."

"Pretty much what we told teachers last week. A slow start. Use the senior students who helped stock the library to induct Year 7, show a few of the teachers around." Kelly adjusted her plans daily, sometimes hourly. Each new setback required a rejigging of priorities.

"Slow works."

"I also want to open to the primary schools. Again, maybe some bigger groups and story time as their first experience or a play with the computers. I've lined up a meeting with the three local primary school principals later tomorrow morning to ask what they've been thinking or would like to happen. Is that okay?"

"Do you need help with the principals?" He downed another mouthful of beer, but she wasn't distracted this time. Much. He was offering help, despite not having a spare minute in his day. He was a good boss, a good housemate. Maybe it was time to admit he might be a good man?

"I'm good. The council CEO rang me after your meeting. He's been chatting with Maeve and Ellen. We figured the community can have access from two p.m. until seven p.m. Wednesday through Friday the first week. We can't open this weekend, but will need to do a few hours on both Saturday and Sunday as soon as possible."

"You're not working sixty-hour weeks. That's not viable."

"This week it's a necessity. But I take your point." And his concern made Kelly's insides go squishy. "The CEO said you'd agreed to schedule a full management board meeting next week. He's used to deferring to Ayesha. It's reasonable for one of the school secretaries to set that up for you."

"I'll see what I can do. More water, or would you like some wine now?"

"Wine, please."

"Play nice with the copper. I've met him."

"He has the Mick Jamieson seal of approval?"

"It's harder won than you might think." He set a glass of wine in front of her. "If it counts for anything, you've got it. I wasn't sure we'd make it."

"What? Open the library, or maintain our peace?"

"Both. Thank you for that."

Kelly had always struggled to accept praise, but winning Mick's changed something inside her. Having both been battle-scarred, they each knew the value of true praise.

Rob Chan, senior Tullamore police officer, was friendly, polite, and when he'd finished following Ralph around the library, wandered back to where they were having their meeting.

"Care to join us for a bit, Rob?" Mick beckoned the man over. "We can offer pastries and a cup of tea?"

Kelly kicked him under the table. *Let the copper walk out the door. He's done what he came for.*

"I bought too many," Mick added, rising to his feet to grab another chair, or maybe to escape another kick.

"A cup of tea would be welcome." The cop came forward with his hand outstretched. "We also haven't met, Ms. Steele. I'm Sergeant Chan."

Kelly rose, plastering a pleasant smile on her face. Mick's turn to roll his eyes.

"Hi." She took the policeman's hand. "Please call me Kelly."

"I'm Rob. There's a lot of excitement from a lot of people about the library opening." He took the chair offered. "Hi, Maeve, Ellen. Nice to meet you again, Susie." The wretched man knew his community well. "So, it's all systems go?"

"Almost," Kelly confessed.

"Can I help?"

"If you've got a few hours spare each week to read stories to pre-schoolers," Maeve said.

"Really?" Rob sat up straighter.

"You sound interested, mate," Mick teased.

"I bet my wife would be. Our youngest starts school this year, and she's missing having little ones underfoot all day." Rob was growing more enthusiastic by the minute.

"Has she done any storytelling before?" Kelly asked.

"A bit in Sydney, when we had our first daughter. With three, plus supporting my move here, it's been hard." He took a pastry from the plate Mick thrust toward him. "She's done some drama training, if that helps?"

"Sound perfect," said Maeve, with an innocence that didn't deceive Kelly for a second. Maeve thrived on matching people to tasks.

"I could ring her now?" Rob had his phone in his hand in seconds. "She could probably come by and meet you today."

"That would be great." Expectant looks from around the table told Kelly she was the only person hesitating to employ the policeman's wife. Okay. No harm talking to the woman. "We're prepared to pay for the police working with children check for the right candidate."

"Beth's still current from volunteering at the child care centre." Rob punched in the number and asked the question. "Will midday suit you?"

"Make it two if you can. I'm seeing the primary school principals at midday," Kelly said. Beth Chan sounded too good to be true.

Beaming, Rob finished the call. "That's great. Glad I was tempted by the pastry, but I should get back."

"Have another," Mick offered.

"One's enough." Rob pushed himself to his feet. "Thanks. I'll catch you later.

There was a moment's silence after he left.

"That went better than expected," Maeve said, winking at Kelly.

"You knew his wife would be interested?" Kelly asked.

"Let's say, I thought there was a strong chance."

"Has anyone ever said you're a marvel, Maeve?" Mick stared at the librarian.

"A gal never gets tired of genuine compliments."

Giggles ran around the table.

Housemate invited local top cop to meeting. Wife's a reader.

Volunteered to do tiny tots book group. Boo gave ticks of approval.
It's finally coming together. We open on Monday.

At the school staff meeting later that afternoon Kelly reflected on the achievements of the last few weeks. Peace with a past that had haunted her for too long, and a library, which against all odds, was about to open. Both of those victories owed something to the man standing at the front of the room.

In two weeks, she'd learned Mick did what he said he'd do. She understood the painstaking work and time needed to build credibility in any role. For someone like herself, sitting in a head-office role and largely invisible to schools, making sure she delivered what she promised was essential to her professional relationships. Doing, not talking, was also central to her personal relationships—that's how she knew Bella loved her.

The flip side of her growing respect for Mick was endorphins on the loose. Sex and running were *not* the same, but she had to repeatedly remind herself not to simply ogle Mick's physique. She wanted to climb all over his muscled, taut, hot body and let what happened naturally happen. Perhaps not in the staff meeting.

She glanced around. She never perved on men.

Well, occasionally she did, purely from an aesthetic point of view, not because of intense personal interest.

Her problem was she'd come to like Mick, admired that he'd remade himself, respected his goals, and saw him live them every day in the way he treated students, staff, Boo, even strangers in the street with respect. He had a genuine interest in who they were, rather than constantly weighing up how he could use them.

Right this second, she respected how he was dealing with Dom's obstruction.

"Dom, we have three items from this meeting for executive consideration. The council CEO is keen to move forward on staffing and management. Can we schedule a meeting?"

"I'll call the CEO, have a chat. I think you're over-engineering things. There'll be a simple solution." Dom spouted more weasel words.

Right, and you have that simple solution. Kelly wanted to scream with frustration.

Dom waved a hand. "I think that's about it for today. It's been a long week."

Longer for some than others. Kelly thought of the energy-sapping days she and Mick were putting in to keep the library moving forward until Dom could schedule his chat with the CEO. She was becoming robotic—rise, run, shower, go to work heigh-ho, work-work-work, home, a meal, then collapse comatose into bed. It wasn't sustainable. It also wasn't conducive to starting an affair.

Whoa! Who said anything about an affair?

"Anyone interested, please feel free to join me for a drink at our regular watering hole." And so ends another week in Dom's kingdom.

At least Kelly wouldn't be returning to the library tonight. Thank all the little fishes in the deep blue sea. An early night with just Mick and Boo for company. Maybe they'd watch a movie, make popcorn. She bet he could make the best popcorn.

"Kelly." Mick caught her at the door. "I'm going to the pub. I'll probably stay for a few drinks, maybe a meal."

"Sure." Although she wasn't sure at all.

* * *

Mick was ready to hogtie Dom and lock him into a room with the council CEO, except he'd discovered the man frequented Dom's pub. Had they agreed on a go-slow, and Mick was the only one not in the loop?

I'm becoming paranoid.

But his searches of the files and his attempts to coax

gossip from other staff members had so far yielded zilch. Mick had noted Dom's delays and prevarications in his diary. The staff meeting minutes would show delayed decision-making, but with two weeks down, it was still possible for Dom to excuse his failings as teething problems or the inability to get everyone in the room at the same time.

Hence, Mick's second Friday at the pub. When he'd rather be curled up on the sofa at the house with Kelly on the first night they'd be home by six o'clock all week.

Kelly's expression when he'd told her what he was doing had betrayed … confusion, disgust?

I'm here for a job.

A job Kelly would endorse if she knew.

Mick followed Dom and a few others to the pub. Bought the first round. Despite his earlier defence of Kelly, he still played big, boofy, ambitious, but not-too-smart bloke whenever he found himself in Dom's company. Tonight he let the conversation about sport and general school hassles roll over him. The council CEO did drop by their table, but Dom distracted him with talk about the progress of a local golf tournament. The council event was a fundraiser to improve community amenities.

Dom was good. Mick had to score him high points for convincing the male community leaders he was a great guy. So far, the womenfolk of Tullamore had remained silent.

With a few more rounds of drinks, talk became looser.

"Ever consider Kelly might be a plant from head office?" Dom signalled the bar staff for a fresh drink.

"Whoa!" Mick jerked back in his chair. "What sort of plant?"

"Don't know, really. Just a thought. Ayesha was a bit evasive when I tried to pin her down on the library before she left." Dom leaned forward conspiratorially. "To be honest, I couldn't believe the mess she left."

"You think head office, through Kelly, might be investigating Ayesha?"

"A few of Ayesha's decisions are worth investigating."

Dom made a clucking barnyard animal sound. "But she's done a great job over the years. I, for one, wouldn't want to see her name tarnished."

"What sort of decisions? I inherited the mess. And to be blunt, we're not fully sorted yet."

"But you open on Monday." Dom nodded when the barman brought his drink. "Ayesha's relationship with the builder hasn't done any real damage."

"Ayesha was involved with the builder?" Mick let speculation seep into his voice.

"There were rumours. But the building's passed all checks, so it's no longer an issue."

"Kelly hasn't mentioned anything."

"She's not in touch with Roslyn Morales?" Dom stared into his drink. From the smell, he'd shifted to rum and cola.

"From what I can see, she's desperate to prove she was the right choice for the head office job." *Forgive me, Kelly.* "Been working her butt off."

Dom laughed. "Yeah, well. And we've had a string of bad luck. That Maeve is quick. I was on the point of making Susie an offer, when I saw Maeve hustle her into the council offices."

More bullshit. But Mick kept that thought to himself, excusing himself to get some air. He reached the hallway to the bathrooms and leaned back against the wall, closing his eyes to suck in fresher air. A body bumped into him. Instinctively, he reached out his hands to steady whoever it was.

"Steph?" he asked. "Are you oaky?"

"Fine," she mumbled. "Need bathroom." She freed herself and wove down the hall toward the women's toilets.

Mick made his way back to their table in the bar, with Stephanie returning a few minutes later, her face pale, her skin covered with a sheen of sweat. Mick's hands fisted under the table.

"Want company on the walk home, Steph? I'm going your way," he asked, keeping his tone neutral.

She looked at him for a long time, then nodded.

"Night all," Mick called. "Anyone else heading out?"

"So soon?" Dom smiled. "Goodnight, Steph. Don't do anything I wouldn't do." He turned back to the table, missing the stunned look on Stephanie's face.

Mick waited until they were outside to ask questions. "Are you okay?"

"Fine." She crossed her arms defensively and turned away.

Forty minutes later, Mick let himself into the dark house and tiptoed down the hall before climbing into bed—alone. Mick resented the evening he'd spent in the pub. He'd have preferred to be back here with Kelly and Boo. What did that say about him?

Dom had suggested Ayesha was corrupt without making a single allegation. Mick recognised the type. Ascribe your actions to others, tarnish their reputations to protect your own. Had there been maladministration over building contracts? Or was that a rabbit hole Dom wanted to send Mick down? He'd start searching those records next week.

The more disturbing element was pumping Mick for info about Kelly. Dom had a history with Ayesha, so he might resent her success, or fear she had some dirt on him. Sabotaging the library made sense in that context, coupled with plausible deniability for any mistake. Kelly had attracted Dom's animosity, and Mick had failed to neutralise it.

The end of week two, and already Mick wanted to escape.

CHAPTER NINE

"I don't want to talk work this morning." Mick remained in the doorway. A cold shower after their run hadn't improved his mood.

"Drinking with the staff sour you for the topic?"

"Dom refused to discuss work specifics with me, although he encouraged the new teachers to download about their classroom problems." He crossed to the sink.

"Providing support?" She leaned her hips against the counter beside him.

"More a shoulder to lean on," Mick replied, with more sarcasm than he'd intended. Kelly would notice sarcasm, just like she'd noticed his grumpiness the week before.

She nudged him with her hip.

Glory be to the angels.

"Yet his drinking companions wake up grumpy every time. I'm sensing a pattern here. Any women stay to the bitter end?"

"A few, including Stephanie Bryant."

"Don't keep me in suspense." She waved a hand in a circular gesture. Please continue.

"Tired and emotional is the polite term. Plastered is closer to the truth."

"Ayesha liked Steph, saw her as a bit of an ally. Both females in an increasingly male-dominated senior staff. She didn't mention a problem with alcohol."

"I offered to walk Steph home. We made it to the car park, and the council CEO's car pulled up. They live a few doors away. Said they'd see Steph got home. I think she and the CEO's wife are a bit friendly."

"All's well that ends well." Now who was doing sarcasm?

Only the women at the gathering seemed unable to handle a few drinks. That was what Kelly had said about the launch after-party. A pattern? Mick would file that with the other information he was collecting.

By Thursday of week three, Dom's endless, plausible excuses about why no action had been taken on library recruitment had set Mick's teeth on edge. He wandered across to the library. Kelly stood on the steps while kids tumbled out the door. The bell had just rung, signalling a change of period.

"Hi."

"Hi yourself." She smiled. And his mood instantly improved.

"I thought I'd do another walkthrough now if that's okay."

"Be my guest. I'll be upstairs if you need me for anything. C'mon, Boo."

"Hi, Maeve. Any sense of community reaction to the library yet?"

"Most are pleased. They like having the kids around."

A scream pierced the air. *Kelly*. Mick took the steps two at a time. Boo's bark reassured him she wasn't undefended. Still, his heart hammered and adrenalin surged through his body. Maeve and Ellen were behind him, but slower.

"Kelly, where are you?" He faced rows of shelves.

"Second row on the right." She didn't sound like herself. Mick rounded the shelf faster than cop training recommended. He allowed himself a quick threat assessment—an upturned box, books at odd angles, and a rogue step stool out of position. Seeing Kelly curled on her side, her face twisted in pain sliced through him. Boo stood at her head. Mick dropped to his knees beside her. "Are you okay?"

"I'm stupid."

"We both know that's not true. Where do you hurt?"

"My pride." She rolled into a sitting position. "Sit, Boo." The dog dropped on his haunches.

"My mum's strategy is to kiss every ache better." He was babbling because she was safe. "Not sure it ever works." Mick's heart was settling back into its normal rhythm. "I need to check."

Her eyes met his, and she bit her lip before nodding permission.

"I'm guessing you were carrying, rather than trolleying, a box of books and tripped over the stool."

"Damn thing was in the wrong place."

"I'd swear they've been programmed to be out of place," Mick agreed. "Which leg?"

"Right." She bent forward, rubbing her ankle. She chose skirts now that school was officially open—straight, finish-above-the-knee denim skirts in various colours. This apple green skirt had ridden up her thighs, and Mick was treated to bare skin and a glimpse of white knickers. He closed his eyes.

I will not look.

"Let me." He ran his hand down her bare calf. Her skin was silky soft; a surprise given he'd watched her muscular legs eat kilometres. He loved those legs. He'd always liked the notion that the knee bone was connected to the thigh bone, and the thigh bone was connected to the hip bone, and heaven could be found between a woman's spread legs. His fingers trembled.

Steady boy.

Lingering wasn't an option despite the temptation.

"Sneaker off." He removed the shoe and short sock. "How does that feel?"

"Okay." Then Kelly waved Maeve away. "I'll fix it in a minute. You have enough to do."

"And I thought my daughter was a terrible invalid." Maeve stacked books back in the box.

"I'm not an invalid."

"Then stop making a fuss over a little hurt"—Maeve grinned—"and let Mick check it out."

"I make that a majority vote," Ellen added, tucking the footstool back into its alcove.

"Wiggle your toes." Mick sat back on his haunches.

She wiggled.

"I'll rotate your ankle. Let me know if anything hurts." He rotated her ankle one way, then the other.

She winced.

"Some swelling, but it's not a bad sprain."

"It's nothing."

She was flustered and annoyed. Flustered by his touch? That made two of them. Holding hands briefly didn't rate against having a hand on the back of her foot and a palm around her ankle. Strong and shapely, and he almost said the words tangled on the tip of his tongue aloud.

"Want me to ask Maeve's opinion of that?" He pushed to his feet.

"I'm conscious, physically fit, and able to look after myself." Kelly rolled to her hands and knees, then tried a yoga push back onto her feet. "Ow!"

"I rest my case." Mick bent and scooped her into his arms, then held firm expecting her to fight. He could get used to having her in his arms, and the insight stunned him. Cuddling, caring, keeping. "You know the drill. RICE— rest, ice, compression and elevation."

"Good lad," Maeve said. "We'll set her up in her office. There's enough paperwork to keep her going for the rest of the day, and you can keep your leg up."

"Light exercise is recommended," she grumbled.

"If you're very good, you can walk home." Mick deposited her in her desk chair.

"Watch it, buddy."

"Afraid I can't, even though it's a very shapely ankle. But I've got work to do," Mick teased.

He could joke because her injury was minor, but her scream had scared him shitless. She hadn't screamed in Hay. Though both her silence then and her scream now had sliced through him, shredding his usual calm.

* * *

"Thanks for dinner." Kelly studied Mick's efficient, toned back bent over the sink. Playing nursemaid didn't seem to bother him, while being injured was akin to being trapped for her.

"A bit more gratitude and less resentment in your tone might convince me you mean that." Mick finished stacking the dishwasher. He'd cooked dinner for her on Thursday night, after her accident, and again tonight.

"I can stand, I can walk, and I can run. And don't look at me like that. I hate being helpless."

"You're a long way from helpless, but it makes sense to pace yourself. This is something I can do."

"You said I could move to the running track tomorrow." Kelly hated when she sounded whiny.

"You don't like the sports oval?"

"It's okay for rehabilitation."

It was perfect for rehabilitation.

She'd walked, then jogged a few laps, while he'd run. Boo had loved dancing between the two of them. And Boo had loved the drive. Mick had transferred Boo's car harness to the back seat of his car and ferried all three of them for the past two days.

"I prefer morning runs, and I like the streets," she admitted.

"The freedom, the potential for a surprise?" he asked.

"I can change direction. I don't feel so constrained. You're right. There's an element of surprise, the potential for a new adventure." Now wasn't the moment to discover she liked running with him and Boo.

"Whereas the oval is bog standard boring?"

"Well, it is."

"You're not, Kelly. Bog standard or boring. We'll try the running track tomorrow afternoon. If that works, we'll go back to mornings on the streets."

"Thank you, Mr. Jamieson." But his compliment wrapped around her heart, creating a warm fuzzy feeling.

The soft buzz of her phone woke Kelly on Saturday morning. She groaned and rolled over. It repeated its signal—a chat group. Probably Lucy and Clem demanding news. Boo nudged her.

"Okay, okay. Won't anyone let me sleep in?" Except she'd insisted last night that she wanted her morning run back.

Are you still alive? Kelly read Clem's message. *Does Boo still like housemate?*

Doing long hours, Kelly stated, staring at Boo. No reproach in her pooch's gaze:

And yes, Boo still likes housemate. Yes, housemate has a name.
                    If I tell you, you'll just Google him.

Kelly's phone pinged in fast response. *We've sent you a surprise. Arriving soon.*

Kelly sat bolt upright and stabbed *Call.*

Out of nowhere, the doorbell rang. Boo raced out of the room, barking in welcome. Kelly killed the call, rolled out of bed, and pulled her bedroom door wide.

"I'm looking for Kelly Steele." Bella's crisp, dry voice echoed down the hall.

"You've come to the right"—Mick grabbed Boo's collar when the dog lunged past—"place."

"Hello, Boo." Bella ran her hand across Boo's head.

"Now, sit."

"Bella?" Kelly's mind lurched. Leaving Bella and Mick alone was asking for trouble.

"I'm a surprise." Bella grinned, then jerked a thumb toward Mick. "Does Boo still like 'what's his name?'"

"We've reached an agreement," Mick said. "Name's Mick Jamieson. Can I take your bag?" Unshaven, barefoot, in black cut-off jeans and a faded Midnight Oil tee, he was enough to make Kelly's mouth water even with Bella as a witness. "Would you like a cup of tea, breakfast?"

"Yes to everything." Bella abandoned her overnight bag, strolled down the hall toward Kelly and kissed her cheek. "Are you joining us?"

"Give me five," Kelly said, knowing it was a mistake. Bella could ferret out most secrets in a minute and a half, tops. "Save your cross-examination until I arrive."

Back in her bedroom, Kelly hit the phone:

Not fair to send Bella to check on me.

By the time she'd pulled on shorts and a clean blouse, she had an answer. Pushing her feet into sandals, she typed a new message:

If it was her own idea, why was her first question 'Does Boo still like what's his name?'

She finger-combed her hair while waiting for the ping. The screen lit up with emojis of hearts and flowers.

Kelly tucked her phone in her pocket and jogged to the kitchen, arriving in time to hear Mick's voice.

"Of course you'll stay here. There's plenty of room." Mick placed a teapot in front of Bella, then collected milk and sugar.

"You can't be missing me already. It's only been three weeks." Kelly walked around Bella to take a seat on her other side, planting a kiss on the older woman's head in passing.

"I came to see Boo." Bella poured milk into her tea. "And for a little espionage."

Kelly rolled her eyes. "You're going to embarrass me."

Mick put a mug in front of Kelly. "Tell her what she wants to know. I've heard that stops the worst forms of torture."

"I can't believe this is happening." Kelly lifted the teapot, then set it down with a thunk. "She wants to know who *you* are."

"Mick—short for Michael—Jamieson, youngest of three children. Two sisters. Parents divorced. Dad a copper. Mum a nurse. I'm hoping I take after Mum. Good chance, since my sisters and my maternal grandfather also had a hand in my upbringing." He took a seat at the table and faced Bella. "I first met Kelly seventeen years ago in Hay. My first posting, and my actions that night dishonoured the women in my family and hurt Kelly. I'm sorry for that."

Kelly kept her mouth shut.

"Is that what we'd find in an internet search?" Bella sipped her tea.

"There's a bit more. Ultimately, I cut my losses and resigned from the police force. But I took George Hogan out with me. Would you like me to move to a motel for the night?"

"No." Kelly's response was immediate.

"Kelly's social worker told me there were some inquiries about her. There was a possibility Kelly would be called to testify."

"You never told me." Kelly's imperturbable foster parent had hidden secrets from her.

"Lahn and I talked about it. Whether or not you could refuse. How it would impact you. Would it be better to see George Hogan prosecuted? Neither of us had much confidence he'd be convicted." Bella turned back to Mick. "You withdrew before we had to make any decisions. Before we'd told Kelly. I'd like to thank you for that."

"What?" Bella's little recitation had Kelly's head spinning.

"There's a terrific French-style bakery a few blocks over," Mick said. "Want me to take Boo and get a selection of pastries for brunch?"

"Did Kelly tell you I have a sweet tooth?" Bella patted Kelly's hand.

"She might have mentioned Sunday is high-tea day." He pushed to his feet. "Boo?" he asked.

"Boo, go with Mick." Kelly watched in a daze when Mick took the lead off a hook and clipped it onto Boo. "Go with Mick," she repeated.

In seconds, the kitchen was quiet.

"Do you remember telling me it was your fault?" Bella sipped her tea.

"You said it wasn't." The absolute conviction on Bella's face had steadied Kelly. "That I might have behaved impulsively, even stupidly, but I didn't deserve police abuse."

"Responsibility is a funny thing. Who takes responsibility for actions, who doesn't? The subtle nuances."

"You and your subtle nuances." Kelly nudged Bella with her shoulder.

"Lahn and I agreed we'd tell you if giving evidence moved from a possibility to a likelihood." Bella studied her. "Do you want an apology?"

Kelly's mind teemed with questions, but one surfaced. "Did you know George Hogan was demoted and resigned?"

"No. Neither Lahn nor I could find many details. The police protect their own. Only I'm guessing they didn't count Mick Jamieson as one of their own."

"No, they didn't."

"Did Mick tell you?" Bella's curiosity was understandable.

"I recognised him on the first day. I went for him, threatened to report him to school authorities. He said they knew. He told me a bit. That he'd considered, then abandoned the idea of getting me to testify. Liam told me more."

"Ah." Bella reached for her hand. "I should have

guessed you'd call Liam."

"Liam said the sisterhood would rip his toenails out if they found out he knew and hadn't told them."

"Why haven't you?"

"Because they haven't met Mick. Because I'm still feeling my way. Because I like him. Like what I see of his actions at school."

Is it possible to go from fear to trust in a few weeks?

As a psychologist, Clem would probably have something to say about that, but she wasn't asking Clementine—yet.

"And Boo likes him."

"Boo's never made a mistake." Kelly leaned to rest her head on Bella's shoulder.

"Have you forgiven Mick?"

"He reminded me I said I'd never forgive him."

"A big burden for a young man who already blamed himself."

"I told him I have. I've accepted that we were both young and stupid in different ways, and that he was punished for what he did. Mick said his father is a cop. His father asked him to drop it."

"Idealists carry the worst scars when the people they love or institutions they believe in let them down. Your mother left you a few scars." And Bella wielded words like scalpels, cutting deep to drain the poison.

"Almost impossible to see. Just a bit of incomprehension left." Kelly had thought of her never-really-there mother a few times lately. Maybe triggered by the very different stories Mick told of his mother? Maybe because Mick hadn't shied away from the brutal truth—"*She abandoned you.*"

"Has Mick let the anger and frustration go?" Bella stroked her hair. "Have you let the anger and frustration go?"

"I'm working on it. I know I'm a different person to the teenager who walked in your door. You and Charlie, Lucy and her grandparents, Clem and her foster parents have all made me a different person."

"You've made you a different person."

"How long are you able to stay?"

"Just the one night. I've got a committee meeting on Monday morning."

"Are you going to report to the sisterhood?"

"I'll leave that for you." Bella grinned. "But I'd love to see your library."

"After morning tea, I'll take you and Boo."

Kelly called into the library after she waved Bella off on the bus on Sunday afternoon. She texted Mick that she'd been delayed, then locked herself in her office and called up a video link to Lucy and Clem.

"Why aren't I surprised that you're available?" Kelly tried for sarcasm to hide her complicated feelings. Love was uppermost because they worried about her, a touch of loneliness because they were too far away for a hug, trepidation about what she had to tell them because she wanted them to give Mick a second chance."

"We knew you'd start missing Bella the second she got on the bus, so of course we're available," said Clem.

"She always has the fastest, most plausible excuses." Lucy turned to stare at Clem, because of course they were sharing a screen. "How do you do that?"

"Do you want me to stand up, turn around, and strip down so you can check for injuries?"

"My, my, I had no idea it was so lethal in Tullamore." Clem returned her gimlet stare.

"I put Bella on the bus. She's expecting you both after work tomorrow. She'll provide food and drinks. She didn't take any photos in my presence, but she's sneaky, so I'm not claiming they don't exist." Kelly was holding on to the fact that Bella liked Mick, and Bella would stop Kelly's friends from descending on Tullamore in a pack.

"What sort of photos?" Lucy asked.

"The name of my housemate is Michael Jamieson." Kelly paused. Bella approved of Mick. Kelly approved of Mick, had approved even before Bella gave her tick of approval.

"Boo likes him. We know that bit." Clem waved a hand. "Cut to the chase."

"The name of the young cop at Abbadon Central was Michael Jamieson."

"I thought you didn't know his name." Lucy looked puzzled.

"How did a cop who conducted an illegal strip search get to be a deputy principal in a school with adolescent girls?" Clem was on the warpath.

"Bella likes him." Kelly played her best card.

"That's not an answer," said Lucy.

"Will you listen to an answer with an open mind?" Kelly pushed back.

"Try us." Clem folded her arms.

"Long story short, Mick reported George Hogan to police internal affairs. For a while, he searched for me to give evidence. Apparently, Bella and my social worker knew about that and discussed how to handle it if an official request was made. Mick decided to leave me out of it when things got heavy. George Hogan was demoted and forced out. Liam confirmed his story—"

Lucy interrupted, "Liam's known all along? He hasn't said a word."

"I swore Liam to secrecy." And he'd kept his promise.

Learning to trust that far was another gift from Bella. She'd insisted on introducing Kelly to her male friends, in drawing Kelly into conversations that were both respectful and challenging. Bella had pointed out in subtle and not-so-subtle ways that not all men were arrogant arseholes, but Kelly hadn't really believed love was possible for someone like her until the last few years. Until she'd met Clem's Jamie and Lucy's Niall and the extended Quinn family. She'd learned that enduring love was a reality. Just not for her.

Sex, she understood, although she'd been a late starter there too. Maybe it was time to catch up. She liked Mick, admired him, and fancied him.

Be honest, Kelly Steele, the idea of bouncing his bones has growing appeal.

Except it was already more complicated than that. She was falling for him.

"Liam is my husband's brother and *my* brother-in-law."

"Whom you've very kindly agreed to share with us. And for which we are unendingly, pathetically, obscenely grateful." Clem had unfolded her arms during the telling and now elbowed Lucy in the side.

"I like it when you grovel." Lucy looked smug.

Clem continued, "When you say heavy, you mean vicious. Cops don't take kindly to whistleblowers."

"They don't. Mick was branded a traitor to his own and resigned." Kelly's shoulders slumped. "He said he was young and stupid. Tried to protect me to the best of his ability."

"What did you say?" Lucy asked gently.

"That I was young and stupid too. Wandering a town I didn't know after dark. Insisting on my rights with an old-school copper intent on asserting *his* power in *his* town." Kelly brushed tears from her cheeks, surprised to be crying. "If·I hadn't hightailed it back to Sydney that night, I'd never have met Bella or you two. You're the best things in my life."

"How did you work out it was him?"

"I recognised him. He recognised me. Mick has nightmares too." Kelly hadn't meant to share that.

"And Boo likes him?" Clem was letting her off the hook.

"Boo trusts him."

"We'll be in touch after we grill Bella," Lucy vowed with a smile. "If Bella doesn't have pictures, will you send us one?"

"Maybe. We're making peace, maybe making friends," Kelly confessed.

"If you're happy with that, so are we," Clem said.
An invisible burden lifted from Kelly's shoulders.

CHAPTER TEN

Mick was waiting in the kitchen—their common ground—when Kelly got back from the bus station with Boo. She was dry-eyed but had to be hurting. "Toasted sandwiches for tea tonight. Lots of hot melted cheese."

"That's your idea of comfort food."

He watched Boo cross the room to curl up in the corner looking hopeful. The dog's relaxed pose told him everything would be okay.

"What's yours?" Mick had considered offering her Vegemite toast, the go-to comfort food in his childhood, the meal that soothed many battle injuries. It was still an option.

"Scottish whisky and potato crisps."

"How old were you when you started that?"

"Twenty-eight. It was Bella's idea." She gave a secret smile.

"Do that a lot, do you?" He'd never seen her drink more than a glass or two of wine.

"I didn't know she drank whisky until that night."

"She's not far, Kelly. You can invite her back when she has more time."

"I'm discombobulated because of …" She circled a

finger in the air.

"Air currents? Storm coming? Salt deficiency?"

"From the first minute I met her, Bella wanted me to be strong and independent, and half the time I didn't see the small things."

"I want to hear this story, so what's it to be?" Mick asked. "I go shopping for whisky and crisps or you make do with toasted cheese sandwiches and red wine?"

"Don't go shopping."

"Right answer. Do you want me to feed Boo first?"

The dog's head swivelled in Mick's direction. Letting Mick feed Boo was a different step forward in Kelly trusting him. Mick waited because her trust in every area was a prize worth winning.

She considered him for thirty seconds in silence. "Thank you."

"I bought another present. Should I spell it out?"

"Does it involve a B-O-N-E?"

"Yep, large, cut in half both ways. Should be enough for more than one meal. Why are you looking at me as if I've got two heads? I thought he'd be missing Bella too."

"That's sweet."

"*Sweet?*" He pretended horror. "Let's take all of this to the back porch. Can you get the glasses, please?" Mick collected the marrow bone. Boo shot to his feet. "Outside, Boo." Mick pushed the door open and nudged a chock under it to keep it open. Boo raced ahead of him. Throwing the marrow bone onto the grass, Mick returned to collect a bottle of cabernet merlot. After setting the bottle on the side table, he sank into the swing seat. "I'm beginning to see the point of these things." He patted the place beside him.

"You already planning your rocking chair, grandpa?" She placed the glasses beside the bottle before dropping into the deep cushions of the seat, her arrival setting up a small rocking movement.

"Rocking has its moments," Mick deadpanned. "I have a grandpa."

"Most people start with two."

"Know yours?" He grinned at her when she gave him the evil eye.

"They've never set eyes on me to my knowledge. Tell me about yours."

"I'll make it quick. Mum's dad. He lived in Western Australia but came to Sydney when the case with George Hogan was over, when life no longer made sense. He took me camping. Total isolation. We walked and talked, and walked and talked until I had a plan to do more."

"You haven't asked why I was delayed."

"You're an intelligent adult in control of your own destiny. Isn't that the mantra Arabella taught you?" He opened the bottle of wine, poured some into a glass and passed it to her.

"I stopped in at the library and video-conferenced with the sisterhood." She toasted him with the glass.

"Sounds serious."

"Before I met Bella, I was in a care home."

"You said you shared a room with two girls, Lucy and Clem." He was good at remembering.

"We've been friends ever since. Lucy and Clem were ten, but in some ways more street smart than me. Lucy's grandparents found her. Lucy—Liùsaidh—was named for her granny. Clem—Clementine—was fostered by a lovely couple. Bella, and Lucy and Clem's guardians made sure we visited, until we were old enough to get phones, and we organised ourselves." She nudged him with her shoulder.

They'd made physical contact more since her accident. She'd let him wrap the bandage for the few days she'd needed it, and they didn't go out of their way to step around each other in the kitchen anymore. If one brushed against the other in passing, no biggie. Except Mick wanted to linger, to turn a casual brush into something more intimate.

"You downloaded on them first when you went back to Sydney."

"Yeah. They got the very first heavily expletive-laden

version of my brief stay in Hay."

"And they weren't surprised by what happened to you."

Damn! Would it never change?

"Cops had featured in their lives, but it's not just cops with entitled men in their ranks—witness Dom Ellis. Lucy and Clem already recognised the type. You have to if you want to be able to protect yourself. They're both happily married now to wonderful men."

"Did they pass judgement on me?"

"They're waiting until they see Bella's photos."

"What photos?"

"I didn't actually see her take any, but that doesn't mean she didn't." She pushed the swing with her foot. "We saved our worst expletives for you."

"For months I had this ringing in my ears, even considered seeing a doctor. Should have guessed it was you." Mick took a sip of his wine, enjoying the balmy evening. "I'm glad you told your friends who I am."

He hoped it proved she wasn't ashamed of having forgiven him. The fluttery sensation in his gut—that he'd found a woman who understood him, who knew the worst thing he'd ever done, and was sitting beside him on a swing seat with her shoulder brushing his—was new to him. Liking was a kind of forgiveness, being able to admit to being attracted ratcheted the tension higher. Desire was constant and tougher to handle.

"Tell me another Arabella story."

"First. Thanks for covering for me at the library today, and for lending me your car."

"No problem. Where did you take her?"

"Around the district, an aimless drive, but we ended up at a park on the outskirts of town for a picnic. Sweeping views, big skies, visible heat haze, country silence—she loved it all."

"She's a fascinating woman."

"She is. And the man she found fascinating died in Vietnam. I studied a photo on her sideboard for weeks, until

Bella finally said "Ask," but she's also sneaky."

"That doesn't tally with what you've told me so far."

"Sneaky about her kindness. It took ages for me to realise she rewarded every small victory I achieved. To me they were victories, but I didn't expect anyone else to even notice them." Kelly picked up his hand and traced patterns in the open palm. "I'd been with her three months when Bella asked me to go out after dark to collect some takeaway. I had a tantrum.

"'Geez, hadn't she heard of delivery. Lash out, lady.'

"She said, 'I was afraid to go out after dark alone.'

"I told her it was none of her damn business.

"'Fine,' she said. She'd go alone.

"I felt so small. I screeched every cuss I could think of, while Bella put on her scarf, then her coat and opened the front door. I grabbed the door out of her hand and slammed it shut, then begged her to get delivery.

"'Only if you give me a reason,' Bella said."

Kelly had settled on the figure eight and was drawing figure eight after figure eight in the palm of Mick's hand.

"'Because I'm fucking afraid. Satisfied?'

"Bella booked me into animal service training the next day. I had a choice of three dogs. Charlie chose me."

"You said you had Charlie twelve years."

"Bella and I bawled for days when we had to put him down. Giving me Charlie was an act of love. The whisky and crisps were to mark his passing and our despair."

"Arabella's a woman who knows how to mark the big occasions."

"She's the reason I didn't self-destruct."

"And you hope like hell she knows how much you love her for that."

"I do."

"I'm sure she does. But she's not the only reason. You're stronger than you think, Kelly. Running's a bit of a metaphor. You love the sheer physicality of running, but running also distances you from traumatic events. It's healthy self-protection."

"You didn't run."

"I'm a stubborn son of a gun. But so are you. And 'run' has other meanings—manage, supervise, lead, look after. You're all of those things too."

"You're a good man, Mr. Jamieson," she whispered, seemingly undone by the compliment.

"Arabella sounds like my mum. Mum called a family meeting after things got really hot with Police Internal Review. Mum, my two older sisters, and me. They voted to get a second mortgage on the house to pay my legal costs. The house is Mum's only asset, 'our inheritance,' she used to tease, but they were prepared to put it on the line to help me." Mick shook his head. "I didn't accept."

"Because getting the offer was enough. Sometimes it's easy to know who loves you. It's not always the people you want to love you."

"Ain't that the truth." Mick thought of his father, his ex-girlfriend. "Want a hug?" The words came from nowhere.

Bullshit, Jamieson. You want to touch her, but tonight she needs a hug.

"Maybe." She cocked her head to one side, testing what lay behind the offer.

Don't blow it. He lifted Kelly into his lap, his arms linked loosely around her. After a few moments, she lowered her head to his shoulder. He lifted a hand to massage her nape, sliding his hand under her hair to knead and press away the tightness from weeks of physical exertion.

"You've been hauling too many boxes."

"Finished now," she murmured.

His finger shifted to a caress, a minor adjustment to the symphony of touch he dreamed of, enough for Mick to draw solace from the silkiness of her skin, the angle of her neck, her sigh of pleasure. Her scent teased him, something floral, sweet with a touch of tartness. It suited her.

Her head lifted. "Are you getting me used to you?"

"Is it working?"

"Yeah. I told Bella I'd forgiven you."

She snuggled back down. Thank you, Dog. Her breathing slowed, and after a while, she dozed. He'd never considered how big a gesture of trust it was for a woman to let herself sleep in his arms.

Mick held her, a comfortable weight of relaxed, secure woman. Gazing at the night sky, he tried to name the stars and planets, which were so easily missed in cities where artificial light screened them. He and Kelly had traversed planets and new worlds in the last few days. A pity to wake her.

"Kelly, it's cooling down." He bent his mouth to her ear, maybe took the opportunity to rub his nose against it. "Time to go in."

She sat upright. "I wasn't asleep."

"Of course you weren't. Boo was snoring. Bring your wine." He took her free hand and led her to the kitchen. "Boo, you coming?"

The dog followed, curling up on his mat.

"I like my cheese really melted. Maybe a bit brown." She sat at the table.

"Can do." He made sandwiches while she toyed with the rest of her glass of wine. "Tell me another Arabella story."

"When I finished my first year with her and got good grades, she got me two season tickets to an avant-garde theatre in the city. Said I could take a guest to every show."

"Bet you took her." He grinned.

"Yeah, we both loved it."

Sounds exactly like my mum. The two women would like each other. He was sure.

Whoa! You're getting ahead of yourself, man.

On Friday morning, Mick lingered in the shower, letting the heat pummel his back muscles. He and Kelly and Boo had run farther this morning, as if by tacit agreement, with a sprint for the last half kilometre that had left him invigorated. Her ankle was fully healed. He was smiling for what felt like the first time in days when he re-entered the kitchen. Progress on his task for Roslyn was painstakingly slow and largely unproductive. Old coppers used to say cases could be like this. Nothing, nothing, and then it broke open.

Through her bedroom door, he caught the music in Kelly's soft conversation with Boo.

The lucky dog was present when she stripped off her running shorts and tee, was probably allowed to lick some of the salty sweat from her leg. Not that Mick wanted to lick her leg. Well, maybe a little. Imagining her sweaty, naked body pressed up against the tiles in his bathroom, her legs locked around his hips was jostling for equal headspace with his full-time job. Her passion-infused voice at breakfast and dinner was a turn-on; talking about inter-library loans, digital collections, online classes, and book groups with other schools showed how far gone he was. The words "dewy decimal" could make him drool. He wanted to cover her mouth with his and convert all her creative enthusiasm into—what?

"Did you let me beat you?"

She strolled into the kitchen, dressed in what he now recognised as her work clothes, a skirt and simple cotton shirt. Only her hair was refusing to behave this morning, creating a fluffy halo around her head. Her contrasts appealed to him, her professional approach to her work and her backside in the air when she rolled around on the floor with Boo.

"Nuh. You beat me fair and square." He transferred the milk to the table. "Why did you accept this appointment?"

"You've waited until the end of our fourth week together to ask me that?"

"Ros said you'd accepted the offer. Respect for Ayesha and wanting the library to succeed." He shrugged.

"Two reasons. One—I've recently been confirmed in my job. I know a lot of theory about school/community libraries, but have never set one up pretty much from scratch." She hesitated.

"So this will help your credibility in your state-wide role." He nudged her along. "And two?"

"I've never made more than flying visits to country towns since Hay. It's time to confront the bogeyman."

"Instead, I'm here."

"We're not the same people," she said gently. "Why are you here?"

"My dream—strange word to be using at thirty-eight"—Mick scrubbed his face with his hands, not many people knew this dream—"is to be principal of my own school, to model ethical behaviour and to create a supportive environment." He stopped.

"Go on"—she touched his hand—"I'm interested."

Mick was interested in more than conversation. In part because they could talk about anything and everything—talking their way to intimacy. She'd taken his hand after her nightmare, let him touch her after spraining her ankle, turned to him for comfort after Bella's visit, and his body was primed for more. He just had to convince her sex was the right move for both of them. "To help kids to be their best selves, to respect each other."

"See"—she beamed at him—"we've both left Hay behind."

Mick wanted to think so. But Dom Ellis brought back memories of George Hogan. Except he was ten times smarter and used manipulation and lies to get what he wanted instead of blunt force, making Dom harder to catch. "I've got an idea." He leaned against the kitchen sink, not daring to approach her.

"Gonna share?" She opened the cupboard to reach for Boo's breakfast.

"I think we should both take Sunday afternoon off. We've worked like slaves. We'll be full-on again next week. We both need a break."

"Okay," she drew out the word.

"Not necessarily from each other."

"What's that mean?" She turned to face him.

"Ralph, our IT guy, told me about a quiet spot on the river, not far out of town. It's good for swimming. Dogs off the leash."

"Why?"

"The spot's too far to walk or cycle. Boo needs time off."

"Right. He's had a busy few weeks too."

"He's going to have another busy week next week. What about my suggestion?"

"Boo likes playing with W-A-T-E-R." She smiled.

"A spelling vocabulary of three. Smart dog."

"He has more. I'll tell you sometime."

"That's a yes."

"You're right. We've worked our butts off. My every waking moment is focused on the library. I've become obsessive about it, and I've roped you in. You do know that without you I couldn't have made it happen."

"Thanks, but I would have put money on you getting it open with or without me, if you had to sit in Dom's office until he made the necessary phone calls. I've enjoyed it for the most part. A good way to meet staff and students in a semi-formal setting."

I've enjoyed you.

He wasn't sure she was ready to hear that, or that he more than liked her. Her straight talking, her brain, her deep voice that reached into the spaces between his bones and sinews and soothed in a way he couldn't explain.

"Then we both deserve a picnic."

I'm starting to care for you, and that's … unexpected.

CHAPTER ELEVEN

"Play." Boo waited for her to give the order before the dog joined Mick at the river.

Mick dived in, swimming underwater until he had to reach for air; a test from his teenage years to see how long he could hold his breath. When he surfaced, Boo was at his side. Mick wasn't an expert on doggy expressions, but if asked, he'd say Boo was ecstatic. Only one thing marred the canine's delight. He kept looking over his shoulder to check Kelly was safe.

"C'mon, play with us." Mick called to Kelly.

The sleek one-piece navy swimsuit suited her, the colour changing her eyes, so he could imagine they were blue-black, and the cut announcing "a swimsuit is for swimming," not flaunting body parts. She was demurely alluring, more of an imported Belgian chocolate of the kind he savoured than the cheap look-a-likes at the local market he'd purchased on some desperate nights after a nightmare. You knew the difference from the second you took the first bite. She couldn't have the remotest clue how sexy she looked or she'd have donned layers of terry-towelling bathrobe, like his gran used to.

She'd shaken out the picnic blanket near the edge of the

river, then created a little nest for herself with a cushion at her back. Now, she snuggled down, and the little wriggle to settle herself in position stirred not-to-be-acted-on thoughts. Snuggle rhymed with cuddle, and ... she was closing her eyes.

"You're going to sleep?"

"Maybe." She made herself more comfortable.

Mick groaned, then bent to whisper in the dog's ear. "Go get her, Boo. She'll love it."

The dog headed for Kelly, who should have placed the blanket further from the river if she didn't want marauders. Boo shook himself all over her.

"Hey." Her eyes shot open, then narrowed on Mick.

"I just figured that was Boo's way of inviting you for a swim."

"You encouraged him." She rolled onto her knees. Mick got an unexpected eyeful of milk chocolate curves narrowing to an enticing cleavage before she jumped to her feet.

"The water really is lovely. And neither of us knows when we'll get a free afternoon again."

"No splashing at me." She walked to the edge of the river and dipped a toe in the water.

"Really? Now you're asking for trouble." He grinned.

"Non-negotiable." She waded to mid-thigh, trailing a finger through the water. "This is lovely."

"Yeah." Mick had to agree. A gambolling dog, a relaxed woman, and a sense of freedom—the first time he'd been off duty since his arrival. Far from town, far from potentially watching eyes.

Boo broke ranks first, bouncing over to Kelly's side to plant his paws on her shoulders. She sank into the river and floated backward, Boo paddling beside her.

"Looks like splashing to me," Mick said, skidding his hand across the water.

Her laughter was a surprise, a full-bodied belly laugh coated with the bass tones that underlined her speech. He dreamed of that voice whispering in his ear while he was inside her. Mick wasn't fast enough to avoid her retaliatory wave of water. He sank deep, to disguise his growing arousal, and slipped around to come up behind her. Then flipped water at her from behind.

She spun. "Smart guy."

She was a better-than-average swimmer, ducking and weaving around him underwater and surfacing with her face tilted toward the sky, her joy transparent. The battle was reasonably even-sided until Boo joined the melee.

"Pax," he offered. She clambered to her feet, water dripping from her body and made her way toward the beach. Before she could reach dry land, Mick moved in front of her. "I want to kiss you."

"Is that a warning or a statement?" She cocked her head to one side.

"Invitation. I'm going to put my hands on you. Will Boo be okay with that?"

"I have to be okay with it."

"Goes without saying. You haven't said no yet." Mick took a step closer and lifted his hands to cup her shoulders. He was driving himself crazy second-guessing how she'd react if he kissed her, but he was desperate enough to make the move.

"I'm thinking about it." She curled her fingers around his wrists.

"Gonna have to stop that." He brushed his lips across hers, lightly, enough to get the smallest taste of her, knowing he wanted more, but prepared to go slowly to win that right. "This kind of thing works better when you're not thinking. Your turn."

She lifted a hand to his cheek. "I want to."

"And that surprises you?" He dropped his arms to his sides.

"It should surprise you too." Her hand was warm against his skin, her voice equally warm, trickling possibilities through his mind.

"It does a bit. But I heard your voice before I saw you. You have a beautiful voice, all deep and husky and melt-your-bones luscious. I was congratulating myself that I'd be living with *that voice.*"

"Is that why you shut your eyes when you kissed me?" she teased, settling the flicker of anxiety in his belly about whether he should have taken this step. "It's all about the voice?"

"Did not." Mick turned his face into her hand to kiss the vulnerable spot in the centre of her palm.

"It's happening too fast."

Did she know she'd placed the hand Mick had kissed over her heart? "What's happening too fast, Kelly?"

"Finding common ground, enjoying your company"— she scrunched up her nose, and he wanted to kiss her again—"fancying you like hell." She huffed out a breath.

Thank the stars.

"Me too."

"My turn." Stepping closer, she pressed two fingers to her lips, then pressed them to his.

"More," he murmured against her fingers. He was afraid to move, to change the mood, to scare her away.

"Like this?" She ran a finger over his eyebrow, gentle rather than tentative, an exploration. He wanted her to explore every square inch of him. She followed up by brushing her thumbs across his cheekbones, pressing skin against bone to test his strength.

"More."

With a soft sigh, she traced his top lip with her tongue, a sensual sweep of lush heat that unleashed a yearning, when he'd anticipated raw desire. She brushed a light kiss to the corner of his mouth, then moved to his lower lip—taking her sweet time. Lingering longer than he had. Long enough for him to raise his hands to her hips, to anchor them both. Long enough for him to feel her relax, for his pulse to race, and his groin to tighten, for him to be steaming hot.

Dragging her back to the sand to plant himself deeply

inside her held equal appeal to standing waist-high in water while she dictated terms. Then she changed the angle of her head, rubbing her nose against his, and the unexpected intimacy shot through him. Still, Mick didn't make a move.

With a thumb and forefinger, she tugged on his ear. "You have very manly ears." She nipped it or nibbled it or did something magical to it that shot an electric shock through him, bringing him pulsatingly alive.

"What are manly ears?"

He closed his eyes. She was touching him. He'd been so consciously impersonal in Hay, reaching for professionalism while knowing his actions were wrong, the memory was seared into him. He'd had no right to touch. Today, there was nothing impersonal about the pads of her fingers smoothing his eyebrows, tracing patterns around his earlobes, the soft touch of her nose, a friendly kiss in Eskimo culture. He liked that Kelly was feeling friendly—no wonder Eskimos honoured the custom.

"Ears like yours." She was whispering nonsense before her teeth grazed his jaw.

"Well, damn." Mick's grip on her tightened. He'd take this slowly if it killed him. It might kill him.

"Open, please."

Her smoky voice rolled through him, a melodic seduction with notes and tones and cadences. She tilted her head. For endless seconds, their mouths clung, testing his control. She used her tongue to tease at the corner of his mouth. He opened to her because he'd go insane if he didn't. Her tongue in his mouth was a minor cataclysm. Having Kelly warm in his arms, enticing him to share kisses was a miracle.

"That's sumptuous."

"That's another girly word, like manly ears, but I guess I can live with it." Mick sank into another kiss, letting himself devour her for just a moment. With his mouth. Still, he didn't move his hands, even though her breasts were resting against his chest, begging for attention.

She pressed a hand against his chest. He drew back instantly. Not far. Their breath mingled in the air between, soft pants of delight and shock.

"I think my brain's turned to mush." Her husky groan wasn't an objection.

"Makes us even." *My brain's mush, my cock is rock hard, and I'm happy.*

"I like kissing you." Had she deliberately wriggled?

"Pleased to hear it," Mick grunted, still trying to catch his breath and his scattered brain cells. Not sure why he wanted to.

"I'll have to think about how pleased." She took his hand and turned toward the shore.

"You do that," he whispered. "We need to take this slowly."

* * *

A cold shower before she went to bed? Kelly was too much of a sybarite to take a cold shower. She also liked the sensation of being hot and bothered. It hadn't happened in a while. Kelly considered pleasuring herself, before realising that Mick would be the focus of her fantasy, and she couldn't trust herself not to wander across the hall and knock on his door.

Nothing wrong with that.

"What have you done, Kelly Steele?"

I kissed him. He kissed me first.

"That was one hell of a kiss."

A delicious kiss, or cocktail of kisses, Kelly could have spent hours repeating. He'd let her build the tempo, but for a split second she thought he'd surrendered control, lost himself in the drugging sensation of mouths straining for more. He'd been aroused, his lovely hard length pressed against her middle. She'd deliberately wiggled, loved his groan, half-agony, half-delight. She was smart enough to see the parallels between tonight and Hay. She'd been the one with the roving hands today, while he'd been passive.

Edit that thought.

She was smart enough to see the differences. Today they'd banished the final shadows. His kisses had been very personal.

Kelly Steele had kissed Mick Jamieson. Knowingly. With conscious forethought. She searched her head and her heart. And she didn't regret it for a second.

He'd let her know he was attracted.

So was she.

Their history made them careful with each other. "*We have to take this slowly*," he'd said, echoing her thoughts.

But they were putting that history behind them, one conversation at a time, one run at a time, one day at a time. They were due some joy, some tender moments on a swing, maybe some wild, monkey sex to celebrate who they'd become.

She'd celebrated Lucy's relationship with Niall, Clem's with Jamie. They were wonderful men. She'd had to bite her tongue not to add "*You do exist, Mick*" to her description of her friends' husbands.

She'd made her first move this afternoon. Small, but she'd opened a door she didn't want to close. *Do you want to have wild, monkey sex with me, Mick?*

Stop!

She composed a message for her girl pack. Her finger hovered. She pressed *Send*:

> *Kissed Mick. Before you ask—on a scale of one to ten, we were using a different scale.*

Messages flew back her.

Bella: *What took you so long?*

Lucy: *Speaking* as *someone who's currently indulging, go girl.*

Clem: *We placed bets. Bella included.*

Bella: an emoji of an athlete holding up a trophy.

Clem: *I want all the juicy details. Where were his hands?*

Kelly laughed aloud, then covered her hand with her mouth, in case she disturbed Mick.

I'm cautious. My apologies to Niall, and put that phone down, Lucy. I'm not broadcasting details for the world wide web, the dark web and AI to gobble up and regurgitate in a porn video.

Bella: *I must have failed in my training.*

Silence from Lucy.

Clem: *You need visuals or voiceovers for porn. Mind you, your voice could work. Start writing the letter now. Want drawings. Don't care if they're just stick figures.*

I love you too.

She'd dream of Mick, maybe touch herself while she did. Happy and giddy and carefree. She locked her door.

No pretend sleepwalking for me tonight.

The last library visitor on Friday night avoided Kelly's eye, ignored the bell, and was reluctant to leave when she tapped him on the shoulder.

"Sorry, I was hoping to finish this book. You don't lend it out."

"You're welcome to come back tomorrow. I can put it aside."

"Saturday morning junior sport." The man grimaced.

"I can still put it aside."

"Monday." He had the grace to look embarrassed. "Sorry for stuffing you around."

"Don't do it again." She coupled the rebuke with her best smile.

Kelly did her usual check that all entrances were locked. She'd set the security codes when she left. She glanced at the large clock in the library's entrance. Seven-ten. Not bad, even with her dilatory reader. Between five and seven, about twenty-five to thirty people had come through. Most of them were tourists, as in, not library regulars but locals who wanted to look inside a building that had slowly taken shape over the previous year. A few came to borrow books or use the computers.

The roster wasn't fully sorted, hence her solo shift

tonight, but the board of management had made significant progress at its inaugural meeting Wednesday night. Mick had chaired and the council CEO had brought his secretary to take notes. The CEO had been the shining light this week, enthusiastic, capable, solution-oriented where Dom was on a go-slow.

"There are a lot of balls to juggle in the first few weeks of a new year. We'll get to it."

If Kelly heard Dom mouth that excuse one more time, she might knee him where it hurt.

She'd offered apologies for this afternoon's staff meeting without a single regret; she was on library duty; the rest of the staff had the meeting and some parent-teacher meetings. The traditional meet-up in the pub would start later tonight. Not that she was even tempted.

She made her way back to her office, Boo padding along beside her. Mick was coming by when his parent-teacher meeting with the junior maths students finished. Pizza for dinner. Hallelujah! She didn't have the energy to cook or clean, or even to make conversation tonight.

She and Mick had been careful with each other all week—a brush of fingers when passing a plate or cup to each other; sitting close enough to each other on the sofa to grab a hand when one of the psychological thrillers they both preferred to violent shoot-em-ups turned scary. He'd taken to dropping a light kiss on her crown when he passed her at the kitchen table. And, heat suffused her body thinking about it now, she'd patted his butt this morning on their way up the hall. She'd almost melted at the look he'd shot her. He was being careful, and insight hit. Mick needed her to make the first move.

Boo's low growl brought Kelly's head up. Dom was leaning against the doorjamb, and she had no idea how he'd gained access.

"Hi, Kelly." Dom eyed Boo with displeasure. "I didn't know you had a dog."

"His name's Boo."

"I'm sure he's a perfectly well-behaved animal." Boo was on alert. "But dogs aren't allowed in the library."

"You're right," she agreed. No point in generating conflict. "But while I'm doing odd hours, single shifts and settling into a routine, Mick suggested I bring Boo along."

"He didn't ask me." Dom took a step closer, his sticky scent clouding the air between them.

"How can I help you?" Kelly didn't give Boo the order to relax.

How the hell did Dom get in?

"I haven't had a chance to drop in during opening hours before now. I thought I'd have a look around." Dom waved a hand back toward the sparsely lit library. "It's coming along well."

"You get a better sense of how it works in the daytime when the kids are here." Kelly picked up a sharpened pencil, tapping its base on her desk.

Why tell me an unnecessary lie?

Boo would have warned her earlier if someone had been wandering around the library. "It's more alive. A buzz of body odours, colognes, curiosity, suppressed giggles in the study nooks and pretending to be above it all."

"My secretary told me you've had some of the seniors showing other kids around?" Dom said, when she'd been following through on a plan explicitly explained at a previous staff meeting. "The feedback's positive."

"It's working well, but we need more staff, quickly."

"Things take more time in the country." Dom gave a shrug. "It is what it is."

"The council CEO has a third full-time librarian starting Monday." Maeve's find, Susie Morgan, and the council had moved faster than Dom on the job offer.

"Sorry we didn't get to her first. A mix-up in the office about priorities." Dom scratched his chin, pretending the news was new to him, when she'd sat at Mick's side during his phone call for Dom to okay the hire quickly. "The other reason I dropped by was because you've been cooped up here all week"—he smiled genially—"and had to miss the staff meeting. I wanted to personally invite you to join the team at the pub for a drink?"

"I might pass tonight. You're right. It has been a big week, and we're opening tomorrow and Sunday—our first Sunday." Information Mick would also have shared at today's staff meeting.

"Well, with an extra librarian, your load should be easier. Get you back to normal next week. An invitation to the pub is standard after Friday's staff meeting, especially for those new in town. A chance to meet people and relax." He imbued the standard invitation with more threat than invitation.

Kelly's phone sounded, and she looked down. "That's Mick. He's outside." Kelly stood. "My signal to leave." She turned to collect her bag, slipping her computer into it. "By the way, how did you get in, Dom?"

"I have access to all school premises." He drew himself up, apparently stung to be challenged.

"After you." Kelly gestured for Dom to precede her toward the front entrance. "Boo." The dog fell in behind. Kelly closed and locked her office, making a mental note to pick up a packet of padlocks at the hardware store in the morning.

CHAPTER TWELVE

When Dom opened the library door, Mick registered several things simultaneously. Kelly had manoeuvred Boo between her and the principal, the dog was on guard, Kelly was carrying her bag when she usually took Mick on a tour before lockup to outline any changes or urgent issues. She was also seriously pissed off.

"Dom. I didn't expect to see you here."

Dom had poked his head around the door at Mick's meeting earlier, waved to the parents and students present, and asked Mick to lock up because Dom had finished for the evening.

"Thought Kelly might not know a few of us meet at the pub for a drink and maybe a meal most Friday nights."

Not a clever excuse when Mick had been at the pub the previous week.

The smile Dom flashed at Kelly was vaguely unsavoury. "A chance for new staff to blend in."

Kelly turned her back, her shoulders taut with tension, reset the security code, then pulled the door shut behind her. "Thanks for the invite, Dom. If I don't get some sleep, I'll fall down."

"Another time." He waved and sauntered in the

direction of the nearest pub.

Kelly waited until he was out of earshot. "They can't even choose a pub on the other side of town from the school."

"To be fair. It's the best pub in town." Mick decided to lance the boil. "Why did you let him in?"

"I didn't." Her glare screamed "How could you think for even a second that I would?" She huffed out a breath. "All good, Boo." She rubbed the dog's back.

"Hi, Boo." Mick touched the dog's head. "Did you order Boo on guard, or did he make up his own mind?" Mick kept his voice relaxed. Maybe he could ask to borrow Boo for reconnaissance some time.

"Dom appeared in the doorway to my office. No warning. Boo's growl was the first I knew I wasn't alone."

"How'd he get in?" Alarm trickled down Mick's spine. Wanting to protect her was getting beyond debts owed to a more personal concern about her well-being. He was joining Boo in her pack.

"He has keys to every building on school land."

"Not technically on school land, but he should have access for emergencies."

"Doesn't excuse him arriving unannounced."

"Agreed. Want me to speak to him?" Mick framed words in his head—"*Listen, you fucker, if I find you in the library again without an invitation, I'll do more than report you for harassment.*" Not a good move at this stage, but not defending Kelly openly was too close a reminder of his past failure.

"You modelled good behaviour. Although I doubt he recognised it."

"Did he scare you?"

"On a scale of one to ten?"

"No male staff member should make any female staff member or student—correct that—any staff member or student uncomfortable, much less afraid, at any time."

"Can I quote you on that, Mr. Jamieson? Because I believe we have a problem."

"Did he scare you?"

"Yes." She waved a hand in exasperation. "Until I saw he took Boo seriously."

"Why does that piss you off?"

"I could outrun him. I could probably knock him unconscious. I took a few self-defence classes. I prefer to run." She stared over his shoulder, clearly weighing her words. "I don't trust him. Professionally or personally." She sighed. "We should make a move."

Stepping forward, Mick wrapped his arms around her, his jaw resting against her temple. Inch by inch she relaxed and rested her weight against him. He'd been careful not to trespass since last Sunday afternoon, but it had tested his self-control. He'd weakened a few times, grabbed her hand watching a crime show, kissed the top of her head. He'd convinced himself it was important for Kelly to hold all the power.

Am I wrong?

Is she waiting for me to make the first move?

Was her pat on his butt this morning an invitation for more? "We can eat at the pizza place or get takeaway?"

"Let's eat there." She pushed back, her hands on his forearms. "I checked. They'll let Boo into the outdoor area. No mess at home."

"Works for me." What worked better was her use of the word "home." She'd called it a house in every conversation they'd had so far. She might not trust Dom, but she trusted Mick in multiple small ways. A wave of tenderness toward her left him in unfamiliar territory. Sharing his simple everyday with her was like being bathed in sunshine after weeks where rain had drowned out sense and sound—a beginning.

The pizza place was heaving, although the bulk of the trade looked to be takeaway. Kelly led the way down a side path opening to a casual, overgrown garden at the back. Thick hedges marked the end point, but somewhere nearby was a jasmine. A plant he'd forever associate with Kelly.

Tables were scattered around the open space in groupings of two and four and eight. Strings of fairy lights were strung from the trees, their light supplemented by candles stuck in cans on the tables. She selected a table in the far corner, where they could sit side by side with their backs to the hedge.

"What about here?" Kelly turned to him.

"Provides a clear view of all entrances and exits." Mick slid into a seat. "You did your research."

"Yeah, well. A habit that can get you into as much trouble as it avoids."

Insight hit him between the eyeballs. "Is that what you were doing in Hay?"

"I'm starving," she said. "Order now. Interrogation later." She pointed to the disc on the table. "All the mod cons of your bigger cities. Scan the disc for a menu, then hover over the QR code to order."

"One large, or do you want your own?" Mick peered at the tray being carried to the next table.

"Depends what you're ordering." She was scanning the menu.

"Your choice. All I ask for is food and a cold beer."

She pressed a few keys. "Done."

"Don't tell me. I'm ready for a good surprise tonight."

"I'll say this once." She pulled two knife, fork and serviette packs from the bucket in the centre of the table, passed him one and set the other to her left. "I'd been in Hay not much more than an hour when I met you. Off the train, checked out the room, wanted to get a sense of the school before starting, so trespassed there, was spotted by the security guard."

"He never reported it." Mick nodded his thanks to the waiter who set two beers on the table.

She traced a finger through the condensation on her bottle. "I was stupid. Instead of running back toward the boarding house, I took off in the other direction. An area I hadn't checked out. Got lost, found myself up a laneway with three hoodies who had plans for my evening I didn't fancy. While hiding from them, you showed up. The rest you know."

"I'm sorry."

"We did that bit," she said softly, pressing her thigh against his.

"And that's it?"

"We can accept we were both young and stupid. We aren't now." She hadn't moved away after pressing his thigh. The contact was good, her closeness allowing them to keep their voices low.

"Where are you heading with this, Kel?" Mick sensed she'd been doing her own calculations and was about to share her findings.

"We're in a bit of a situation. Dom Ellis trashed Ayesha at the official opening last year. I've heard him subtly belittle and undercut her since we've been working on the library, despite your spirited defence of her at the first staff meeting. I think he spiked a drink at the party after the official handover; bringing a woman into line, like he tried to make me his coffee maid at the staff meeting."

"Did he threaten you tonight?"

"I'm in the Ayesha category. Tonight he wanted to show me who's in charge, to make me wary, to ensure I didn't step out of line. Longer term he'd be happy to undermine my authority and reputation"—she paused—"and he'd be the first to reach for his phone camera if I found myself in a compromising situation. He's a danger to female staff—in multiple ways."

"Keep Boo with you all the time in the library."

"That's against the rules."

"Stuff the rules." The pizza was set between them. "Or rather, we'll amend the rules to cover extenuating circumstances. That's what we have."

"It's more than that, Mick." She laid a hand on his arm. "It's corruption of public office, misuse of power every bit as egregious as George Hogan. Were you explicitly sent here to stop him?"

"Holy fuck! What makes you ask that?" If she could see through him so easily, would others? Although so far no one else had shared a negative opinion of Dom with him.

"You decided when you were barely an adult to fight corruption, I can't see you turning a blind eye to it now."

Mick's decision was instinctive; he wouldn't keep her in the dark about his moves this time. In Hay, he hadn't been able to explain his actions, to reassure her at any point. "Dom's smart, well-regarded, surrounded by a loyal team and careful."

"Potentially spiking drinks at staff parties at the pub isn't careful."

"Have you heard any complaints? I haven't."

She chewed on a mouthful of pizza for a while. "He's careful who he targets so he gets no complaints."

"You're telling this story." And Mick was listening. He transferred another slice of pizza to his plate. "Who makes a good target in this case?"

"Someone desperate for a job, anxious about their reputation, or too low in the hierarchy to be able to stop abuse."

"Good list." It tallied with his. Thank you, Dog—Kelly didn't fit any of those categories.

"I'm betting Ayesha had the backbone to call him on his behaviour, and somehow he forced her out."

"I can't verify or deny that. I just don't know." But he'd check if Ayesha had contacted Ros in the last few weeks with new info. Unlikely, because Ros would have updated him. Ayesha had a staunch defender in Kelly. Would Kelly defend the man Mick was now? *I wish.*

"But you're looking at his conduct."

"I'm looking at his conduct, and so far, all I'm seeing is smoke and mirrors. No concrete evidence. He's good at covering his tracks."

If Dom crosses a line with me, I'll complain." She was serious.

"Be careful. He's made a few comments about you. Harmless, except they're not." Mick covered her hand with his own.

"Public place, Mick. Small town." She glanced at his hand and disengaged hers. "If Dom's after me, we don't want to give him ammunition to attack or undermine either of us."

"Fuck, Dom. But you're right. What we do in our private life is our business." And Mick had no intention of stepping back from her.

"What private life?" Her voice dropped to the softest, sexiest whisper, and a smile curved her mouth.

"I'll show you." Mick didn't need to be asked twice.

She pushed him against the front door the second it closed. "I've been waiting all week for this."

"Just a week?" Mick's hands streaked down her back to cup her backside and lift her closer. "Don't overthink it. We're attracted, unattached, we like each other."

"We want to erase our first meeting," she murmured.

"You're overthinking again."

"I can call a halt at any time?" She drew her head back to look at him. "I have no intention of calling a halt this side of Christmas."

His heart smiled, if such a thing were possible. "Say no, if my hands or my mouth or any other part of me makes you feel uncomfortable."

"We have to think about what we're doing at some point."

"Not now."

"Not now." She nodded.

"Do you have an instruction for Boo?"

She glanced at the dog. "No looking."

"Good idea." Mick was positive they wanted to make love, just didn't know how to start. "We agree we want to do this?"

"Yes." She answered clearly. "Do we need to take it slowly?"

"Nuh! Done that."

Thank you to the little green men in space.

"But so I don't trigger any annoying or distracting reminders of the past, how about we each take one side of the bed, turn our backs, strip down and climb in?" Mick squeezed her butt, signaling his intention.

"Do you want me to turn out the light?" She was laughing at him. It was going to be okay.

"I think we can be adult enough to leave the light on." Mick strolled to one side of the bed and turned his back. He threw hope in the air. "Next time we can undress each other."

"That's a very confident statement."

"Just putting it out there." Mick wanted it clear this was about more than a one-night stand.

"What about we talk each other through this?"

"You're purring like a contented feline contemplating mischief." He dropped onto the bed, his knees shaky. She was in his room, almost naked, almost in his bed. He almost had his hands on her.

I'm overthinking.

"I'm suggesting verbal encouragement." Her scent already teased at the edge of his imagination; her smoke-hazed voice added another erotic layer. "When I sat on my side of your bed, my skirt rode up my thighs. Oh dear."

"Tell me about 'oh dear.'" He glossed a hand over his cock, which had been showing interest since Kelly had grabbed him inside the front door.

"There's a damp patch on my knickers."

"Maybe you should take them off?" His mouth dried.

And maybe I should remember I'm letting her lead.

"What order do you take your clothes off, Mick?"

"Depends if I'm in a hurry." A button popped off his shirt before he dragged it over his head.

She giggled. "Did you just rip your shirt off?"

"Are you cheating?"

Please cheat because then I can.

"I have excellent hearing. And we have all night."

"That's a blessing," Mick muttered.

"Did you say something?"

"What are you doing, now?"

"Standing naked on my side of this bed and wondering what's taking you so long."

"That sound you make between a giggle and a purr gives me goosebumps." Mick slipped his belt, flicked open the button on his jeans. "And makes me wonder why we've waited so long." He stood to ditch his jeans.

"Maybe I can do something to make you so desperate for me, you'd rip off your clothes. I'd like to see you desperate."

Mick had never heard that little catch in her throat before. "Are you touching yourself?"

"Would you like me to?"

"Let's turn around now."

"Are you naked?" The velvet chocolate of her whisper slid over his body, a seductive touch, leaving him hard and aching.

"Almost." He shucked his jocks. "Right. There. On the count of three. One, two—"

"Great backside. It looks good when you're running, or bending, or doing not much of anything—"

Mick pivoted. Kelly was smiling at him, teasing him, and waiting for him.

"—But I like it even better butt-naked. I cheated. I turned around before you."

"You're beautiful."

"Show me." She held out her hand, making it easy.

Mick circled the bed to take her hand. Holding her hand settled some of his nerves. "We won't need this." He pulled the summer waffle blanket off the bed.

"You're changing the ground plan." She lifted her free hand to his cheek. "Weren't we supposed to crawl across the bed to reach each other?"

"I want to kiss you." Would she remember he'd asked that question after their swim last week?

She pressed two fingers to her mouth, then placed them on his lips. "Yes, please."

Where to start? How to show her that gaining her intimate trust changed something in him? Lifting both hands, he cupped her shoulders, and was ambushed by her scent, fresh with a touch of tartness, like her. Bending to nuzzle at the sensitive place between her shoulder and neck, he welcomed the tremble that brought her body closer to his. He did it again, finding her skin satiny soft, using her sigh to slide his hands down her back to tuck her body between his thighs, letting her feel what holding her did to him.

"More," she said, her hands starting their own journey.

Mick trailed kisses along her jaw, giving special attention to her chin. She led with her chin, tilted it up slightly when she had a point to make. He loved that she signaled her intention, gave him time to reflect.

She got her hands on his butt and rocked herself against him. "More."

"I haven't had time to explore your breasts yet." He shaped her breast and gently squeezed.

"All night, Mick. We've got all night. This first time we should go fast. To get it over with." She whimpered.

His mouth on her nipple might have had something to do with her breathy little half sighs. He turned his head, his cheek resting on the curve of her breast. "To save any embarrassment?" Mick slid his hand between them, gently fingering between her thighs.

She pushed herself against his fingers. And he listened for the voluptuous moan that told him he'd found the spot that sent her a little crazy.

"I'm not embarrassed, Kelly." He pressed his mouth to her ear. "Aroused, excited, and primed to come." He rocked far enough back to create a small space between them.

"Maybe I should pull myself off first to ease the edge."

"Can't wait that long." She grabbed his hips and dragged him back. "Where do you keep your condoms?"

"This side of the bed. And a point of clarification"—he punctuated his clarification with more kisses—"I bought them online. We don't need a local chemist or supermarket assistant knowing our business."

"Smart boy. So, there was method in you joining me on this side of the bed." Mischief lit her eyes. "Wrap it. I'd put one on you, but truly, I don't trust myself not to pounce first and think later."

"Where do you want to be?" He sheathed himself.

"Here." She gave the sexiest throaty murmur, and his brains went to mush.

"Good to know. I meant, do you want to be on top?" He was her willing slave.

* * *

Kelly and he were finished with the pavane they'd danced for the last few weeks, advance and retreat. She was trembling, but it was a laughter and anticipating good-sex vibe kind of tremble. The steps from anger to ceasefire to lasting peace to having the hots for him had been unexpectedly easy. He'd been honest with Kelly, about his past and his current role in Tullamore. His steadiness of purpose had captured her attention. Looking at his ripped body wasn't a hardship either.

"Are you coming?" He bounced onto the bed.

She leaned forward to slide a finger down his sheathed cock. "Bet on it."

"Bet at least on a trifecta." His tease was also a promise.

Crawling across the empty space, she straddled his thighs. "Let's start this way, but I'm amendable to whatever you have in mind." Then she inched higher, her body moving instinctively to cup him with her thighs.

"You don't know what I have in mind."

Kelly rocked against him.

"You're wet." He undulated against her, his head thrown back. "Keep doing that. Oh yeah, I like that."

Not embarrassed, and prepared to show me he's vulnerable.

In that moment, Kelly dropped her final barricades, and the sneaky, sexy beast gave her an unlooked for treat, using his fingers to make her come. She sank onto his chest. "I needed that."

"You also need less recovery time than me. Roll over. My turn on top."

Kelly liked him straddling her, unkempt, disheveled by their lovemaking and happy. They were both happy. "I like it here."

"Then it's unanimous." He caressed her breast. "Now I want to catch some of those bits I missed earlier."

"We haven't finished the fast bit yet."

"I'm not trying to set a record." He cupped her second breast, stroking and massaging, but the smile curving his mouth undid her.

She gripped his arms, pulling herself up to nibble at his bottom lip. "I want you inside me."

"Like this?" His tongue in her mouth, mimicked the act of love, while his hands ran down her back and back up her flanks, until she was desperate.

Kelly tugged on his hair. "Mick?"

"Mmm." He lifted his head, his expression dazed and hungry. Protectiveness caught her by the throat. Kelly wanted him to always be safe, always be loved, to love him.

"Stop talking and love me."

He let her sink back to the bed, then rose above her, sweat-slicked, focused on her.

Fire and frenzy, that's what she craved. His taste mingled with his scent in her mouth. His back, his knee, his torso poised above her were new and exciting textures she reached for. When he crouched over her, she stroked a hand down his cheek, the slight bristle stirring feelings of tenderness. He nudged his way into her.

"That's delicious. You're delicious."

"Delicious is another non-manly word." The muscles in his arms bunched tight to support his weight. "I should be saying you're delicious." His gaze was a physical caress. Tender, passionate, and her body rocked against him.

"Even maths teachers must know some adjectives." She'd never teased a lover before. Never used the word lovemaking or love even in her head.

"What about tasty, luscious." His next nudge-thrust was deeper, and he groaned. "You're wet, and you feel so damn good."

Sensation radiated outwards until her fingers and toes tingled. "I can feel you in my—"

Heart. I nearly said heart.

"What about stunning?" He was relentlessly erotic. "That's an adjective." His thrusting developed a devastatingly consistent rhythm. "Yeah. I like to make you pant. Those breathy little sounds undo me. Tighter, Kelly. Hold me tighter."

Close to the edge, she fought for control.

"Now, I'm coming now," he roared.

She let herself soar, tiny spasms coalescing into a breathtaking explosion. Making love to Mick wasn't meant to be so perfect. "Holy hell," she screamed.

He swallowed her cries, while rolling them over so she lay on top. "I'm prepared to swear it was holy, as in divine. It'll be hard to beat, but I'm prepared to try."

"Already?"

"A cuddle might get me in the mood faster."

Kelly curled down beside him, one leg thrown over his thighs, her hand caught in his, both resting on his chest. She was boneless, breathless, and amazed that Mick and she could make such magic. He was a constant surprise; as a lover and as a man. A delicious, lovely surprise, and she couldn't stop smiling.

Look at me.

"Feel free to make any suggestions at all that might help

your mood," she said, surrendering to the unexpected delight of teasing her lover.

She'd expected the sex to be good, instead it was ... overwhelming. Too many senses to separate, but Mick was woven through all of them.

CHAPTER THIRTEEN

"Interesting selection of videos on rotation in the entrance hall." Mick was in the library in the middle of the day, lured there by mutterings from the maths staffroom and among some of the kids.

"Do you like them?" Kelly pretended an innocence Mick didn't buy.

"Your tone is the aural equivalent of batting your eyelashes at me." Mick kept his voice low and his gaze on the video. "Great female mathematicians, female scientists, musicians?"

She shrugged. "They're the only videos I've got. I thought the entrance hall was a good place to showcase some of the books we've got."

"As in 'See this woman in the video, have I got a book for you' sort of thing?"

"Exactly."

"Do you have books on all those women?" He'd done a fair bit of unpacking and shelving himself and would have registered the maths histories.

"Unfortunately, no, but they're easily searchable on the internet." She pointed to a computer set up on a desk in a corner of the space. A few girls in school uniforms were clustered around the screen.

Mick pointed to the large screen. "Maryam Mirzakham, Iranian, research topics include hyperbolic and symplectic geometry. I've studied maths, and I'm not sure I could explain that in words of one syllable."

"That's the point. Some women understand and are experts in subjects men aren't."

"Never doubted it." Mick grinned. "Eugenia Cheng, mathematician in higher category theory. Also a pianist."

"I was positive you'd know there's a strong connection between maths and music skills." She watched the series of video clips move on. "And then there's just plain musical genius. Cynthia Robinson, American trumpeter and founder of Sly and the Family Stone."

"What's the reaction?" Mick was here because of the discontent among the male executive. It was about time someone upended their complacency.

"The Head of Maths said he thought my selection was unrepresentative and misleading. There are more male maths geniuses by a factor of ten, he claimed, than females."

"I'm guessing you had your answer ready." Mick wished he'd been present.

"I said his senior class could name at least twenty males and not one female, so I thought I'd start them off."

"Can I ask how you came to be chatting to his senior maths class about the greatest mathematicians in history?"

"They've booked one of our meeting rooms. Or rather, a deputation of senior girls has requested a permanent booking on one of the study rooms. Monday to Thursday, and two hours on Saturday afternoon—girls only."

"What did you say?"

"I asked why? Turns out they think they're dumber than the boys, so want to do some work where they're free to talk to each other and help each other."

"Are there subjects where they feel they're particularly dumb?" Mick had a new bit of evidence. Or did he? Dealing with adolescent feelings of inadequacy was an insubstantial beast, peer pressure and social media were all the mix.

"Maths is one."

The senior maths teacher had been among the loudest mutterers. "Six of those girls were in the top ten for maths at the end of Year 10."

"How do you know that?"

He shrugged. "I've been looking at patterns. When did they ask?"

"The beginning of the week."

"I like your way of fighting back. You're not putting anyone down. Just offering possibilities."

"I like their way of fighting back. Any individual or group can book a room. It's only if we have huge demand that I, or one of the other librarians, has to decide on competing interests. There's no competition at the moment."

"Let's move this to your office." Mick escorted her to the back of the library. "Tell me your but."

"It's not a real solution. Usually I mix this video up— males, females, people from all the nations on earth, and it attracts little interest. This school seems to have obliterated all examples of female excellence."

"You noticed." Mick wasn't surprised.

Kelly was attuned to misogyny, and intimately aware of the body's reactions to stress—fight, flight, freeze and fawn. She'd admire the girls' decision to fight and she'd protect them with her last breath.

"So did you. They should be getting fairer instruction in class. If the class splits so that all the boys are the best performers and the girls are the worst, it's the weirdest class I've ever encountered. And if that's the truth, the teacher should be giving the girls extra attention."

"I could drop in occasionally."

"Again, not a solution. Why didn't you take the senior class?"

"Catch them when they're young, and you've got a chance of holding their interest. I want the Year Sevens to discover the magic of numbers and"—he looked embarrassed—"yeah, well. I'll be bringing them to see this."

"You're a natural teacher, you know." Her compliment warmed him in a different way to her body in his bed. "Why are you so keen to get out of the classroom?"

"You should know the answer to that better than most," he replied. "The tone of a school, the possibilities for students stem from the quality of the leadership. I want to create something positive."

"This isn't about atonement for what happened to me. You wanted to make a difference in the police force as well." She moved closer, brushed against his side, and dropped her voice. "Why agree to this undercover stuff?"

"Because I did think I could atone—make amends—initially. I accepted one job, then a second. I said I was finished. I wasn't given a choice with this job."

"Someone must have strong reasons to question Dom's conduct."

Mick hadn't consciously used the word atonement in his conversations with himself, but he was still considering its role in his decisions since Hay two days later when Bev, the longest serving secretary, came into his office.

"Do you have a minute?" Bev had already entered and shut the door behind her.

"How can I help?" Mick gestured to the seat in front of his desk.

"My niece is one of the students in the extra classes for the girls at the library. Mary Bellow. My sister married a Bellow."

"She's a smart young woman. Wants to be a doctor." According to Kelly, Mary was a future chief medical officer.

"Mary was the prime mover in asking Ms. Steele about study sessions."

"Are you here on Mary's behalf?"

Mick hadn't heard about any more pushback on the

library sessions since the last staff meeting. He'd endorsed them, and had dropped in a few times to provide a sounding board for problems. Making it clear his endorsement of the study club was more than lip service.

Bev pulled an envelope from her pocket and slid it across the desk. "I've noticed something odd about the allocation of extra duties." She held his gaze. "Thought a second set of eyes might tell me if I've made a mistake." Bev knew as well as he did the allocation of extra duties was on Dom's list.

Mick flicked up the flap on the envelope and slid out some pages. Excel spreadsheets, the top few pages listing playground duty rosters, the last few identifying other responsibilities. "What sort of odd?"

"Female staff appear to get longer playground duty than male staff, and they're assigned to the playgrounds furthest from the staff room. Female staff generate more recorded complaints than the males, get allocated more administrative work because they're 'competent.'" Bev's expression was bland, her voice neutral while she basically accused Dom Ellis of bullying.

Ruddy hell!

"Can you give me an example?" If what Bev was saying was true, and the evidence was on the spreadsheet, Mick could do a system search to locate the original file. He could get Dom on the code of conduct. Not much, but added to the belittling of the senior girls, Mick was starting to build a picture.

"Ms. Steele has lunch duty near the sports fields." Bev folded her hands neatly in her lap. "Librarians don't usually get playground duty, because they're on duty in the library during breaks."

Fuck! Dom was punishing Kelly, or Ayesha, or both.

"Thanks, Bev, I'll have a look." He wasn't offering her much, but it seemed to be enough.

"Thank you." Bev rose, then hesitated. "Your regular visits to the office are appreciated."

Mick could take that any way he liked, that the secretaries appreciated his friendliness or his support. But, Mick had noticed Dom was less pre-emptory in issuing instructions to female staff members when he had a male audience. Dom liked the cover provided by one-on one scenarios.

Mick passed Kelly the iced water he'd poured them both.

"Thanks." Kelly smiled. "You seem distracted. Problem at work?"

"Why didn't you tell me Dom has assigned you a shit playground duty when you shouldn't have to do it?"

"Because I knew you'd be pissed off." She sipped the water slowly. "And that he'd give it to Laura or Josie, who already have their fair share of crap jobs."

"I am pissed off. It's unfair, spiteful and small-minded."

She grinned. "In my head, I've reimagined it as an extra exercise session for Boo, a chance for him to get out of the library on a Wednesday and play with some kids for a while."

"Wednesday?" Mick growled.

"Uh-huh." She swirled the remaining water in her glass. "The day I work late. Dom knows I don't like him. Just his petty way to show he's the boss."

"He's pissed that you've made the library a roaring success." Mick knew it was more than jealousy.

"Maybe. He'd like me to make a scene. So, he could argue I'm claiming special treatment as a head office ring in. Putting an official complaint on my record would give him a hard-on. He'd prefer to see me pissed as a newt and disgracing myself in some way."

"You don't sound too fussed by it."

She stood and sashayed toward him, sliding one hand around his back to squeeze his butt. He went rock hard. "I'm trusting you to bring him down."

"What about my career?"

"Are you telling me your career matters more than your

integrity?"

Mick had a choice, to make a joke or to trust her, to let her closer to him than anyone had been in years. "Possessions don't matter much to me. When I lost everything, I learned what's important in life, or was reminded of what I'd taken for granted."

"Now you're sounding impossibly altruistic." She was challenging him, as aware as he was of how important this conversation had become.

"Hypothetical." He wanted her to admit she and he shared this insight. "You've got sizable savings in the bank and you get a call that Arabella needs urgent financial help. What do you do?"

"I bet you think you're clever." But she was smiling again.

"At the risk of sounding like a sanctimonious prick, I'm grateful for learning early what counts. Say the words, Kelly."

"You're a sanctimonious prick."

He snorted.

"People matter. Love matters. Having at least one person in your life who listens to you, who hears you, who makes you feel safe, so you can go out in the world and be brave matters." She rubbed herself against his groin.

Mick forgot about Dom, his students and his career when her hand slid around to his crotch to make friends.

* * *

Kelly yielded to the lure of Mick's increased tempo, his hands shaping her breasts, his body driving her higher and higher. "Yes," she cried, the orgasm ripping through her, leaving her body tingling in low, intimate places.

She didn't want to move. She never wanted to move. The lassitude of being absolutely, gloriously, sexually sated was an addictive pleasure. In the aftermath of her release, he shuddered beneath her, jack-knifing to wrap his arms around her. She clung to him, savouring the affection in his touch, the sheer annihilating intimacy she experienced each time they made love.

He rolled her over until he straddled her. "Want a lift to Dom's place tonight?"

"I want to come home and take up where you just left off." Kelly scrunched up her nose, and he rocked gently against her. Desire swirled through her, a dizzying current that made her want to forget everything except what they shared in this bed. "Dom's party counts as an official duty, right?"

"You got the email. Dom's barbeque is to allow all staff to mingle in an informal setting. The term's almost over. Not everyone has the time or likes going to the pub. This is a chance to unwind."

"You don't want to go either?"

"More, I'm not looking forward to answering questions about Ayesha that I can't answer."

"Are people still asking?"

"They've restarted in the last week. Not sure what's prompted them or who's the source. I have the same information you do. Although, Dom suggested Ayesha was in a relationship with the builder."

"Don't know the answer to that. Can I take Boo?"

"That bad, huh?"

Bad would be a repeat of the other social functions Dom had organised, and the muscles across Kelly's shoulders and neck tightened. Easy to be ambushed in a house where you don't know the exits or escape routes, and she hadn't had those sorts of flashbacks since she got Charlie.

Kelly watched the final houses disappear in the side-view mirror. Street lights petered out a kilometre further out, then they were on their own. Kelly sent a message:

Compulsory party at the principal's. Think Wake in Fright!
Boo not invited. Relying on Mick to cover my back.

The large ranch-style home was set back from the drive. Impossible to guess the acreage of the property in the dark, but the house was long, low, and tonight, brightly lit. Aside from that, the location reminded her of a row of garages in Hay—isolated. No one would hear you shout in the dark.

"It's a large house for a single man," Kelly commented.

"His wife and kids arrived with him. Only lasted about six months." Mick joined the cars parked in a line across from the front door.

"Country appointments can be tough on a marriage." Kelly worked harder this time to keep her voice neutral.

"Second marriage."

"Are you warning me?" Kelly glanced at his profile. She'd shared a house with him for seven weeks now, been his lover for more than two. Neither of them talked of taking the relationship further. And why was that? "About Dom being on the prowl? About being careful what I drink?"

About us never mentioning my departure in two weeks and two days from now.

"You've already made up your mind about Dom Ellis," he said mildly.

From sharing a house, Kelly didn't rank Mick as a big drinker. Even before she'd looked inside the small chill box he'd packed for tonight, Kelly knew he didn't plan to drink and drive. Kelly would stick to mineral water.

"Were there kids from the first marriage?"

"Twins starting college this year. Wife chose her family over following Dom to subsequent appointments. Amicable divorce."

"You know a lot about it."

"He's a chatty sort of bloke. His second wife, kids five and three years old, also missed her family. Went back to Dom's last town."

"I'm sensing a pattern here."

"Patterns everywhere"—switching off the engine, he turned to face her—"if you look."

"How long do we have to stay?"

"As the new deputy principal, I need to stay for a bit."

"Fair enough."

Still, he'd tucked their drinks bag behind the big bath overflowing with ice and bottles. Away from prying eyes? Contamination?

Two hours later, Kelly withdrew into a corner and inhaled the vibe. It was a repeat of the function at the pub. Staff with wives and husbands left around nine-thirty. Only singles remained—amend that—only people who had arrived without a partner were still partying. Kelly circulated endlessly, nursing her single sparkling mineral water. Still, as the evening dragged on, more males than females remained.

She'd trained herself to match faces to names—a teacher's skill. But after seven weeks and regular classes in the library, she knew everyone. Steph Bryant had partied late on the official library opening night and had stuck pretty close to Dom. Tonight Steph leaned against a wall, and her broody, watchful expression troubled Kelly. Suddenly, Steph pushed herself off her wall, walking unsteadily toward Dom at the punch bowl.

A short sharp exchange, Steph's face was contorted in anger or despair. She waved a hand in the air. Dom's back was to Kelly, so she couldn't read him. When Dom turned, he had two glasses of punch in his hands, a fixed smile on his face, and he brushed past Stephanie, heading toward …?

Kelly followed him with her gaze. Josie and Laura were fresh out of college, on their first appointments, excited, enthusiastic, and already developing a slight crush on a principal who'd open his home to welcome staff. Kelly wandered in the direction of the young women, ostensibly randomly, stopping to exchange a word with whoever she passed. Mick's path intersected with hers before she reached Dom.

"Don't touch the punch," Mick whispered close to her

ear.

His expression was bland, but his eyes were alert. Cop eyes. Kelly would bet Bella's library that Dom Ellis would be monumentally pissed off when the truth came out.

"Warn them." She jerked her head toward the two women. She wanted to snatch the glasses from Dom's paws and upend them down his gullet.

"This heat's a killer. We've just made a fruit punch." Dom passed one to each of the women. "By the way, you're welcome to stay tonight." The principal waved a hand expansively at the size of the house. "Plenty of room here. Not a good look to be picked up by the cops for DUI."

"Then why hand them another alcoholic drink!" she muttered, before turning to Mick. "I can't watch this road crash any longer. Can I plead more work tomorrow and leave?"

"I should stay a bit longer, wave the flag so to speak. Can you bear another half-hour to an hour?"

"I've got a better idea. I'll offer to drive Steph home in her car. You can collect me from her place when you're through, or I can walk from there?"

"Okay." His turn to study her. "I'm guessing the alternative is telling Dom what you think of him in loud words of one syllable."

"You're reading me right. I'd mix it up with a few expletives learned in dark alleys."

"Whisper them to me later. I love it when you talk dirty." He scanned the room. "I'm being watched. Text me Steph's address, and I'll collect you."

* * *

Mick kept a slightly goofy smile on his face, pleasantly sloshed but on the right side of legally being able to drive. Almost no one else in the room was sober. With Stephanie, Kelly and a few other women gone, they were down to about half a dozen men and the two newbies, Josie and

Laura. Mick ambled from the veranda back to the living room, chatting occasionally, and helping himself to some punch. With his back to the crowd, he poured it into the sample container he'd brought for the purpose. After Steph's behaviour at the pub, he'd come prepared. Pushing it deep in his trousers pocket, he made his way to Dom's side.

"My dance, I think." Mick insinuated himself between the two women.

"We're not dancing." Laura giggled, or maybe Laura and Josie both giggled.

"How about I dance you out to the car," Mick said.

"Hey, you're not deserting us now, are you?" Dom's expression was still benign, but there was an edge to his words.

"Ready to pass out." Laura sagged against Mick. "Better do that in my own bed."

"Where you go, I go." Josie slurred her words.

"Are you sure you're up to driving, mate?" Dom was suddenly the concerned host. "You can all bunk down here."

"I'm good," Mick replied. "On call again in the library tomorrow at sparrow's fart. Don't know what I was thinking."

Dom stepped back. "Then I'll see you all next week."

Mick called out, "Night all. Thanks for the great party, Dom."

The fresh air hit Laura and Josie like a knockout punch. By the time they reached his car, he had to help them fasten their seat belts. Once in the driver's seat, he texted Kelly:

Leaving now.

Thirty seconds later, he got his response:

39 Pine Street. See you soon.

"Where am I taking you?" Mick programmed in the addresses, a few streets from each other. Josie was the logical first drop-off, then a few blocks further to Laura's. Both needed help opening their front doors.

When Mick pulled up at 39 Pine, Kelly emerged from a dark corner of the veranda. He pushed open the car door. "Sorry it took so long."

"If your drive here was anything like mine, I'm guessing you had to pull over a few times."

"Was Steph ill?"

"Twice on the drive. Once since. She's sleeping now. I needed the time to help clean her up and get her to bed. Stephanie said she must have eaten something before she went to the party." Kelly was non-committal.

"Must have eaten at the same place as Laura and Josie." Mick had a theory, part of the reason he'd wanted to stay. He hadn't realised Stephanie was also a target.

"The punch was spiked."

"I don't know that for a fact." But it was a strong probability.

"Give me your educated guess," she said.

"Did you ask Steph if she thought her drink was spiked?"

Steph hadn't shared more than work-related problems with Mick so far, and Steph was guarded around him. *Crap!* Had she, like Kelly, twigged that he had an ulterior motive for being here? Usually he was careful around women. Edit that—he'd become careful after Hay when he realised he'd have to tell any woman he got serious with why he'd left the force. More than one had turned away.

Kelly knew. And he and she were lovers. And that was … lovely.

"I asked Steph if she needed a doctor." Kelly's fist closed—frustration or anger? "She said she was fine."

"Stephanie has been here a few years. It can't be her first-end-of-term-off-with-a-bang party." Although it was unlikely Steph wanted the school staff to see her plastered. He recalled the pub, the night he'd offered to walk Steph home. She'd apologised the next Monday, trying to hide her embarrassment and pleaded a twenty-four-hour bug.

"Did you get a sample of the punch?" she asked.

"Are you sure you didn't do evidence training?"

Mick stuck his hand in his trousers pocket and pulled out the vial. He'd send the sample in the departmental bag to Ros, marked urgent and confidential. Bev would be able to handle that, no questions asked. His first firm ally in the school, apart from Kelly.

"We don't have concrete evidence," he added.

Keeping secrets would hurt her, but Mick wouldn't raise false hopes by speculating on unproven evidence. And with Dom escalating, Mick had promised himself he'd do whatever it took to keep Kelly safe. Kelly leaving Tullamore confident and happy had become non-negotiable. If that made him unworthy of her trust, he'd deal with it.

"At the library function last year, I thought Steph and Dom might be close. Tonight, I thought they had a fight. Well, she had a fight. His back was to me, and he cut her short."

"Makes sense to shut down a fight when you're the host and their boss." Playing devil's advocate wasn't Mick's preferred approach to eliciting information.

"Crap host if at least three of his guests are legless and vomiting their guts out." She was right.

Mick put his hand over the fist she'd made on her knee. "If it helps at all, I agree."

"I don't drink much at the best of times," she admitted. "I don't drink in places where I'm unsure of the territory, or I'm an outsider."

"Good rule."

But she'd had a drink with him. More than once. Boo had been present, but still ... A confession and a compliment in exchange for a few words of support. He'd take any and all crumbs of encouragement. In his head, they were lovers, not just convenient bedmates for the duration.

"I hate being helpless." Her voice had gone dark.

"You might believe you're helpless."

In a dirty garage in Hay, Mick had had a hand in creating her self-doubt. The knowledge stopped him from telling her he was falling for her, had fallen for her.

"No one who knows you does. You have a core of steel, Kelly. When you're trapped, you fight back. Even when someone holds you physically captive, your mind isn't helpless, your heart isn't helpless. I knew that in Hay."

"I run away."

"You regroup. That's a necessary survival strategy." He didn't add that for a long time she'd had to do it alone.

"Thank you." She flattened her hand beneath his. More encouragement.

"To go back to your earlier point. Is it possible Dom and Steph had a thing, Dom broke it off before Steph was ready, and she wants to start it again?" If that was the case and Stephanie was an informant, then her evidence against Dom might be muddied.

"Not that she told me," she said, before falling silent, but Mick had the sense she wasn't finished. "Boo wouldn't have been welcome at the party. I relied on you tonight."

"That's nice to know." He pulled into the driveway beside the house.

She waited until they reached the front door. "We both know I shouldn't have to."

Mick wrapped his arms around her and held on. A hug. He needed contact. Her confidence in him made him feel like he could move mountains, should move mountains. He resented the fact any woman had to be wary. He nursed an especial loathing for the threat to Kelly's sense of self. His mother and sisters were strong; he'd relied on their strength when he hit rock bottom. Kelly's family and friends relied on Boo when she was far from home. Needing a guard dog twenty-four-seven was no way to live a life.

Kelly was decent and honourable, committed to public service—an old-fashioned term, an old-fashioned value, but one Mick prized. She deserved to live fear-free. Hugging her wasn't enough. Mick needed to love her tonight, to give her everything he was.

"Want make-up sex?"

"What are we making up for?"

"For spending so much of our time on school business when we'd rather be reassuring Boo that your cries are ecstasy, not extremis."

"Funny man." She slipped her hand inside his shirt; his perfect fantasy lover come to life.

CHAPTER FOURTEEN

Mick lectured himself on the way to the library to collect Kelly. Wednesday—when she was forced to do a punitive playground duty—and he'd done some extra maths with his Year Seven stragglers to stop himself from bursting into Dom's office to yell "This stops now."

Brilliant, Jamieson, defeat Dom with brute force, and get yourself suspended.

He buzzed that he was on his way. When she opened the door, he stepped inside and opened his arms. Drenched himself in her scent, in her goodness, in her belief in his ability to disable Dom. So far, he'd failed.

At home, Mick put his briefcase on the table and pulled out the report. "Ros was fast. The toxicology report has confirmed a mix of GBH and ketamine."

"That's dangerous. What are you going to do?" She obviously expected him to do something, and in this he had to fail her. Again.

"Add it to the infuriatingly small pile of concrete evidence I have, and hope I get more." The flimsiness of the evidence coupled with his conviction of Dom's guilt was doing his head in.

"You can't charge him?" She tried to hide her

disappointment, which added to Mick's frustration.

"Let's be brutal about this. It's impossible to know who spiked the punch bowl."

"Dom took no action when some of his guests were showing all the signs of being drunk and unable to manage themselves." She slammed the fridge door shut and slapped the bottle of water on the table. "Were the only victims women?"

"From what I saw, yes. Not a single male touched the punch. But Dom's still got plausible deniability. He could blame one of the women. A joke gone wrong? Someone who left early? 'Someone who slipped in, Officer, because there was such a crowd around tonight? You know what it's like. Kids with a warped sense of humour trying to get one up on their teachers.'"

Mick had wasted hours in the middle of the night, flat on his back, considering options, when by rights he should have been tucking himself in behind Kelly, nuzzling her neck, and holding her close.

I'll make it up to you, I promise.

"You're right." With her elbows on the table, and a frown crinkling her forehead, she accepted his logic.

"I've got fuck all for the last seven and a half weeks. Sexist prejudice against some female teachers and senior girls. Nothing concrete on recruitment. Bad record-keeping isn't an indictable offence. Spiked punch. A flimsy ragtag of accusations Dom can avoid with a good lawyer. I'm sorry."

Kelly would expect more. And hell! He was trying to prove something to Kelly. He was doing a final job for the department before he got his own goddam school. A school he'd dreamt of last night with Kelly by his side. How crazy was that?

I haven't told her how I feel.

Some stupid part of him was convinced he had to stop Dom before he could talk to Kelly about possibilities, about whether or not they had a next. Dom was the Shelob intent on protecting his territory using any means he could, including attacking Kelly.

"Not your fault, Mick. Bella taught me not to feel responsible for someone else's wrongdoing."

"How does that work out?"

"Not always well. Witness my mini tantrum with the water bottle. Can I get you a beer while I throw some steaks on the barbeque?"

"I'll help." *Leave it alone, Jamieson.* Let it cook, and you'll get an answer. He could feel it in his bones. "How about we banish Dom for tonight?"

"Sounds like a deal." She grabbed two beers from the fridge, topped them both.

"What's your fantasy holiday." Mick's question wasn't entirely random. He'd started to play with the idea of asking Kelly to join him for a few days break over Easter. Just them, and Boo, somewhere private.

"To visit some of the places I've read about in books?" She pulled the steaks out of the fridge, then hid them in the microwave to bring them to room temperature. Never trust a dog with an unguarded slab of raw meat.

"Name some."

"Nicolson's Café Edinburgh, the Elephant Bar." She was throwing him bait.

"J. K. Rowling and Harry Potter, right?"

"I'm impressed. Vesuvio Café, San Francisco."

"Mum's addicted to books. Remember. Jack Kerouac, Allen Ginsberg and the Beat Generation." Mick smiled in reminiscence. Why hadn't he asked Kelly about books and holidays before now? "Mostly second-hand or markets, but 'It's the quality of the words that counts and dog-eared means it's been treasured.'"

"A mum quote?" she asked.

He nodded.

"Might have been a dog. Boo chewed on everything when I got him."

"Hence, the term dog-eared. Mum didn't care, so long as *her children* didn't deface any." Mick rolled his eyes before reaching for the fridge door.

"Venice." She got glasses from the cupboard.

"Lots for Venice, but I'd pick Inspectorre Brunetti and the Donna Leon books." Mick enjoyed both the detective work and the tour of the city he'd found in them. "Have you been to any of these places?"

"Not yet. What about you?"

"Bummed around Australia for a year after I left the force. Started with Grandpa, then saw some of Tim Winton's Western Australia."

"I've seen his documentary on Ningaloo Reef. Magical. It's on my bucket list."

"Mine too."

He could picture Kelly there in her prim, delicious swimsuit, that he'd coax her out of on some quiet beach. Show her the decadence and delight of swimming naked. Make love to her in pristine waters. One piece of concrete evidence, then the dominoes would fall. With a bit more work and luck, Mick could make that happen.

* * *

"Why don't we add an extra element to our getaway location?" Kelly sat in his lap and was pleased at the reaction. "Where's your fantasy place for making love?"

"Is anywhere the right answer?" He slipped a hand under her skirt and finger-walked up her outer thigh, each inch higher, draining Kelly of the evening's frustration until her body was humming with anticipation.

"Not sure that's allowed in Nicolson's Café." She gave his ear a tug.

Kelly liked touching him, any excuse to touch him. He was disappointed with himself. Not fair, when he'd been given so little to go on by Ros and was operating with a school who'd either learned unquestioning loyalty, or who feared that disloyalty was always punished.

"I reckon we could manage a quickie in a dark corner of

Vesuvio Café."

"Only if you practise keeping your mouth closed when you come."

"Pot calling the kettle." He brushed his thumb over her pantie gusset.

"I don't scream." She rocked against his hand.

"Not always, but you make those little murmurs, sort of hiccups where air is caught in your throat, you sigh and go all soft and cuddly." His finger reached under her pants to stroke her. "Like you're making now."

"Maybe this is a good time to practise then? Are we on a bar stool or one of the benches?"

"You wanna make love on a bar stool?" He slid two fingers inside her.

Her breathing hitched. "I'm prepared to discuss the logistics."

"A corner booth would be better. You could wear one of those big skirt dresses, no knickers. I'd probably go commando, light trousers, a little loose." He increased the tempo of his caress. "Snuggle in the corner."

"Don't stop," she whimpered, rocking against his hand. "I can see you've given this con … sider … able—that's lovely—thought."

"You make me think, Kelly. Of making love in Vesuvio Café." He lifted her to straddle him. "Although Ningaloo Reef would be my first choice. I want you naked on the beach." He cupped her buttocks and nudged at her vagina with his still-covered cock.

"I've heard it's become very popular." Kelly rested her head on his shoulder, struggling to form coherent sentences. He did that to her. "Are you planning on erecting a beach tent for us?"

"I'm planning to sit you on the end of this table and screw you witless." He rose with her in his arms and perched her on the end of the table.

"Please do." She missed him, and he was less than a foot away.

He kicked off his shoes before ditching his trousers, then his hands reached under her dress to peel away her knickers.

Lovemaking with Mick was passion and laughter, tender touches and whispers and groans. A shared agreement to set aside problems they couldn't solve quickly. It was comfort, and all the words Kelly associated with Lucy and Niall, and Jamie and Clem's relationships. Love? She'd never trusted the words; no, that wasn't true. Never trusted if words weren't matched by actions. Mick and she had covered a lot of ground in their journey from enemies to bedmates. Was this love? Mick hadn't given her words, but his touch was loving, and he kept his word. Kelly hadn't anticipated a man like him.

* * *

Mick rolled his shoulders, deciding there wasn't much more he could do this week. He massaged his temples, his eyes aching from reading files and reports he'd hoped would turn up something, anything. Dom was careful, more careful than the staff Mick had investigated on previous postings. They'd finished week seven of term; eight weeks of sharing a house with Kelly.

Easter was in another two weeks. He had the sense time was running out. Kelly was due to leave at Easter. Neither Kelly nor he had skated anywhere near the conversation called "What's next?"

He usually took his time on the walk through the park to the library. Its pockets of open space were balanced by clumps of trees and bushes. Benches nestled deep within those trees provided cool comfort on a hot afternoon. Soft scents—not all of which he could identify—surrounded and soothed him. He could sift and file what he'd learned before meeting Kelly.

"Mick," a soft voice called.

He spun around, unsure if he was the target.

"Over here. In the lily pillies. There's a bench."

"So there is." Mick made his way into the peppery-scented bushes, hidden from watching eyes. "Hello, Maeve."

"I want to ask you a favour." She sat upright on the bench, a large carry bag balanced on her knees.

"How can I help?' His mind was racing, considering and abandoning reasons for this ambush.

"It's confidential."

Mick turned his head to look her full in the face. "Sounds important."

"It is to me and mine." The strained voice was alien to the competent, friendly librarian he mixed with daily.

"Go on." He faced straight ahead, giving her space and privacy, but a cop corner of his brain was jumping with that sensation of the case about to crack open. *Steady*.

"My eldest girl's a teacher."

Mick waited.

"She applied for a position here eighteen months ago. Head of Science. She's experienced, worked across the state and overseas. Has held senior positions in city schools."

"You must be very proud." Mick's heart sank. He'd examined the recruitment records. He'd found full details of those interviewed, the reasons for the ranking, and the final job offers. The records about those who didn't make it to interview were less complete. A list of names, the culling sheet countersigned by Dom Ellis and Ayesha Patel. Not an ideal recruitment process, but on the face of it, not maladministration.

"I'm proud of her for a lot of reasons. Not just her success, but her wish to come home and help me with her dad. He's not well."

"She was unsuccessful?" *Stupid question.*

"Unsuccessful we can live with. Not getting an interview is the galling part of it. Not being given a plausible reason for no interview. A very competitive field." Maeve almost spat the words. "I know exactly who was interviewed and who got the job. None of them was in the same class as my girl. And that's not bias talking."

"What do you want me to do?" Bias didn't tally with the Maeve that Mick had come to know over recent weeks. She also wasn't vindictive, making Mick question whether he'd missed something. He'd assumed Ayesha wouldn't sign anything that wasn't legit. Had he been wrong?

Maeve opened her large bag and pulled out a USB. "Read this. Tell me why she wasn't called to interview. How she might improve her application." Maeve was mocking. "She's going to try again. The bloke who got the job wants to move back to Sydney."

"Why me?"

"I've got a friend at the school. She told me what happened at the first staff meeting. What's been happening since. How you treat staff and students. Some people notice. I've seen you in the library. With the kids. Morning and afternoon. You remind me a bit of my daughter. Ellen and I couldn't start work without Dom's say so. Somehow he failed to pick up the council CEO's calls."

"I'm not sure I can help." Mick stared at the USB. He was holding evidence—potentially the first bit of concrete evidence, which might prompt questions about mal-administration for both Ayesha Patel and Dom Ellis. He'd clone and send it private express post to Roslyn tomorrow. Follow up with a phone call.

"We've got nothing to lose. My husband's not getting any better. I need my daughter home. She needs a job before she can come home."

"I can't promise anything." Making promises he couldn't keep was a sure way to disaster. "I'll have a look and give you my thoughts." He tucked the USB in his pocket and rose to leave.

"Another thing."

Mick turned back.

"My daughter's about thirty-five. Not a sweet young thing. Able to look after herself." Her chin set at a defiant tilt.

"Is that an accusation?"

"Not one I can substantiate. Dom Ellis has a lot of supporters in this town."

Mick collected Kelly at the library, asked her about her day, and answered her questions about his, although part of his mind was turning over this new information Maeve had given him. At home, they headed straight for the kitchen. Kelly dropped into a chair, and he passed her a glass of cold water.

Only then did Mick raise the topic of Maeve's daughter. "Has Maeve ever mentioned her daughter to you?"

"The science whiz? She's very proud of her."

"Is that all she's said?"

"Pretty much. She's held down some pretty impressive positions." Kelly rolled her glass across her forehead. The simple gesture made him grip his glass tighter, rather than sweep her into his arms and into bed. The hum of desire was constant. The pleasure of being in her company a thirst he hadn't quenched, didn't think he ever would.

"Maeve's daughter applied for a job at the school and missed out," he said, both pleased and relieved to discover Maeve had decided to trust him.

"Someone fiddled recruitment?" Kelly didn't mention Dom's name, but it hung in the air between them.

"I'll have a close look at the records. See what I can find."

Mick would check again. But after weeks of nothing, this might be another domino falling. His instincts told him he might finally have something. A dud Head of Maths and unfair playground duty assignments were minor misdemeanours. If Dom was fixing recruitment, it ratcheted things up to a whole new level.

Two days later, on Sunday afternoon, when Kelly was

rostered on at the library, Mick set up the videoconference. He'd tell her soon. Keeping a secret from her on this was a betrayal of what they'd started to create.

Tossing around accusations before he had concrete proof was a mug's game.

Tell the truth, Jamieson. Kelly idolises Ayesha. Kelly might tell me to go jump if I suggest Ayesha helped rig recruitment, and is on the run to prevent her actions becoming public knowledge.

And what a pathetic outcome—administrative malfeasance rather than sexual misconduct.

It was the tip of the iceberg on Dom's sins, not the killer blow Mick needed.

"Mick, this is Ayesha. I don't believe you've met."

Mick scanned the face of the woman sitting beside Roslyn in the regional office. She looked more anxious than angry. Mick wanted to make his own assessment. Despite suggesting Ayesha was unreachable, Roslyn clearly had some way to contact the missing deputy principal, and his questions about probity in recruitment had galvanised Ros. She'd messaged him this morning to say Ayesha was devastated to discover her name had been forged on the cull sheets and would talk to him via video link.

"Nice to finally meet you, Ayesha. There are so many people who sing your praises here."

Not me—not yet.

"I don't deserve that," Ayesha said bluntly. "I've let them down."

"In what way?"

"I know some of those women who were culled out. Maeve's daughter, for goodness sake. She'd be such a coup for the school."

"So, where are we?" Mick asked. Without Ayesha's co-operation, they still had nothing, and he wasn't convinced she was a reliable witness.

"Dom blackmailed me into leaving." Ayesha deflated with the confession.

Mick held his silence, waiting for Roslyn to step in.

"How?"

"First let me say, I didn't know Dom forged my signature on those recruitment documents." Ayesha twisted her hands together. "He'd locked me out of recruitment. I was relieved, given my workload, then I started to ask myself why males got all the top jobs. And fairly ordinary males at that. But country towns rarely attract the best performers."

"They attracted you, Ayesha," Roslyn replied.

"I moved for my boys." Ayesha looked into the camera. "I was widowed young. I thought a country town and school would give my boys a different experience, a chance to heal in a different environment." She sighed. "They're at university now, and I threw myself into the library. Wanted a distraction from missing them."

"The library's a huge success," Mick said.

The library was the key. Dom's attempts to sabotage it were personal, toward Ayesha, toward Kelly. Two strong women? If Kelly's faith in Ayesha was right, then Ayesha might have challenged Dom.

"Dom weaponised the library against me." Ayesha was bitter.

"I'm not sure I understand." Mick wanted words of one syllable that would exonerate her.

"Tenders were sought for the building. Dom and the council CEO handled those. After the successful company was announced, I became more involved. I met the owner of the building company. Daniel and I became romantically involved." She blew out a breath.

"I was busy. With plans for the library, with teaching, with my new relationship, but I became worried about the senior year girls. Their grades were falling—all of them. I didn't have any senior classes myself, but I checked all the documents and marks for the HSC. I spoke to one of the girls I knew well. Her older sisters had been in my sons' classes. She was brighter than her siblings, yet her marks were poor and going backward."

"You're right. This year has started out the same way."

After the senior girls' comments about maths, Mick had done a comparison of grades across previous years. Maths and Science showed the greatest discrepancy, the greatest drop in girls' performance. Again, too insubstantial to pin down.

Ayesha flinched. "I spoke to Dom about my concerns. Said I was going to alert Roslyn and do a review of why."

"Let me guess." Mick hated that he could see this so easily. "He blackmailed you over your relationship. Said it had started before it did. Presented you with signed documents suggesting you'd failed to declare a conflict of interest."

"Yes," Ayesha admitted. "But by then, Dom had started undermining me. He'd identify problems, raise them at executive meetings, and ask me what had gone wrong. He'd been steadily eroding my credibility with senior staff, so that when he threatened me, I thought no one would believe my version."

Mick let Ros ask the obvious question. "Why not call me?"

"Dom promised he'd change the teachers for the senior girls. I thought he was jealous of me, of the praise I was getting for the library. I thought if I went, it would stop. It never occurred to me he'd falsify other school records. I was exhausted putting out brush fires of gossip, missing the boys, Daniel was here."

"And the systematic belittling of office staff?" Mick pushed because every small transgression mattered, and the signs were impossible to ignore. Self-preservation in a deputy principal wasn't a pretty sight. Kelly would have called Dom on it.

Be fair, Mick.

He could hear Kelly's voice. Ayesha was subject to the same, if not more, insidious undermining than the other staff or students.

"I rang one of the secretaries after Roslyn spoke to me." Ayesha brushed a tear from her cheek. "The treatment of office staff. That's escalated this year. Toward the end of last year Dom's requests were often borderline unreasonable, but accompanied by a smile or a joke. And Dom's not alone in his management style."

Ayesha was defeated, when Mick wanted her to be angry.

"What about the sexual exploitation of young female teachers?" Mick had no concrete evidence, but his gut told him it had happened, would happen again.

"A teacher left last year. She resigned from the service. I asked her if there was any way I could help her. She said it was her own fault she'd got caught up in a romantic liaison."

"You believed her."

"I didn't have any reason not to."

"Do you know the name of her partner?"

"No. But it could have been one of Dom's 'boys,' if not Dom himself." Her hands twisted together on the desk. "If that's the case, she would have had no way of coping with the power imbalance."

"I can follow up and find out," Roslyn said.

"I didn't go to the pub; my social circle was more the parents I met when the kids were growing up. I'm sounding blind and naïve, which is a terrible excuse."

"You said you were exhausted." Mick returned to Ayesha's earlier words. Another pattern. Delegating many and minor tasks to silence women. Ayesha could confirm that.

"In retrospect. Yes. Dom tended to assign extra duties to any teacher who asked too many questions," Ayesha said. "To be blunt, at the end, I was tired and scared. I didn't want my relationship with Daniel smeared. Didn't want my kids involved. Still don't."

"That's understandable," Ros said. She was more forgiving than Mick, or more patient.

Kelly might side with Ayesha. Female solidarity. Mick couldn't fight that.

"So, what are our next steps?" Mick asked.

"I need to think, to talk to Daniel and the boys, maybe

consult a lawyer." Ayesha was exhibiting signs of shock.

Ros shook her head, a small signal, but she was asking Mick for more time for Ayesha.

Fine! But it wasn't just about Ayesha. Kelly could be next.

Mick continued, "If you do nothing, you could still face questions over the recruitment practices. Dom could still broadcast his claims."

And if you do nothing, then Dom is free to continue his destruction. From where I sit, that makes you complicit.

But what the hell do I know? I'm not the victim here. Whatever I do, Kelly comes first.

CHAPTER FIFTEEN

At the gate, Kelly released Boo from his lead then followed him around the side of the house. Finding Mick nursing a beer on the back porch, she bent to kiss him—and wasn't it lovely to know her man would be waiting ready to listen and act?

Steady on, Kelly. You're getting ahead of yourself.

"Sorry I couldn't meet you this afternoon," Mick said. "You're later than planned. Beer, water or wine?"

"I'll get myself a wine, if you'll make the call."

"What call?" He tugged her onto his lap to deepen the kiss.

"Pizza or Thai takeaway. Your choice."

"Pizza. Has something happened?"

Planting a kiss on his forehead, she pushed to her feet. Safe harbour was Mick reading her mood and opting for one of her comfort foods. "You are a very kind man because I know for a fact Thai fish cakes are your all-time favourites."

"How do you know that?" He pulled out his phone.

"The double order and the frozen extras are the giveaways. You're right. Something has happened. I need to talk to you and neither of us needs to worry about dinner."

He made the call while following her into the kitchen. Then waited while she poured a glass of wine and sat at the table. He stood behind her chair to massage her shoulders. "You're tight. Anger or frustration? Can I guess the cause?"

"You'd probably guess the right who." She was weary to her bones. Sexual exploitation was all about power, and neither she nor Mick needed to be reminded of that. Neither of them could walk past it either, and that was a bond worth more than rubies. "You might not guess the what."

"Tell me."

"Laura came to see me before closing time. She wanted my support and maybe my advice."

He continued his slow, clever kneading. She reached up a hand to cover one of his.

"Sit with me." Her throat was scratchy, and she tried to summon a smile. "Laura showed me some photos. Of her naked in bed with Dom."

"What did he want?"

"Interesting first question, but on the money. He wanted sex on demand. After all, she'd asked for it once. Placed him in a compromising position."

"How is she? Does she need a doctor? Safe accommodation? She can come here." His reaction settled all the jagged endings of Kelly's rage.

"She wants answers and justice, but she's ashamed, humiliated, embarrassed."

"I hope she's bloody angry," he said. "Bastard. Why come to you? Not me? Not a local doctor?"

"I'm a woman. Closer in age than many of the female teachers. An outsider. Likely to believe her version of events. She said she trusted me."

"What does Laura want you to do?"

"She doesn't know if they had sex. She certainly didn't consent. Said she had a crush on him because he seemed so nice, but never seriously contemplated taking it further. They were having a drink at the pub. He offered to drive her home. She woke up in her own bed feeling like shit."

"Dom slipped her a Mickey Finn?" Mick had risen to pace the kitchen.

"No evidence or witnesses—" The ringing doorbell interrupted her.

"I'll get it." Mick pressed a kiss to her crown on his way out. Boo moved closer and put his head on her feet. "Don't move."

Mick intuitively understood Kelly was paralyzed by the retelling. She hadn't expected to be. Watching him collect plates, napkins and cutlery was like watching a scene in a film. Completely disconnected from her. He plonked the pizza box on a breadboard and slid a slice onto each plate. "Eat. If you can."

Kelly forked up a bite and made herself chew. "He sent her the photos yesterday, suggested they get together next week. She threw up."

"Has she answered him?"

"Laura wants to press charges. Taking photos without permission. Posting them on a carriage service without permission. Non-consensual sex, although she's not convinced they had sex. Blackmail." Kelly pushed her plate away.

He closed the pizza box and moved it to the kitchen bench. "What did you say you'd do?"

"I said I'd talk to you. Get your advice and tell her tomorrow."

"You had to convince her?" he asked.

"She said she'd seen you at the pub, mixing it with Dom's boys. She's not one hundred percent sure about you," Kelly admitted. He'd needed to be seen at the pub with the boys, his beers hid his reconnaissance missions, but before she'd known his reasons, Kelly had had questions. Laura's hesitation showed the damage.

"But you are?"

Kelly hated seeing the doubt in his eyes. "Yes. You don't share a single square inch of common ground with Dom. You're undercover, with few signposts. Laura's just given us a signpost." Nausea swirled in her belly. Eating had been a mistake. "Would he do the same to Ayesha? No." She answered her own question. "She's too old for him."

* * *

"Maybe, but I think Dom's got some hold on Ayesha."

That was the closest Mick would skate to telling Kelly he had some intel on the older woman, a pathetic attempt to prepare Kelly for bad news.

"I'm not confident we can prove it," he added.

Mick wasn't confident Ayesha would go through with an official complaint.

"What sort of hold? Ayesha wouldn't know how to misbehave?"

Mick did battle with his conscience. "Innocents are the victims of choice for bullies. Anyone can be worn down by relentless attacks."

"That's Dom's pattern. Undermining the senior girls' confidence, publicly belittling older female staff, including Ayesha, and taking sexual advantage of younger women. He's an unchecked misogynistic bully."

"I said there were always patterns." Mick forced a smile.

He'd checked his phone bare minutes before Kelly's arrival. Still no word from Ros. He'd like to have Ayesha's name on a signed affidavit, but at the least he needed confirmation she'd bring a complaint.

"But we're wasting time. We need to get Laura out of town tonight. There's a late bus to Dubbo. I'll get Roslyn to pick her up at the other end. Will you help me persuade Laura?"

Kelly pushed to her feet, her response unhesitating. "What will you tell Dom?"

A few weeks of Kelly's loyalty in his life and in his bed weren't anywhere near enough.

"Laura called in sick. Said she'd eaten something. Needed a day or two." Mick was improvising. "Given I organise the replacement teachers, she'd call me first."

"Then what?"

"Then Roslyn, the department, and the police take over. We have to move fast."

Ayesha better get her act together by then. What were Mick's options? He hadn't told Kelly about Ayesha's signature on the recruitment documents because one, Dom was a wily bastard, and two, Ayesha was also a victim. Even if she never lodged a complaint, Ayesha would be a victim. His gut told him Kelly wouldn't support Ayesha's silence, his heart was afraid. He'd spent years with no one except immediate family taking his part.

Kelly had been in Ayesha's shoes.

Kelly would always take the side of a victim. Damned if he told her about Ayesha, damned if he remained silent.

Mick pulled up two blocks from Laura's boarding house.

"Why have we stopped?" She'd been gripping her hands since they'd left the house—left Boo behind.

"Change of plans, if you agree."

"What's the change?" She was listening.

"You send Laura a message, ask if you can speak to her on your own. Then let her know you've told me, and my advice is to leave now. Meanwhile, I'll book a bus ticket to Dubbo in a false name and call Ros. Tell Laura that's what I'm doing, and if she agrees to leave, send me a message. I'll text when I'm entering the back lane. You both slip out and into the car." Dom was in town most nights. Mick couldn't risk him seeing the car outside Laura's place.

"You're scaring me, Mick." Anxiety made her bluesy voice scratchy.

"I'm being cautious. If I park out the front, and Laura takes a while to convince, I could be spotted. Makes it harder to claim she rang in sick tomorrow morning. Dom has tentacles everywhere. Being principal gave him immediate entrée to the business chamber and landed gentry, and he's capitalized on it for all he's worth."

"Makes sense. Dom's a smarter, meaner version than George Hogan." Kelly had stared the beast in the eye. "I don't think she'll take much convincing. She's angry enough and frightened enough to take off on her own. If she sees you've taken it seriously, she'll grab the chance."

"I'll give you ten minutes to get there and get inside. After I've sorted the bus ticket, I'll ring Ros and ask her to give you a video call in twenty. Laura might not know Ros personally, but she'll recognise her. Ros can reassure Laura we're legit."

"You've thought about this." She placed a hand on his thigh, and Mick covered it with his, the connection a balm to his tortured thoughts.

"If Dom gets the slightest inkling of what's up, he'll strike whoever's closest. If I'm pushed, in a few days, I'll say Laura told me the doctor said she needed more rest, and she wanted to go home. This close to Easter, I authorized her departure."

"Let's do it." She started to free her hand.

"One more thing." He squeezed her hand. "Do you have emergency contacts on your phone?"

"Yes."

"Put me at the top of the list." Mick needed to protect her.

Right now, I can't decide if that's because of our history in Hay or because I'm in love with her.

He didn't have time to think about her hesitation. "While you're in Tullamore. While we're dealing with Dom."

I'm sounding desperate.

She pulled out her phone, made the program change, and turned toward the door. She stopped with it half-open, glancing back over her shoulder. Her smile made him feel like a hero. "Thanks for this."

For what?

He watched her walk away. For being selective with the truth? That was a kind of betrayal, and his only excuse was that he'd thought the truth would hurt her.

Wrong, Jamieson.

Before tonight, he only had evidence pointing to Ayesha's guilt, to Ayesha being complicit in maladministration. Sure, Dom was her co-signatory, but given Dom's meticulous attention to detail in the falsified records, there was every chance he'd planned for discovery where only Ayesha would wear the dirt. There was no justice in that outcome. Kelly might never forgive him.

* * *

Two tense nights later, Kelly was exhausted. She struggled to fight through the murky miasma that was suffocating her. She was going through the motions each day, but part of her head was in Dubbo. What were the police doing with Laura's evidence? Another part of her head was back at Abbadon Central, helpless with no one to turn to. Only at night wrapped in Mick's arms, with Boo on his mattress at the foot of the bed, did she feel safe.

"Boo needs another run, and I'm just not up to it tonight. Please take him, Mick."

"A short run. Twenty minutes at top speed." He sounded unhappy. "Before I go, I want to make sure every door and window is locked. Come with me."

Kelly followed him from room to room, confirming each window was locked; not wanting to believe the precautions were necessary, but accepting their history meant Mick needed to do this. He'd been edgy since Laura had gone to Dubbo, or maybe before that. He said he'd had some work calls on Sunday, and she hadn't asked him about them.

"Try to relax a bit." He stepped closer and pulled Kelly into his arms. Warm, safe, hers to love, and she'd never allowed herself to believe she'd find someone who was her soul mate. "Lock the doors behind me, and keep your phone on you."

"Relax doesn't work with 'lock the doors.'"

"Try. I checked with authorities; Dom isn't entitled to keys to residential properties."

"Shit, I didn't think of that."

"Dom asked me about Laura again today. I said she'd sounded terrible when she rang yesterday morning, and we'd agreed she'd take two days sick leave. Said I'll check with her tomorrow morning, if I don't hear from her tonight. That I'd keep him updated. He seemed to buy it. I guess I'm just antsy."

"Go for a run. A shower will help me relax. Boo, run with Mick."

"Could you hold the shower until we get back?"

"I'm sticky and uncomfortable. I'm also behind locked doors. You've confirmed Dom doesn't have keys. I can't live in fear, Mick."

"Maybe I just want to share." He waggled his eyebrows. "Take your phone to the shower."

She rolled her eyes.

"What? You might slip."

"I've never slipped in a shower in my life." After locking the front door behind her man and her dog, Kelly headed for her bedroom. When had she started thinking of Mick as *her* man? They'd made no promises. She had less than two weeks left in Tullamore, and neither of them had even ventured in the direction of what next?

Except for a whimsical conversation about fantasy holidays. She'd love to explore more of the world, more of life with Mick. She'd slipped from grudging respect to liking to lusting after Mick.

I love you. Am I brave enough to tell you?

Rolling her shoulders, Kelly trawled through a mental list of cooked meals in the freezer. Chicken casserole it is. Already cooked. First the decadence of a long, hot shower. Autumn came earlier in the evening out here in the central west, and the nights were starting to get colder. She'd steam away her low mood, and the fatigue born of anxiety and the tension that had built over the last nearly nine weeks. Knowing that a George Hogan equivalent held power over the lives of children was too close a reminder of her helplessness in Hay. And she was grateful to her bones that Mick had engaged her support in taking Dom Ellis down.

Setting fresh jeans and a long-sleeved tee on the bed, she wandered into the bathroom and stripped down before stepping into the shower, and tucking her phone on the ledge of the shower screen. Not her usual practice, but she'd promised Mick she'd keep it close. She shivered, then laughed at her collywobbles.

The hot water cascading down her back was heaven.

The right choice, Kel.

Her muscles slowly unravelled under the pummeling of the spray. After soaping herself down, she turned to face the nozzle. Closing her eyes, she let her head fall back, so the warm water could stream down her face and across her chest.

"Well, hello, Kelly." Dom blocked the bathroom door.

Don't panic.

"How did you get in?"

"Back door." His gaze wandered over her, more vengeful than covetous. Rape was always about power, but it was also a tool of hate for some men.

"I locked the back door." The instinct to cover herself was almost overwhelming, but Dom wanted her fear, wanted her begging. The steam was creating condensation, acting as a light veil between her nakedness and him.

I'm sorry, Mick. I should have waited for my shower.

"I noticed that." He stepped further into the room, grabbed her towel and threw it behind him into the hall. "Very unfriendly for a small country town. Friends drop in on each other all the time."

"We're not friends." She readied herself to fight. Went through the mental preparatory steps Clem had taught her. "How did you get in?"

"I have keys to all departmental properties in town."

Dom held up a set of keys, revealing the thin synthetic gloves he was wearing, and fear threatened to take over.

I'll be damned if I let him see it.

"This is not technically a school property. And you have no rights when people live here. I'd like you to leave."

I'd like to get close enough to knee you in the balls.

He waved a phone. "Time to get out, Kelly."

"Pass me a towel," Kelly issued a counter order.

He laughed. "You're going to pose for a few shots for me."

Photos! The gloves were about not being caught. Blackmail, not rape. The same technique he'd used with Laura, when Kelly thought Dom saw her as another Ayesha and wanted to undermine her work in the library. Kelly closed her eyes briefly, to steady herself. She wasn't done, and Mick and Boo weren't far away.

Making a big show of returning the shampoo and conditioner to the ledge, she fumbled, and in her fumble hit the emergency call button on her phone.

"Hurry up."

Relief surged through her when Dom didn't appear to notice anything. "Mick's due any minute."

"You should be so lucky." Dom snorted. "I saw him heading for the river with that stupid dog of yours. He never runs for less than forty minutes." If Dom had been timing their runs, that gave her an advantage.

"You've been spying on us?" Slowly, she turned the taps off, rubbed the excess water off her arms and legs. Her mind raced. How long did she have? What did he want? Photos? She could deal with that, stay calm, and keep him talking until help came.

If you put even a finger on me, all bets are off.

"Watching you. Making sure everything's going okay with my new staff." His twisted mind sickened her. "Let's get a few shots of the beauty ending her bath." Chuckling, as if he'd told a hilarious joke, he leaned forward to push the shower screen open. He snapped a few shots. But he was watching her still, his gaze largely on her face, searching for fear. He fed on fear.

She wouldn't give it to him.

"If you answer my questions, this won't take so long. Where's Laura?"

Then Kelly saw it. *He* was afraid. That's what had brought him here, flushed him into the open. "At home in bed. Mick says she's not well." She stayed inside the shower stall.

"I asked Josie to check. I was concerned." Dom shrugged. "Laura's gone. According to the manager of the boarding house, you're the last person to have seen her. And that was two nights ago. Where is she?"

"I have no idea." Kelly held her hands up in surrender. More than ten minutes. Mick had been gone more than ten minutes. And it had been, what? A minute since she'd pressed *Call.*

"You can do better than that." Dom held up his camera.

"She rang her parents. They were worried about her health. Suggested she see a doctor in Dubbo." If Kelly charged him, she might disable him long enough to get out.

"I don't believe you. Mick took her home after my party, took some compromising photos of her. He's been trying to blackmail her."

Kelly readied to charge. Dom stepped sideways**,** anticipating her move, his bulk blocking the doorway. Rage burned through her. Although rage didn't stop her heart hammering in her chest. Didn't stop her fists clenching.

No! No! No! You will not shift responsibility onto Mick for your crimes.

"I've contacted the department to lodge a complaint against him." He waved the phone in front of her again. What reaction was he seeking? "Might not stick. Laura's getting a bit of name. Even came on to me."

"You're a disgusting liar."

"Think you're the only one he's screwing? He took Steph home after a night at the pub a few weeks ago. Likes to sample the merchandise, does our Mick."

"I don't believe you." She let her voice tremble. He'd just given her a useful piece of information. Dom didn't know that the council CEO and his wife had taken over from Mick in the car park when Steph needed a lift home. There were independent witnesses who could exonerate Mick, and they would. Unlike George Hogan's coterie in Hay.

"I'm going to step back, and you're going to walk into the bedroom. Quietly. I think we need some bedroom shots." He waved the camera in the direction of her room.

"No." Was he planning on replicating the shots he'd taken of Laura? She could smell Dom's sweat, smell something underlying that—menace. Dom badly wanted to hurt her but wanted Mick to wear the blame. "*It was Mick's fault, all Mick*" would be Dom's defense. She wouldn't allow it to happen. Mick was coming, and Kelly refused to be helpless.

Mick had told her she wasn't helpless, even when trapped like now.

"I'm happy to give you a reason to move along. A backhander. After all, it's Mick doing this. Mick's phone."

"Mick took his phone with him on his run."

Get him to talk, Kelly.

"This is his business phone. Ayesha's old mobile. The one I signed out to him when he first arrived. Turns out, Mick's a bit of an amateur photographer."

"You'll never make that stick."

"Try me. There's only the two of us here, so it's my word against yours." He pushed the bathroom door wide behind him. "I've been keeping notes on you, had to put a few on your official record. Insubordination, refusal to follow instructions, refusal to carry out duties, bad influence on the students."

"You need to meet with me and my rep if you have any serious accusations." But Kelly's stomach muscles clenched at the precision planning behind this attack.

"Appointment scheduled for Monday. You sent the request to the union rep."

"You're mad."

"I'm thorough. You'll find that out when it comes to your disciplinary hearing. I can make that go away, if you tell me where Laura is and why she left."

Kelly thought she heard the front door, almost inaudible, but surely that had been a click? "Laura's in a safe house in Dubbo organised by Roslyn Morales. She's given a statement to the police about being blackmailed to provide sexual favours."

"I told you Mick was trying to blackmail her. It's all on his phone." He held up the phone again.

"She named you."

He lunged for Kelly, but before he could grab her, Boo burst through the door and leapt between them. Mick was close behind, and Kelly could hear the siren drawing closer. She sank to the floor, curling around herself. Then she began to shake.

Run, Kelly.

"It's okay. You're safe now." Mick wrapped large towels around her, but Kelly didn't believe him.

Somehow, she was back in Abbadon Central, a town she'd fled to because of her mother's rejection.

Run, Kelly.

Like then, she hadn't been smart enough, fast enough to get herself out of trouble. Her heart beat against her ribs. She pressed a hand to it.

Run.

The refrain was on repeat in her head, her body twitched like a baby rabbit's, the compulsion to flee into the night stronger than her heart beat.

Run.

"Here, Boo." A male voice, but there were men in the room, moving about, and words swirling just beyond her reach.

Run, Kelly.

Boo pressed against her side. She turned her face into his body and blocked out everything else.

CHAPTER SIXTEEN

Mick took the chair beside her while Rob Chan questioned her. Boo took the other side. Kelly's grip on the dog's collar seemed to be all that was holding her in the room. Mick wanted to lift her into his arms, but wasn't sure she wouldn't sense his fury. He didn't want to contaminate her with his self-disgust. He'd missed the signs Dom was on the edge.

"I was in the shower when Dom Ellis broke into the house." Her voice was flat, and Mick was helpless to undo the last half hour.

"Did he touch you?" Rob asked.

Kelly had met Rob before. His wife, Beth, was doing the reading for the preschoolers at the library, and Mick didn't know if that made it easier or harder for Kelly.

"Yes."

"Jesus." Mick roared.

She turned to look at him. The first time since he'd arrived. Mick had let her down.

"Dom didn't lay a finger on me, but he violated me with looks and thoughts and words. He was in my home."

"Can you tell me more?" Rob kept his voice low.

"My guess is Dom's been doing this for years. He weighs

up everyone he meets to decide how and if he can use them. Mick and I are patsies. He's apparently scheduled a disciplinary meeting with me and my rep on Monday. Any accusations I make against him are payback for him just doing his job."

"What's he got on me?" Mick asked.

"Dom signed Ayesha's old mobile out to you at the beginning of the term. The compromising photos of Laura, of me, and who knows what else are on that phone. *Your* official phone. He's already reported you for seeking to blackmail Laura for sexual favours."

"Jesus wept."

"A bit flimsy. If Mick's never touched it, it won't have his fingerprints on it. Location tracking can prove it wasn't where Mick was." Rob shook his head.

"What do you think, Mick?" Kelly asked.

"That Dom's smart enough to have lifted my prints and transferred them to the phone. He's also smart enough to have secreted the phone in my office, and to have planted it here from time to time."

"He used keys a few weeks ago to sneak up on me when I was alone after hours in the library. He didn't expect Boo. Tonight, he waited until Boo left with Mick. Then he used keys to break in."

Mick's hands formed fists.

"How do you know that? Could you have left a window open?" Rob was busy taking notes.

"Will you tell him, or will I?" She glanced at Mick.

"I was a cop. I was posted here because of some concerning patterns in the last few years. Ayesha's sudden departure set off alarm bells. I checked the house before I went for the run. Every window and door in this place was locked. Kelly hasn't stirred anywhere without Boo for the last few weeks."

But I didn't do enough.

"I heard rumours," Rob said. "Mostly from kids about girls being unfairly treated."

"Dom Ellis told me he had keys to this house and used them to get in tonight." Kelly was unequivocal. "Dom said he wanted answers to a few questions, and the photos on Mick's 'official' phone were his surety of getting his way with me, with Mick."

"Why did he attack you?"

"I told him Laura had lodged a complaint against him."

"The cops in Dubbo are dealing with it. I hoped they'd have kept you informed," Mick said.

"The paperwork came through late this afternoon. A warrant for Dom's arrest on charges. In respect to Laura Favretto; misuse of a carriage service involving photos taken without consent and blackmail. In respect to Ayesha Patel, blackmail and fraud. Tonight, adds B & E, intimidation, and assault."

"Ayesha's pressed charges?" Kelly looked to Mick for an answer.

He'd let her down; the knowledge was a gut punch. By not telling her what he knew of Ayesha's case, he'd betrayed what they'd been building. He'd chosen to withhold key information.

"Right. Well." Mick pushed himself upright. "I uncovered evidence of corruption in recruitment. The documents were countersigned by Ayesha. Initially, there was a possibility she was complicit. On Sunday, I interviewed her via video with the regional director present. Ayesha denied ever signing the documents and admitted Dom had blackmailed her into leaving. She wanted to think about pressing charges on the forgery. That's all. Dom defeated Ayesha. She wasn't angry enough to fight back. I had no case."

"According to my info, your regional director, Roslyn Morales, introduced Laura to Ayesha. Whatever they talked about convinced Ayesha to lodge the formal complaint." Rob filled in the gaps.

Kelly wouldn't look at him.

"Dom also accused Mick of drugging and sexually

harassing Stephanie Bryant," she said.

"When was I supposed to have done that?" Mick dragged a hand through his hair.

"The night you offered to walk her home from the pub. *Only* in that case you told me the council CEO and his wife took over. You gave me the ammunition to fight him." She sounded battered. Her rich voice croaky with tears.

"Is that enough for tonight?" Mick begged Rob.

"I'd say so. We've got him in a cell. He's called his lawyer—the mayor." Rob's eyebrows rose, conveying his knowledge of the town's hierarchy. "I'll be off then. Kelly, I'll talk to you again tomorrow."

"I'll see you out." Mick followed the cop up the hall, shook his hand, and locked the door after Rob left. Then he rested his head against it. He'd failed her, like he had in Hay. Had let a vicious bastard treat her as a nothing, an object, not as a sexual object—Dom Ellis saw women as objects to be manipulated and used. Naked photos were a tool. Sex was a tool. Mick wanted to smash things. Instead, he went back to Kelly's bedroom. "How can I help?"

A bit bloody late, Jamieson.

"Why didn't you tell me about Ayesha?"

Telling her he'd been afraid she'd support Ayesha, not him, was a cop-out. *Poor pun.* "When you got home, you told me about Laura. Laura became the priority."

"For every minute of the last two days?"

"You've been worried about Laura," he insisted.

I didn't want you to be disillusioned. I didn't want to hurt you.

"At the beginning I had a suggestion that Ayesha and Dom had falsified recruitment records. I didn't think you'd be okay with that."

"You could have shared your doubts about Ayesha."

"Right! The day Laura came to you, Ayesha told me Dom had forged her signature on those records. Dom blackmailed her into leaving, citing corrupt behaviour with the library's builder, her lover. Despite that, at the end of the meeting Ayesha hadn't agreed to lodge a formal complaint on either account. I decided you'd had a tough enough day without me knocking your idol off her pedestal."

"Let's *be* honest." The fire in Kelly's eyes reminded him of when he'd dropped her off at the boarding house in Hay. "You wouldn't have told me regardless of what happened to Laura."

Only in that case you told me about the council CEO. In his head, Mick admitted the justice of Kelly's accusations. He hadn't planned to tell her. Had already decided that the attack on Laura trumped the lesser crimes and would place blame where it should be.

He'd missed the parallels between Ayesha and Kelly. Hadn't anticipated Dom would forge Kelly's signature, or try and blackmail her about her relationship with Mick. Kelly was right. Mick had left her undefended because he was afraid.

"We had Laura. Ayesha refused to fight once. I don't know her well, how badly he scared her. You admire her." Mick was losing Kelly. Fear curdled his gut. Despite his cack-handed attempt to protect Kelly from disillusionment about Ayesha, from physical harm, he was losing her.

"I can cope with finding people have feet of clay—"

"If that's to my account—"

"You chose not to tell me. I knew Dom wanted to punish me, but I thought he saved his meanest little games for women of a certain type. I'm not his type. Blackmailing Ayesha is a clue Dom might try to blackmail me too. Over mal-administration, non-performance of my job, my relationship with you."

She was right, and Mick had no excuses left.

"What would you like to do?" Frustration robbed him of answers; he'd disappointed the woman he loved, not the schoolgirl in Hay. He could separate the two in his head and his heart. He didn't love her because of Hay, he loved her because she was the other half of him.

"I want another shower."

"Of course. Need help?"

"Just Boo. Thanks." She stayed where she was.

Mick returned to the kitchen. Had he lost the right to comfort both of them? He pulled out his phone. "Arabella. It's Mick Jamieson. Kelly's been attacked." He heard the indrawn breath.

"I'll come straight away."

"She's not physically harmed." Mick swallowed hard. "He humiliated her. She was in the shower, and he broke in."

"Where was Boo?" She sounded puzzled.

"It's been a rough week. We agreed I'd take Boo for a short run. It happened while we were out."

"It's not your fault, Mick."

"Then whose bloody fault is it?" he roared.

"The man who broke in," she said simply. "I'll be there before morning."

"Thank you. Stay as long as you want, as long as you need to." Mick's mother had steadied a world gone mad after Hay. Arabella was Kelly's adoptive mother. He waited until he heard the shower turn off, then waited a bit longer before knocking on her door.

"Come in." She was already in bed, the covers pulled up to her shoulders with Boo standing guard at her head. *Keep away* was tattooed in invisible ink on her forehead.

He carried the tray to her. "Whiskey with an *E* because it's Irish and Vegemite toast. Jameson's, hope that's okay?"

She nodded.

"I know the Vegemite toast doesn't rate alongside potato crisps. But we don't have any crisps."

Please talk to me, Kelly.

She flashed a wan smile. "And Vegemite toast is the cure-all in your family."

"Yeah." He handed her the whiskey glass. "You say when." He barely poured a finger into the glass.

"When."

"I rang Arabella."

She studied him, and Mick couldn't read her. All these days and nights when he'd held her in his arms and slipped into love with her. Was in love with her. They'd been forming a special bond, or he had. And now he couldn't read her.

"Arabella will be here in the morning."

She set her glass down, tears brimming in her eyes. "That's that, then." Her voice was dead. She turned her back on him. Her silence screamed "Don't touch me," but holding her was the only way he'd be able to tell her he was sorry.

He loved her, he would always love her.

He had no choice but to leave.

* * *

When Kelly answered the door on Thursday morning, Bella opened her arms. Kelly walked into them. She'd spent the night awake, trying to understand what had happened. What had broken between her and Mick, and if it was her fault. Telling him he'd failed to protect her was unforgivable. She'd hurt him. When he didn't climb into her bed last night to hold her, she'd been too proud to beg. Kelly had begged her mother all those years ago to love her. Her mother had laughed. "Why should your life be any different to mine?"

You abandoned me.

She had to bite her tongue not to shout the words.

"Hush now. Don't talk yet." Bella rocked her.

"I want to go home." Kelly heard Mick's indrawn breath behind her and turned to face him. "I've contacted Rob Chan this morning. He can talk to me in Sydney. I've spoken to Ros. I've been released early. I've already packed."

"Please go through to the kitchen, Arabella. We'll be with you in a minute." Mick stood silent while Bella walked around him and down the hall. "I'm not arguing with you. But Arabella's been on the road all night. She needs some food and some sleep before you can expect her to go back on the road."

"I'll drive." Kelly just wanted to run and never stop.

"Not good enough."

"I need to go."

You're running, Kelly.

"We need to talk about this. You can stay. You don't have to go into work. We'll have some free air in a week, a few days off over Easter. Why are you leaving?" He was uncertain—desperate, and his distress made her ache inside.

"We made no promises or plans beyond the end of this term," Kelly said, knowing she'd compromise in an instant if he loved her.

"What about making friends, enjoying being together in and out of bed?" He took a step closer.

Kelly waved him back. "Friends tell the truth."

"I haven't lied to you."

"You withheld critical facts." A single small fact and she was overreacting. But he'd called Bella. He'd seen Dom ogling her naked body and hadn't touched her since.

He looked like she'd slapped him. "I didn't tell you about Ayesha, because I didn't know what she'd do. If she'd fight or run?"

"I have a state-wide job based in the heart of the city."

I'm running away.

"You want a small town posting so you can create the kind of school you've dreamed of. You deserve that promotion."

You've sacrificed a piece of your soul to get that promotion.

The menace of Dom Ellis hovered in the air between them. "A long-distance relationship won't work."

He raised a hand and let it drop. "All true, but why save those objections until now?"

"I haven't saved them until now." Kelly tried patience, when her heart was breaking. "That's the trajectory we've been on. Nine weeks doesn't change goals nurtured over years."

"What's going on, Kelly? Renegotiating goals is a piece of cake if it's what we want. You said you once dreamed of living and working in the country."

"That was knocked out of me."

"Not fair." He took another step toward her.

Please stop.

"You need a small country high school to test your theories."

"The truth, Kelly. I need the truth."

"You haven't completely forgiven yourself. You're playing protector. Twice you've met me and twice you've witnessed me being humiliated, violated. You've convinced yourself you care for me"—Kelly struggled to contain the tremble in her voice—"because I've forgiven you."

"You're wrong."

Now, she read hurt bewilderment in his eyes. "Am I?"

"You're right on one level. I did have the memory of Hay etched into my psyche. I did need to see you and know you'd forgiven me. But we sorted that in our first few weeks. We both carry scars from the past, but we've made ourselves into different people. Haven't you moved on?"

"I thought I had. It's why I accepted this job. I had Bella and Charlie, Lucy and her grandparents, and Clem and her foster carers to help me. Meeting you has shaken that belief."

Kelly wasn't explaining herself well. Still, she couldn't free herself of the manacles that had snapped shut on her ankles last night.

Run, Kelly.

Dom's hate-filled eyes when he'd lunged for her; the tiled floor as cold and hard as the garage in Hay; Mick ringing Bella to come and take her away. They added up to abandonment.

"I'm afraid we're caught in some weird love your captor experience."

"Stockholm's Syndrome?" He closed his eyes; his face etched in pain, and she wanted to take back every word.

"You're wrong. I'm not your kidnapper. I haven't taken you hostage. You were in my power for about forty-five minutes seventeen years ago. Fear sent you back to Sydney. Are you saying you're afraid of me now?"

"No." She could be emphatic. Not fear, but a form of self-preservation. Run before she was pushed. Calling Bella had sounded like a nudge.

We should be able to deal with this.

He'd agreed with her assessment weeks ago.

"We're friends, lovers."

"It's not enough." It was more than she'd had with any man, and until last night, she'd thought it was enough. But Vegemite toast and Irish whiskey weren't a lasting substitute for his arms wrapped around her.

"We need time to think. Dom Ellis is the smart twin to George Hogan. You didn't protect me then. This has been about protecting me now. You've done it." He wasn't correcting her. "But you're still fighting that war. That doesn't mean you care for me."

"I love you."

His words were beautiful, and he'd never said them when he'd slid into her body, when he'd made love to her as if she was the only woman on earth.

"You've never said."

Neither did I.

But she remembered her mother saying she loved Kelly, and that had been a lie. Bella didn't say the words, but Kelly knew. With Mick, the timing was wrong. She wanted him to say the words, but not now, not when he hadn't said them before Dom attacked her. Back when he'd delighted in touching her.

"I wasn't sure I had the right to."

"That sums up our problem." Kelly was hollowed out. "Tell me you don't have all those words your sisters threw at you in your head? About how disgusting you were, how misogynistic, how you didn't deserve any woman becoming your lover?"

"They were defending you even though they didn't know you." His hands formed fists.

"Tell me you don't still despise yourself?"

"I despise the man I was then. And I can admit that until I met you, I hadn't really healed. I needed to know you were safe. I didn't know that until I met you. I'm not explaining well—"

"I understand. Forget the psycho-babble about closing the circle. Despite Bella, despite Boo, I knew there were two bogeymen still out there who might ambush me one day, so I needed to be ready. You defanged George and remade yourself. Why wouldn't I fall for you?"

Please disagree with me.

"I love you."

"Sex was the only kind of love my mother understood." She dashed her tears away with one hand. "Maybe it was just sex?"

He flinched. "You mean you don't love me."

"I'm not sure." *And that's a lie, Kelly Steele.* "Given our past, we have to be beyond sure."

"I'm sure. Make no mistake, Kel. I understand you've had your choices stolen from you in the past. This is your choice to make. I love you. Give me a chance. Give us a chance."

"I have to go away." Kelly couldn't process everything he'd said, couldn't see past his reluctance to touch her, her fear he didn't really want her.

"I'll go out, leave you in peace." His expression was grim. "Let Arabella shower, and ask her if she needs to sleep. Text me when you're gone." Without a backward glance, a word to Bella or Boo, he walked through the front door.

Kelly turned and walked toward the kitchen, tears pouring down her cheeks. Two hours later, she put her last bag in the car. Not all her possessions, but she was taking Boo. Would Mick make this so easy, if he really wanted her to stay?

"In you go, Boo." Boo followed Bella's instructions, jumping onto the blanket spread on the back seat for him. Bella attached his harness.

Kelly took the driver's seat, swallowing her tears on the drive toward the coast so she wouldn't wake Bella. Mick had abandoned her.

Why did it feel like she was abandoning him?

CHAPTER SEVENTEEN

Sydney, or at least the expressway on its north western side, arrived sooner than expected. Kelly focused on the view out the side window. She'd driven most of the way, left Bella to nod off, swiped tears from her face that no one else saw. Bella was handling this last hour. The traffic seemed impossible, people swept past in huge swarms, barely aware of each other or the world around them. Her nose twitched. The smell was different. Even the colour of the sky. Who knew you'd get used to the quieter rhythms of a small town so quickly? Boo pushed his nose between the front seats, sensing her distress.

"You're missing him too, aren't you?" Kelly swivelled to bury her face in his neck.

"If you're missing him, why are we driving away?"

"Because I don't want to trap him," Kelly whispered.

"Trap him how?" Bella rarely showed exasperation. "I didn't see some poor animal pinned in a cage. Mick's impressive because he's had to fight to be who he is."

"He didn't tell me about Ayesha."

"I'd bet money Clem and Lucy would have hesitated to criticize your idol, and they have no doubts about your love and loyalty. You'd have bitten their heads off."

"I'm not blind to my idol's faults."

"Don't I know it." Bella chuckled. "You've pointed out mine often enough."

"You're on his side?"

"That's not worthy of you, Kel. By the way, Lucy and Clementine are waiting at home."

"Okay." Kelly wasn't up to answering questions. She didn't think her friends could help with this problem.

Bella pressed the remote for the garage door, drove in, then cut the engine. "Take your bag in. I'll bring Boo and give him some food."

"'Kay." Kelly didn't move.

"I'll show you how it's done." Bella's face was streaked with concern. Her adoptive parent slid out her side of the car before opening the door for Boo. "C'mon, fella. We've got some friends to see you."

Kelly waited until she had the garage to herself. "You can do this."

But it was worse than when she'd run away from home. Then she hadn't known what a stable loving home was. Bella had taught her that. She'd found more with Mick. Safety, companionship and passion beyond her wildest imaginings.

"I can do anything," she whispered, "doesn't mean I want to."

Her friends and Bella would be in the kitchen. Kelly scooted past the half-open door. "Be with you in a minute. Just need to dump this." She held up her bag. She took less than a minute. Long enough to drop her bag inside her bedroom door and backtrack to the kitchen. She plastered a smile on her face. "You shouldn't have left work so early." She corrected herself. "It's lovely to see you." They were already on their feet.

"Come and sit down." Lucy hugged her.

"We've got supplies." Clem took her elbow, handling her like an invalid needing care, before settling her at the table.

It was only then Kelly noticed. An unopened bottle of single malt Scottish whisky held pride of place. It was flanked by four extra-large packets of salted crisps. Mick had offered Jameson's, an Irish whiskey, and Vegemite toast. She loved him.

"Niall will collect us when I call. He's designated driver to make sure we get home." Lucy reached for the bottle.

"What's he doing?" Kelly blinked back the tears that had started with thoughts of Mick.

Lucy waved a hand in a circle. "His muse is upon him. He's making me a surprise for my birthday, so is happy to have some alone time."

"Jamie and his siblings are having a meeting about their dad's health. He's not sure what time he'll be free." Clem lined up four whisky tumblers.

Bella brought a crystal water jug and a cut-glass bowl of ice to the table. "Pick your poison, girls. I might take my first glass straight."

"Show-off." A tear trickled down Kelly's cheek, and she wiped it away.

"Tell us what you want us to know." Bella brushed a kiss to her crown before taking the fourth chair.

"I love him with all my heart." She couldn't not tell them the truth.

"But?" said Clem.

"I think he feels responsible for me."

"How is that a bad thing?" Lucy was doing a tag team with Clem.

"Because wanting to fix what happened to me in Abbadon Central might be responsible, but it isn't everlasting love," she snapped.

Couldn't her friends see that?

"False responsibility is a thing in psychology. Taking responsibility for things you couldn't have changed. Not your fault, but you still feel guilty?" Clem studied her, creases appearing between her eyes.

"Maybe." Kelly took a sip of the single malt too fast, and

the burn sizzled down her throat.

"Don't you think seeing a monster trapping you naked in the shower might have been a more immediate challenge to his protective instincts?" Clem never let self-pity get in the way of logic in her work.

"Ouch!" said Lucy.

"Mick didn't need to be thinking of the past to feel guilty for underestimating Dom Ellis." Clem gentled her voice. "Or to be devastated at what happened to you."

Kelly scrubbed tears away, but more kept coming.

"Do you feel responsible for Bella?" Lucy reached out a hand to cover Kelly's.

"Not responsible." Kelly glanced at her adoptive mother. "But I make decisions that include her well-being. I worry when she's not well." She hiccupped. "If she's out alone after dark."

"You do not." Bella sounded exasperated.

"I do, actually," Kelly confessed, crossing to the bench to collect some tissues.

"So, is Mick feeling guilty, responsible, or devastated?" Clem resumed her attack.

"I'd hate to be your enemy." Kelly plopped down on the chair and started to mop her eyes. *Devastated.* She'd be devastated if someone attacked him.

"You'll never have to find out." Clem flashed a beatific smile.

"I don't think Mick knows. It's all happened so fast. Does he love me, or has he got himself caught up in a way he never intended?"

"I'd say that young man has worked out his priorities and doesn't just go with the flow." Bella added a bit of acid. "He's not about to saddle himself with a woman out of sympathy or from some misplaced protective urge."

"Bella, my protective urge isn't misplaced. You're precious to me."

"Harrumph. Are you precious to him?"

"I'm giving him space to find out."

"You're scared," said Clem.

"Damn right, I'm scared. I've never felt like this before."

"So, you're the one with the misplaced protective urge. You're saving him from himself."

"He wants to be the principal of his own school, a country school. I've just won my dream job, a city job."

"Intelligent people have been known to negotiate and compromise." Bella saluted with her glass.

"The most successful couples protect each other publicly and privately." Clem threw out another Molotov cocktail.

"Mick called you to come and get me." There, she'd said it aloud. Mick had decided she should go. "That proves he doesn't love me."

Bella carefully placed her whisky on the table. Lucy and Clem remained silent. "Mick rang me to tell me my child was hurt. I said I'd be there. Would you have called his family, his mother, if he'd been hurt?"

"I said I was going."

"Not an answer." Bella was gimlet-eyed.

"Yes, I'd have called his family," she snapped.

And I wouldn't have been abandoning him, just gathering more support.

"*Mick* invited me to stay as long as you needed me, as long as I wanted to stay. He wasn't planning to send you anywhere," Bella finished.

"He didn't tell me that." But it was typical of Mick's concern for others. "Then why hasn't he rung?"

"Whisht lassie, as Grandpa would say. When you knock a fella out, you've got to give him time to get back on his feet." Lucy popped a handful of crisps into her mouth.

"You run, Kel. You run physically, but that's camouflage for something deeper, for running before you get hurt, before anyone can hurt you. For most of your early life, you had to run." Clem sighed. "I had to run."

"I didn't run," Kelly protested.

Bella raised a disbelieving eyebrow. "Mick explicitly

asked you to stay."

He had. And she'd run because she was afraid he didn't want her, didn't love her. She'd sabotaged what they might have had.

"You're an idiot if you think he rejected you," Bella said gently.

"I abandoned him." The insight hit hard. She'd committed the crime she'd accused Mick of. "What am I going to do?"

"Finish sharing this pity party with us, because, hey, weeks since we saw you, Kel. Tomorrow's a new day. Whatever you decide, we'll help." Clem raised her glass, waiting until the other women raised theirs. "Here's to us."

"Tomorrow," Kelly whispered. Not knowing what she'd do, but knowing she'd do something. She'd never told him she loved him. How could she expect him to know? Bella had texted him on their way out of Tullamore. Kelly sent her own.

Arrived in Sydney.

If he answered, she'd know. He sent a thumbs-up emoji. She cried herself to sleep.

"Hell, I'm timetabled late tonight." On Friday, Kelly woke groggy, disoriented and almost regretting the alcohol consumed at her pity party. Except that was the purpose of pity parties. She grabbed her phone.

Mick, can you ring Maeve and see if she'll cover for me tonight? I'll swap her for—

What? Kelly wasn't in Tullamore, had left Mick with the short straw. He'd need to explain to Maeve and everyone else why Kelly had fled town and organise her replacement. She groaned. Another little kick to her conscience. She'd also abandoned Maeve and Ellen and Susie and Beth.

Instead, she rang her boss at the Education Department's Head Office.

"I'm back-to-back today. I can't see you until Monday

morning."

Impatience danced in her blood. Kelly was itching to run—this time in the opposite direction.

Boo nudged her, his nose cool against her skin, asking the question "Will you run with me?"

The familiar streets held nostalgic appeal, remnants of some long-ago period of her life, instead of nine short weeks ago. From the way Boo danced around her and kept looking over his shoulder, he was missing Mick too.

Mick, Boo missed you on our run this morning. She pressed *Delete.*

Showering and dressing signified a sense of purpose; a marginal improvement on fuzzy head and the echoing emptiness at the core of her. She'd wronged him, saying he couldn't separate the past from the present, when Kelly was the one letting a woman she hadn't seen since she was sixteen years old, and who'd barely tolerated her before then, influence her choices.

"Don't speak until I've had at least three cups of tea." Bella set an enormous teapot on the table and plopped onto the chair opposite.

"You could take up running." Kelly offered an old joke.

"And you could take the Trappist vow of silence."

"My boss can't see me until Monday." Kelly added sugar to her tea, and Bella's eyebrows disappeared into her fringe. "My blood sugar's down." Kelly excused her gesture.

"What are you going to do?"

"Keep adding sugar until I level out?"

"Not an answer."

"Stuffed if I know. I miss the library. Not just Mick, but the library. The kids coming and going, the pre-schoolers with their eyes fixed on Beth while she reads them a story. Tiny tots with their mouths hanging open, their eyes wide, barely moving because they don't want to miss a word. I've already composed two texts to Mick this morning."

"Sent them?"

"No."

"Why not?"

"Because yesterday I told him I was leaving." Kelly rolled her eyes, an adolescent response to a dumb question. "Sending him messages about Boo looking for him on our run or asking him to call one of the other librarians to cover for me doesn't seem like the way to conduct a separation." She set the teapot down with a bang.

Bella winced. "Last night you were going after him."

"What if he really doesn't want me? Especially after everything I said to him?"

"Only one way to find out. Could you make me a piece of dry toast, please?"

"That bad?"

"I still don't want to talk. It hurts my ears. And if you make one remark about age and alcohol, I'll ring Lucy and Clem and tell them unrequited love makes you nasty."

Kelly's phone rang, her stomach somersaulted, and she swallowed a quick breath before she registered Roslyn Morales's number. "Ros?"

"It's Ayesha. I'm in Ros's office, and she's lent me her phone. She told me what happened to you. I'm so sorry."

"It's not your fault." Kelly could sympathise with Ayesha's dilemma, but if the deputy principal had been more suspicious … Face it, if Ayesha had agreed to press charges when Mick first confronted her, Dom's attack on Kelly might have been prevented. Everyone expected Mick to do the dirty work.

That includes you, Kelly.

"I'm not responsible for Dom's actions. I am responsible for not inquiring closely enough into certain incidents at the school. Ros and I are discussing those now. I've also apologised to Mick." Ayesha paused. "I hope you'll feel better soon."

"Thanks for calling." Kelly pressed *End*.

"What?" Bella tipped the teapot high, draining it.

"We'll need more tea. And dry toast." Kelly busied herself at the kitchen bench and found herself composing another message for Mick.

Ayesha called, says she's sorry. She's my library guru, not my how-to-live-your-life-with-integrity guru.

"Don't keep me in suspense, or are you composing another message for Mick?"

"Why would I do that?" She placed the slice of dry wholemeal toast in front of Bella. "Ayesha said she's sorry. To me, to Mick, for not twigging to Dom's behaviour earlier." The kettle flipped off and Kelly added hot water to the teapot and brought it to the table. "She's an exceptional librarian, but it takes a special person to be a whistleblower."

I'm sorry, Mick, I love you. Boo loves you. I suspect Bella is already a bit in love with you.

CHAPTER EIGHTEEN

Mid-Saturday morning, the last Saturday of term one, and Mick wasn't expecting callers. He'd fielded endless questions in the last two days, often the same ones again and again.

"Did Dom have some sort of mental breakdown?"

If only it were that simple.

Had it only been Wednesday night Dom had attacked Kelly? Hell, the images of Dom looming over Kelly still brought Mick out in a cold sweat. Thursday morning, she'd left, and taken the best bits of him with her. If he could have, he'd have followed within hours, camped outside Arabella's house until Kelly agreed to talk to him. Arabella had sent a text saying they were safe, easing one fear. Kelly's text gave him nothing more.

Instead, he'd had to face the school. He'd called an urgent staff meeting, then a school assembly. An incident overnight, the principal was helping with inquiries. And they'd limped through until Friday afternoon. Another week of term. Ros was looking at solutions. Mick was concentrated on keeping the school together. Missing Kelly was a physical ache.

I love you, Kelly. That's not going to change.

Only the insistent ringing and knocking had him rolling out of bed and dragging on jeans.

"Keep your shirt on," he yelled from halfway up the hall. Whoever it was on the other side leaned on the bell. "What the …!" He dragged the door open. "Mel?"

"You recognise me!" She stood hands on hips, a bag beside her.

"I've been busy, sis." He dragged a hand through his hair.

"You've been brooding." She grabbed the bag, pushed past him and started down the hall. "Which one's my room?"

"Why are you here?" He followed her, halting when she swung back toward him with a raised eyebrow. She did raised eyebrow better than anyone he knew. "Not that I'm not pleased to see you." He massaged the back of his neck. "Thrilled really."

She grinned. "You're a jerk, but I love you anyway."

"You can have this room." He pushed open the door to the room Arabella had stayed in weeks earlier and was reminded of Kelly, of her sitting in his lap after Arabella left, her fingers curled around her shirt until she'd fallen asleep, of their first kiss at the river, her lips soft but searching, her admission that she'd cheated and been watching him strip before they made love.

Mel threw her bag in the direction of the bed, not waiting to see where it landed. "Kitchen next. I need food and drink."

"You need to tell me what you're doing here." He followed her into the kitchen. She had an inbuilt homing device for kitchens or fridges or something.

Mel spun on her heel and wrapped her arms around him. For a second, he was stiff in her arms, then he slumped against her and let himself be held.

"How did you know?" Mick stepped back and rolled his shoulders.

"Liam Quinn called me." She studied Mick with a

concerned expression. "Remember the lawyer who checked you out for Kelly? Gave you a clean bill of health."

The possible subtext of the words felled him harder than George Hogan's backhander. "Kelly's not coming back."

"I don't know." Mel brushed a kiss to his cheek. "I'll make the coffee."

Mick sat at the table, but he couldn't string enough ideas together to make sense. "When did her proxy brother call you?"

"Did you say poxy or proxy? Long story." She placed coffee in front of him, rifled through her backpack and produced a pastry. "Only slightly squashed. Doesn't affect the taste."

"I seem to have all the time in the world."

"I told you I know Liam Quinn. Met him back in my radical student days when we shared tree houses and lay in front of logging trucks. We lost touch, but I bumped into him in court about six months ago. Kept in touch. He's married. New baby. Picked up a whole new extended family. But you know that bit."

"And now he's the family mouthpiece?" Mick choked on a bite of pastry.

Mel rose to slap him on the back. "When Kelly landed in town, she told the sisterhood—Liam's word—that you're a fine man who hasn't forgiven himself for an illegal strip search in a seedy garage."

"Kelly told me."

"Did she tell you she thinks your sisters made you feel like an unforgivable arsehole?"

"Yeah."

"Well, fuck you! That's the last time I buy you pastries."

"I told her you and Em set me straight all those years ago. Told me how Kelly would be feeling. I did despise myself. And yeah, I have been seeking to atone for what I did to her. But I don't despise myself anymore. She helped me realise it."

"Then how in Dog's name did you get into such a

clusterfuck?"

"The perp—the bloody principal—Dom Ellis, had her trapped in a confined space. Naked. The bastard saw her naked." Mick could still see her, his proud, brave Kelly reduced to huddling on the floor, vulnerable, violated.

"How did you get here so fast?"

"She hit her emergency alarm." *Thank Christ.*

"Why were you her emergency contact one?"

He ran his hand over his head, gripping the back of his neck. "I asked her to."

"And she said, 'I'm happy to have my greatest enemy as my priority contact'? Odd behaviour for someone who doesn't trust or like you."

"She trusted me until I gave her reason not to."

"What reason?"

"I decided not to tell her about the previous librarian, Ayesha, being implicated in falsifying documents. Ultimately Ayesha was being blackmailed by Dom, but I wanted to wait until Ayesha's signed complaint was in the bag. I made the wrong call."

"Why?"

"Kelly's a huge fan of Ayesha's. I thought she'd be devastated by Ayesha's abuse of her position. Maybe blame me for uncovering that, when I hadn't found evidence of the larger crime against Dom." There, he'd said it.

"I learned Ayesha was a victim the day a young teacher told Kelly she was being blackmailed and we had to get her out of town. Ayesha hadn't agreed to make a formal complaint, so I kept it to myself. Dom Ellis has a lot in common with George Hogan. Misogyny is a big part of the problem here—Jesus, even when we called Dom on it, it was all the fault of various women."

"Just when we think we're making progress on equality, someone has to slap us back in line. I take my share of responsibility for telling you women have to be eternally vigilant."

"Kelly and I got muddled in the unravelling of the

present and past. So, she doubted me. No"—he exhaled loudly—"she said by not telling her, I didn't give her the weapons she needed to defend herself."

"That's what you're beating yourself up about. You failed to protect her. Again."

"It's not the same, Mel. It tore me apart to find Dom had trapped her naked in a bathroom, but I wasn't complicit." Despite his legal case against George Hogan, guilt lingered, ready to pop up and ambush him. "I've gone over and over it again in my head. I checked every door and window. I checked that Dom was not on the approved list of keyholders."

"And you convinced her to list you as emergency contact."

"She doesn't trust what we have."

"Has she rejected you?"

"She said we might be captive to circumstances." Which was logical on one level and crazy on another. If they'd met as strangers, with no Hay in their past, she'd have let him comfort her after Dom's attack. She'd still be with him.

"What do you think?"

"It's bullshit."

"Do you deserve to be loved?" Mel linked her free hand with his.

"You're terrifying, you know." Mick shook his head, although for a long while he'd questioned whether the kind of woman he wanted as a partner would have him. "Yeah. I deserve to be loved."

"How are you going to fix it?"

"Buggered if I know," he admitted.

"Two heads are better than one." She propped her elbows on the table and studied him over her coffee cup, eyes narrowed. "May need to call in the big guns."

"Mum?"

"Let's see what we can do. Are you going to eat that pastry?" Mel asked.

"You have it." Mick handed it over. "Dom made

separating the past and the present complicated, especially when he targeted Kelly."

"Explain." Mel licked the sugar from her fingers. "What! You know I need sugar for wargaming."

"Thanks for coming."

She smiled. "Big sisters are the best."

"Dom rubbed my face in petty corruption. I'm sick of it. I didn't want to do this undercover job in the first place. I said I was finished. I'm tired of the dark." Saying it, Mick knew it to be true. He wouldn't be doing any more troubleshooting for the department. "But the more I learned, the more Dom reminded me of all the women I've hurt in my life; the damage I did to Kelly, the life I stole from her, the disappointment in your eyes, in Em's and Mum's."

"You disappointed me for the ten minutes it took me to slag you off. Then I worked out how your actions prevented it from being worse, and you nailed him. At enormous cost to yourself. I'm proud of you Michael Barrymore Jamieson. I was when you resigned from the police force. I am today. I think there's more to it than that."

"What?"

"Mind, the account I got is second or third-hand, but consensus within the sisterhood and extended family suggests Kelly thinks you called her old lady to come and take her away because you were pushing Kelly out."

"I called Arabella just like I would have called Mum for you or me. I begged Kelly not to leave." When his sister looked smug, he added, "Feeling pleased with yourself for getting me to admit that."

"Love looks good on you."

"I'd be careful calling Arabella Steele an old lady to her face, if I was you." He hesitated before adding, "Kelly has her dream job in Sydney."

I may as well confess everything.

"A dream job in Sydney, a dream lover in Tullamore. Tough choice for a gal." She winked. "Make it easier."

"How long can you stay?"

"Just the night." She pushed to her feet, wrapped her arms around him from behind, and then kissed him on the top of his head. "Come home with me."

"I can't abandon them here. People are walking around like they're punch drunk. So many people were conned by Dom. They're struggling to make sense of it. Even the people who didn't have a high opinion of him to start with have been blind-sided."

"I expected that answer. You fix things, Michael Barrymore Jamieson. I'm so proud of you. But I've got one last question. Where do you want to be right now? You don't have to answer me, just yourself. Now, I'm going to have a shower and wash the dirt of the road off me." She headed down the hall.

"Wherever Kelly is. But I'm not sure I can fix this, sis. No matter how much I want to."

* * *

"It's Saturday for Pete's sake. Ring Lucy and Clem. Give your brain a rest, Kelly. Go to the movies." Bella had been hassling Kelly every half hour since lunch.

"All right, already. I'll go." Kelly rolled her eyes.

Three hours later, Bella greeted Kelly on her return. "How was the movie?"

"I have no idea," Kelly admitted.

"Name, actors, language spoken?"

"Nope. Nothing ringing a bell."

Last Saturday afternoon, she and Mick had made love. She'd arrived home from her shift at the library expecting to tackle her share of the household tasks. Instead, Mick had handled everything, cleaning, laundry, the week's shop. He'd even had a lasagne in the oven, champagne on ice, and flowers on the kitchen table. Housetrained didn't begin to cover all his skills.

I never met your mother, Mick, or your sisters. I want to thank them for training you so well.

On Sunday afternoon, she ordered high tea for herself and Bella and drove down to collect it; an old ritual when she'd started establishing new ones with Mick.

I miss you. It's an ache I can't seem to make stop.

Monday was an exercise in patience, but she finally scheduled meetings with the relevant people on Monday afternoon and Tuesday.

I want to come back, Mick. I'm working on it.

She also wanted mountains moved in a minute, when the education department insisted on doing things by the book, on relevant authorities being consulted, on a paper trail that identified who'd agreed to what and where.

She hadn't signed any official employment documents. Yet. She'd given herself forty-eight hours wriggle room before she needed to sign anything. Not that she doubted herself anymore, but Mick might have decided that the history they shared was too big a burden to overcome. She'd told him so, put words in his mouth—Stockholm Syndrome. She was an idiot.

An idiot in love. But she'd abandoned him, not just emotionally, but to a whirlwind of Dom's creation. Mentally, she reviewed what was in the fridge and freezer at Tullamore.

Mick, please eat the fridge, and don't work too hard. Another *Delete.*

Wednesday—nearly a week since she'd seen him. Kelly left Sydney at four in the morning, hoping to avoid the Easter Friday holiday traffic, although most of that would be the other way, country people coming for that last holiday on the coast before winter closed in. Bella was up, even though Kelly had said her goodbye last night and told her to stay in bed.

"Thank you." Kelly hugged Bella tightly. "For always being there."

"I didn't say it the other night, because Clem was on a roll, but I love you. You deserve to be loved. I can give you long lists of why, but you care, you're loyal, and, in my experience, you've never let hate dictate your life."

"What about my running away?"

"You ran to us because you were confused. You're running back because—"

"Because I love him. Because I want to see if we have a future together. Because I want to stop running from my feelings."

"My money's on you."

"If I'm in the house when he gets home, he can't throw me out."

"Nah!" Bella gave her a slight shake. "Four bedrooms. No need to throw you out, just bar the door to his room."

"Did I ever tell you about the time I broke into—"

"Pleased to hear you're thinking creatively."

"I'd best make a move." She hugged Bella again. "Thanks for letting me steal your car."

"It's not stealing if you ask, and I say yes." Bella stepped back.

Kelly had forever to reflect on the drive back. She'd been in a fog last Thursday. Had missed the changes in the landscape heralding the approach of autumn. This time, the huge skies signalled a welcome. For so many reasons, this was the right decision. She had to try.

* * *

Mick had been lost in thought, an endless hamster wheel.

The term ends tomorrow. I can be in Sydney by Friday night. And then what?

He had to give Kelly the space she needed.

If it killed him.

It might just kill him.

Halfway up the garden path, he stopped. The front door was open. He hadn't got as far as thinking another intruder, when Boo barrelled through the door, dancing around Mick's legs.

"Hi, Boo," he whispered, kneeling to bury his face in the dog's neck, absorbing the animal's unconditional welcome. His brain played catch-up, shifting from planning a long drive to Sydney to the realisation Kelly had come back. Why? "I'm pleased to see you too."

"You must be hot and tired. Can I get you a drink?"

Mick looked up. She stood in the doorway, leaning against the jamb. Jeans and a long-sleeved tee, a deep indigo, reminding him of how easy it was to get lost in her eyes, of the times he'd saturated himself in their soft glow when they'd made love. Part of the reason he'd never said he loved her—she used touch, and he'd followed her lead. She looked nervous. Beautiful, but nervous. He never wanted her to be nervous around him again.

"A beer would be welcome."

"I'll meet you in the kitchen." She turned away.

That simple? Mick followed her into the house, dumped his bag, jacket and tie in his bedroom, before joining her in the kitchen. His relationship with Kelly wasn't simple. It was intense, passionate, joyful, and he was prepared to fight to keep it. Did her arrival mean she might too? Or had she called to get the rest of her things?

She handed him a beer, then took a seat at the table, a white wine in front of her. "I've organised dinner."

"What's going on, Kelly?" He should have said "*Don't keep me in suspense.*"

She played with the stem of her glass. "I heard Ayesha's returning next term as principal."

"You've got good sources of information."

"Ros said they offered it to you, and you refused. Her second offer is the deputy position here until the end of the year." She glanced at him, having named her informant.

"Yes."

"What have you decided?"

Two could play at that game. "Why do you want to know?"

"Just making conversation." She took a quick sip of her

wine, swallowed and her mouth opened slightly. He imagined leaning close enough to brush his tongue over her bottom lip. She might bite, but the pleasure of tasting her again would be worth it. "I've got Thai fish cakes for dinner."

"Sounds good." Protecting her heart had been essential for Kelly Manners Steele's survival since she'd been a kid. Despite Mick's desperate need for some reassurance about why she was here, he was asking for too much too soon. So he backtracked to smaller issues. "I asked Steph what her fight with Dom was about at the party?" An insignificant incident in the scale of things.

"Did she guess the punch was spiked?" Kelly was back to twiddling with the stem of her glass.

"Yeah. She was worried. Steph guessed drinks were spiked from time to time to set up situations where women could be coerced into sex. Then essentially blackmailed or cajoled into more sex. A steady stripping of self-esteem. She didn't see it that way until recently, didn't twig to the spiked punch at parties, because she's not usually a punch drinker, said the women were willing. Stephanie was willing.

"But in the two years she'd been here it had never been so blatant, so confident—he—Dom—they—were untouchable. Even with a new unknown deputy on hand, and new young teachers who could have come from anywhere, who could have had family members who were lawyers and judges and doctors, who'd crucify him if they found out."

"Why did Steph tackle him now?"

"She was thrown off the merry-go-round. Her particular groomer is the Head of Maths. Steph was in love, so was prepared to blink if she saw something uncomfortable. Except she was more than uncomfortable when the senior girls' maths grades began to fall. That was her undoing. Her bloke said he was moving on, had lined up a full-time job for the start of the UK school year in September, but was leaving sooner to give him time to get settled in. He wouldn't be taking her with him."

"I hope that job in the UK disappears." Kelly at her fighting best, and he'd missed her instinctive understanding of right and wrong, missed her outrage.

"Ros has provided official advice to her UK equivalent." He rose to lean against the kitchen sink, setting his glass beside him.

"Why has Stephanie only told you this now?"

"I'm a man. I was being matey with Dom. Steph didn't trust me."

Getting Dom arrested had changed that. Learning he'd helped Laura get out of town safely when Steph hadn't twigged to the young woman needing help had made her rethink priorities, or so she'd said.

"And you, poor sod, didn't enjoy a single minute of those nights in the pub with Dom." She flashed a weak smile.

"I resented the fact I wasn't with you." Mick wasn't going to hold back, or pretend he didn't care. "And in the end, it's women who've provided the evidence against Dom, for blackmail, even for the misuse of public office."

"We're a fierce lot, us women."

"Thank the Lord." He waited a heartbeat. "Why did you turn your back on me that night?"

* * *

"That night I wanted nothing more than to crawl into your arms and stay there." Kelly stood and sauntered toward him, putting a bit of sway into her hips. Hoping he'd read her non-verbal invitation as part of her apology.

I want to touch you.

"Why didn't you?"

"Because I saw your face. You were so angry."

Understandably angry.

"Not with you."

"With yourself for failing to protect me." Kelly pressed

a hand to his chest, and the contact gave her courage. "For being present when I was physically humiliated."

"I hated what Dom did to you." His hand covered hers, and the warmth in his hand and his gaze gave her the courage to continue.

"I hated what Dom did to me. I hate more that I let him resurrect my last conversation with my mother and the garage in Hay." She paused. "I hated that for most of that night I was back in Abbadon."

He inched closer, his grip tightening.

"But I'm not sixteen anymore. I'm not alone."

"Why did you leave me?"

Not the library, the school or Tullamore—*me*, and Kelly let hope trickle through her.

"Because I don't want a bodyguard. I don't want a man who stays with me out of a sense of obligation, of guilt, of shame." Kelly tried to read his heart in his eyes. Then her shoulders slumped, and she admitted her fears. "We agreed at the beginning that we'd work out our past together. You called Bella."

"I didn't trust that my support was enough. I'd failed. I called the one person who's never let you down, who kept you safe."

"I thought you'd called Bella because you didn't want me around anymore. Bella asked me if I'd have called your mum if you were hurt."

"What did you say?"

"I wanted to say 'Damn you for being right.'"

"I love you." His words exploded the tight knot of doubt inside her, lighting every corner of her. "A man who loves you, anyone who loves you, is allowed to be angry and guilty that they couldn't keep you from harm."

"Bella and Lucy and Clem agree."

"Because they feel the same way?"

"Yes."

"You trust their love."

"I finally worked out, I trust us."

He exhaled loudly.

"Why did you let me run?" she asked.

"My dad abandoned our family, but it felt personal to me. The cops didn't just cut me loose, they tried to destroy me. I asked you to stay. I was hurting too. Why did you run?"

"I push people away before they can abandon me. I'm sorry I did that to you."

"I thought we had more time. Because you had no control over your early life, it had to be your choice to stay. Everything snowballed. I didn't want to rush you."

"Rush me."

"Neither one of us told the other how we felt."

"You did, Mick." She pressed a finger to his lips. "I fixated on the fact you hadn't said the words before that night. I was wrong. In Sydney, I remembered something my social worker said years ago. 'If someone loves you, they'll never ask you to put yourself in danger.' The opposite is also true. You did everything in your power to keep me safe.

"You knocked on the library door. You insisted I keep Boo with me. You never came up on me without warning. You were there to banish the demons when I woke in fright, you publicly defended me, you gave me your time, your brain power and your emotional support to get the library up and going. You tried to save me from disillusion."

"I'm no saint."

"You're a good man who doesn't big-note himself, just does the right thing." She pressed her fingers to his lips to silence him. "You took Laura to a place of safety, you asked Ros to remove Dom the second the police took the charges seriously. On that night you locked the doors, you set up the emergency signal on my phone, you ran faster than I knew you could run to reach me."

"I love you, Kelly."

"I believe you do." Kelly linked her arms around his neck, her fingers tugging at the hair at his nape. She reached up and laid her mouth on his. Coming home, and she savoured the sensation, before running her tongue along his bottom lip, teasing his mouth open. Sumptuous, the word chased itself along nerve endings bringing her alive. "I love you too."

"I want to swallow you whole."

"Be my guest," she whispered against his lips.

"Ask me again?" He sat on the chair with her in his lap. "Ask me again what my plans are?"

"What are your plans?"

"I don't want to troubleshoot anymore, and it's unfair for the department to keep asking me to bear witness again and again to abuse in public office."

"It's more than unfair, it's corrosive." She kissed his honourable jaw. "Especially when you're an outstanding school leader lots of communities would kill to have."

"I shouldn't have to wallow in the mud when I can create dreams." He grinned. "I've sounded out Ros about a transfer to a Sydney school."

"Sydney schools have longer lists for promotion."

"But Sydney has you."

"You'd give up your dream for me?"

"Not give up. Delay. And it's only one of my dreams. I love you, Kelly. Having you in my life is more important than any promotion."

If she hadn't been sure already that he loved her, that offer would have clinched the deal.

"I don't deserve you." She gripped him tighter. "Except I do. Dom Ellis got away with outrageous behaviour for years. Like George Hogan. Recognising that forced me to go back, to see it from your side. How hard it is to stop such abuse. Steph, Ayesha, young women, even the supposedly good male teachers were too scared or too lazy or too intimidated to call him out. You called out George Hogan." She shook him. "You did what I vowed to do all those years ago. Not because of our shared history. In spite of it. I spoke to my boss while I was in Sydney."

"Mmm." He nuzzled her throat.

"I sounded him out on the idea of me completing this year in Tullamore."

"What?"

His stunned reaction was another gift on this wonderful day. It hadn't crossed his mind to ask Kelly to adjust her life for him. He put her interests above his own.

"You look shell-shocked. I'm sorry for that. Head office had to find a replacement for the term I was here. They're prepared to give me leave for the rest of the year to get the library set up on a solid footing while Ayesha grapples with the fallout of Dom's betrayal of the school community."

"I can't ask you to do that." But his grip had tightened.

"You're not asking. I'm offering. I bet Ayesha has begged you to stay while they review the executive positions here, try and restore community confidence."

"Did she tell you that?"

"She rang me to apologise. Said she'd seen things that should have made her think, but she didn't, but she wouldn't make the same mistake again. She'd spoken to her partner Daniel by then. To her boys. They wanted her to fight. She thinks she owes you her job."

"She doesn't." He dismissed the suggestion.

"You're tempted to stay here?"

You'd love to stay here.

"On a number of levels. But not without you."

"You had the courage to call out George Hogan, to stand up to Dom Ellis. Ayesha would be lucky to have you.

"To have us both. I want a life with you." Boo nuzzled Mick from behind. "And Boo. He likes me."

"Boo loves you." Kelly slid off his lap and took his hand. "And you understand me so well. Pity it took me longer to work it out. I had to be in charge."

"I wasn't sure, but my gut told me hammering at your door or texting you multiple times a day wouldn't work—not that I didn't nearly press *Call* a hundred times a day. Too many people have taken your choices from you. I want you to choose me."

"I have."

"But more importantly I want you to be sure."

"I love you. Take me to bed."

"I thought you'd never ask again." He scooped her into his arms and headed for his bedroom.

"Wait," she said when they reached the door. "Before we start this Easter holiday, let's agree. We stay here for the rest of this year. Then see what suits both of us?"

Hours later, Kelly pressed *Send*:

Staying in Tullamore. Boo's given his blessing. Mick says please visit.

AUTHOR'S NOTE

I'm often driven to write a story because of a triggering incident. In this case, it was the multiple stories of illegal police strip searches of young women at music festivals. There needs to be more outrage. But I write romance, so I decided to play with the idea of two young people caught in a situation where neither really had control. Both carried the trauma. And then they meet again. How have they changed? How did that shared experience change their lives? Can they make peace, maybe more than peace? I hope you enjoy Kelly and Mick's story.

I'd like to thank Yezanira Veneccia for her editing skills and Emily of Emily's World By Design for her creative covers. This book would never have seen the light of day without the ongoing support of Melissa Keir, Inkspell Publishing. Thank you, Melissa.

Don't Miss a Sneak Peek at the Next Book in the Choosing Family Series

An Accidental Flatmate

Chapter One

The lock clicked. Instant relief. Casildo pushed open Anna Turner's temporarily vacant apartment door. Vacant being the only word that mattered. He stepped into the fully-furnished, light-filled, central-Sydney, with carpark, apartment belonging to his best friend Hunter's newly wedded wife.

"Thank you, jaddatee." Cas believed blessings came from his dead grandma, so it seemed only fair to invoke her name.

Anna and Hunter had flown off to their honeymoon destination this morning. Cas hadn't planned to accept Hunter's offer to stay in Anna's apartment. In fact, he'd said, no thanks. But circumstances and a plea from his older sister had made finding immediate accommodation urgent. He chuckled. Lucky Hunt had given him a key. Tonight he'd brought a hold-all with a few essentials. Tomorrow he'd collect the rest of his gear.

The apartment had been largely empty since Hunter and Anna became inseparable, so the rich perfume of melted chocolate teasing his nostrils was unexpected. Amazing how scents could linger, or how the olfactory system could play tricks on you. Anna's go-to drink in an emergency was hot chocolate. Cas ambled down the corridor, the scent growing stronger with each step.

At the loungeroom door, he stopped. Beatriz Gomez— but not Beatriz Gomez as he'd ever seen her before. The scrupulously neat and professional advertising account manager always looked stylish; alluring, rather than conventionally beautiful, but tonight she'd curled up in the corner of a sofa in a multi-coloured, free-flowing, kaftan-type outfit. Her closed eyes and dreamy expression told him her earbuds blocked extraneous noise. Cas's arrival fell in the category of extraneous noise.

Her hands were wrapped around a cup. Hot chocolate. Good to know his sense of smell was still reliable. This version of Beatriz begged to be touched, cuddled really, but they'd never been on those sorts of terms. Cas had never thought of her in those terms. Until today.

Okay, I've had the occasional fantasy.

What guy with a pulse wouldn't? Part of it was her aura of "not available" which had become a silent roar in the last few years. Happy couples, like Hunter and Anna, signalled "not available", but with Beatriz he'd never heard a whisper of a boyfriend, girlfriend, lover. And they worked in a field where gossip spread faster than a new virus.

Not available works for me.

"Beatriz," he called.

No reaction. Not by a flicker of an eyelid did she register his presence. He grinned, although her presence was a problem. She was one of Anna's closest friends. Had she stopped by to check the place was secure, stayed for a hot drink? She looked remarkably settled for a casual drop in.

He moved directly in front of her and raised his voice. "Beatriz."

Her eyes shot open, the hand holding her drink jerked, upending the contents, she cried out and shot to her feet simultaneously. Her toenails were rainbow coloured, as in one yellow, one green, one purple and so on. He'd never be able to look at her regulation short boots the same way again.

"What the—" She tugged the earbuds from her ears.

"Sorry." He held his hands up in surrender.

"Is something wrong? Has something happened to Anna and Hunter?" Her expression leapfrogged shock and hurtled towards concern.

"As far as I know they're flying off into the wide blue yonder, not a care in the world."

She was holding her stained, no longer floaty garment away from her torso, her forehead crinkling into a frown. "Then why did you break in?"

"I didn't break in." He held up his key. "Hunt offered the place to me."

She shook her head vigorously backwards and forwards. "Anna gave me first dibs."

Coming Soon…

Be Sure To Catch The Books In The Choosing Family Series….

MASQUERADE

Fool me once…

Money won't bring LIAM QUINN'S father back, but it'll save his mother's home. A high-paying law partnership is in his sights. To win it, he needs to successfully land a project. Problem is the project requires absolute confidentiality, and he's just discovered his estranged identical twin is appearing life size on a billboard across the city. The second catch is a return to environmental law. His earlier career imploded after his lover was revealed as a mining company spy.

Researcher and soon-to-be-published romance author KATE TURNER needs a disguise. Maybe more than one. Her famous playwright father despises 'trashy' novels. Her ex-boyfriend mocked her 'dirty little secret', then stalked her when she left him. Her identical twin coaxes her into appearing on a billboard to prove she can be notorious and anonymous at the same time. No one connects the billboard model to the dowdy researcher Kate has become, and no one knows about her author pseudonym and second disguise as Ms. Sexy Romance.

Kate and Liam's lives collide when she's hired as Liam's research assistant. Liam's boss laughs off the billboard. Having doubles is the perfect cover for confidential field work.

A masquerade, a road trip, a steamy attraction, the sudden appearance of Liam's old lover, and Ms. Sexy Romance's unexpected arrival in the wrong place at the wrong time, and Liam and Kate discover the steps they took to protect their hearts might break them.

--"A Jennifer Raines romance will make you sigh in the best possible way!"-- Best Selling Author, Grace Burrowes

EXCERPT

Liam gestured to her report, open in front of him. "Simple summaries of assorted environmental disputes across Australia. That's not a lot to work with."

"Have you read my report, Mr. Quinn?" Kate emphasised his surname, annoyance at the snub for her research trumping her anxiety at exposure. She'd back her research skills against anyone in this room.

"I've scanned it." His shoulder lifted in an offhand shrug.

Arrogant moron. Another man living in an echo chamber, so sure his worldview was right not even a drone buzzing overhead would alert him to imminent attack. Was he hostile because his identical twin Niall had kept the billboard campaign secret from him? Or generally hostile to new ideas? "Then you're being deliberately offensive."

"Not yet," he answered, leaning forward—a panther preparing to spring.

Dismayed to be so attuned to his slightest movement, she stiffened her spine.

Liam had her second-guessing her defence strategy.

Until Liam, Kate had trusted that Ms. Dowdy Researcher couldn't be linked to the billboard—the final stress test to confirm no one, especially not her besuited, controlling ex-boyfriend, would recognise Ms. Dowdy as Anna Turner's twin.

Quinn, by design

She's antiques royalty, he's relentlessly modern

Master carpenter NIALL QUINN's passion is creating bespoke furniture. Everything else comes second until his ex-fiancé ditches him when he gifts another creation to a friend, and he discovers his brother has been carrying his dead father debts. Niall's self-respect demands he pay his share. He's landed a prestigious exhibition of his work with a top gallery, possible in part because of the support of an antiques dealer who's been mentor, patron, and generous landlord. Niall's hoping the exhibition will establish his reputation and boost his bank balance.

LUCY McTAVISH's grandfather, antiques supremo Cameron (Cam) McTavish raised her. His death leaves her totally alone. Lucy drained their personal accounts to provide twenty-four-seven in-home palliative care for Cam. The thought of poverty paralyses her, a crippling reminder of life before Cam found her. Laden with debt, she plans to sell Cam's workshop to ensure his antiques emporium survives.

When the will is read, Niall Quinn holds the keys to Cam's workshop. Lucy's convinced he conned her grandpa in his last days and demands he restore antiques for her. Niall is blindsided by the bequest, but worries about yet another debt and agrees to the work.

Lucy and Niall circle each other. In sharing stories and drawing closer, Lucy figures out debt is her childhood bogeyman resurrected by Cam's death. Niall has real debts and, unaware of his exhibition, she looks for clients who'll pay him for the work she'd been demanding for free.

With the exhibition drawing closer, it's crunch time. Will Niall choose his exhibition or Lucy? Does Lucy want a man who won't share his dreams with her?

Award winning author Jennifer Raines' stories combine a love of romance with contemporary conflicts. Her writing is both relevant and heart-warming. Each story is a journey across the world. Jennifer likes to think her readers get occasional hints of the deep passion of a Nora Roberts or the unshakeable loyalty of a Grace Burrowes where love conquers loneliness, distrust and fear.

EXCERPT:

"I didn't ask for that." She made a face at the oversized sandwich he'd set in front of her.

"It's lunchtime." Niall took the chair opposite her.

Her guilty glance at her smartwatch told him she'd lost track of time, while her unfashionably baggy clothes told him eating was a faint memory. Loss of appetite was another by-product of heartache.

He'd been there too. "I hate to eat alone."

"I thought you lived alone." She cut one half of her sandwich in half and added pickles. Eating his food was another nod to politeness. Referring to his living arrangements was her opening salvo in hostilities.

"What else did your granda tell you?" Niall waited for her to swallow her first mouthful, then took a bite of his own, setting himself the task of keeping her in his kitchen long enough to finish her sandwich. Food was his currency for sympathy, although Lucy McTavish's unannounced arrival declared she wasn't here for comfort.

"Months ago, Grandpa talked about meeting a furniture restorer at an antiques auction."

"I've done the odd bit of restoration." Niall was pretty positive Cam had offered those pieces as a sop to Niall's dignity. While the profit from their sale had covered the rent, over time, Niall worked out Cam had become his patron rather than his landlord.

And wasn't that a feckin' indictment. At thirty-four, he needed an old man's patronage because his passion for making bespoke furniture had yet to deliver a decent living.

"Three pieces." She placed her left hand on his table as if drawing strength from the age and beauty of the timber. "Three pieces of furniture were delivered to McTavish's Antiques five months ago."

"Cam said they earned a good profit." Niall wrapped both hands around his Blue Italian Spode cup, watching as she raised the Flora Danica, Royal Copenhagen to her mouth; a distraction while she framed her answer. Like most of his cups, the matching saucers were lost in the mists of time.

"They did." Her chin jut signalled a full stop on McTavish profits.

"Cam said he told you about our arrangement." Niall's doubts were growing. Furniture restorer was a half-arsed description of him.

"He told me he offered you accommodation in return for restoring furniture. Three pieces of furniture over eight months gives you a higher hourly rate than a top-class hooker." The insult rolled off her tongue, the barb sinking deeper than she could have known. Unaware, she popped the last morsel of the second quarter of sandwich into her luscious, bow-shaped mouth.

BETRAYAL

They are wary of trusting, but ... passion has its own rules.

Marketing manager, ANNA TURNER promised reliable, affordable childcare to co-workers under pressure. Proud of negotiating the perfect lease for her employer, a hostile takeover of the building steals her ideal premises.

Architect and property-developer, HUNTER THOMPSON, smells betrayal on his father's breath. An old pattern, but this time his old man plans a hostile takeover of a building owned by the family who raised Hunter as a second son. Hunter out-manoeuvres his father, buying the building himself.

Attending an industry cocktail party, Anna hears Hunter say her magic word, "architect". Revealing her ideal childcare centre plan to him, Anna discovers Hunter tore up her precious lease. Anna is breathtaking in her rage. Intrigued, Hunter offers a new lease, with the opportunity to work together.

Hunter can't risk long term. Anna doesn't do hook-ups—ever. Hidden within their whirlwind romance and growing trust, secrets resurface with devastating consequences. Anna's mantra—*'I share myself, you share yourself, if you want to get into my bed'*—may not survive.

Wary strangers find passion on a shared project, until secrets from their past ambush them. Fans of Grace Burrowes stories where love conquers loneliness and fear, will fall for Jennifer Raines's heartwarming romances.

EXCERPT

"Who bought the building?" Bea prepared for her meetings with meticulous care.

"H. S. Thompson was all the managing agent would give me. Who names their child after a famous dead journalist, for Pete's sake?"

Bea held up a hand. "So, why didn't you send an apology for this shindig?"

"Antonio wanted a presence and reminded me it was my turn to come. 'Cocktail parties loosen tongues and increase personal contacts,'" Anna repeated Antonio's encouragement.

"Networking—naughty and nice?" Bea grinned. "Bet you didn't tell him you were gonna wear your *Killing Eve* dress. He's an understanding boss, but Antonio was present when you took that last dude down, and it probably wasn't what he had in mind tonight."

"I'm wearing it tonight to exorcise my rage, so I can renegotiate from a place of calm." Anna waved her hand from her head to her belly in a gesture of serenity. "But, you're right, I should go."

"On the basis that researching the buyer trumps gladhanding strangers?"

"On the basis I might bite someone's head off when I'm meant to charm. Like the guy looking this way." Anna had been aware of the guy for a while. Now, she put her hand on her friend's arm and adjusted their positions. "Make it casual, Bea. Over my shoulder, about two o'clock. The guy with the lean and hungry look." Anna's pulse raced, a lick of interest curling through her body.

"He's just looking at this stage." Bea's husky contralto oozed intrigue.

"Who is he?"

"I don't recognise him, but he wouldn't have got past security without an invite." Bea took a sip of her drink. "Mid-thirties, tall, dark, broody rather than handsome, and on his own. He's perfected the stiff-backed, imperious, don't-mess-with-me look. Out of place in a crowd like this. Do you want me to find out?"

"Yes." Anna sipped her icy mineral water and waited a heartbeat. "No."

"Well, that's clear." Bea flashed her dimples.

Available now in Ebook and Print- At all Major Book Retailers

ABOUT THE AUTHOR

Australian Jennifer Raines writes contemporary romances set mainly, but not exclusively, in Australia— think Malta, Finland, New Zealand or ? A dreamer and an optimist, her stories are a delicious cocktail of passion, mutual respect and loyalty because she still believes in happily-ever-afters.

Jennifer fell in love with romance as a teenager. Starting with historical romance. Everything in the school library and then a personal treasured collection of Georgette Heyer, hard copies, paperbacks and Ebooks. Comfort food, she calls them, like Vegemite toast, for those times when she feels low. Her library of comfort food has grown over the years but Georgette Heyer was an early star, under the blankets after lights out using a torch.

Jennifer is a member of Romance Writers of Australia. Three times a finalist in the Emerald competition, including in 2017 (*Common Cause*, renamed *Lela's Choice*), 2018 (*Taylor's*

Law) and 2022 (*Quinn, by design* – Choosing Family Book 2). She's a member of Romance Writers of New Zealand, winning the Pacific Hearts competition twice, including in 2019 with *Grace Under Fire*, the sequel to *Taylor's Law*. She's also a member of Romance Writers of America and has been a finalist in chapter competitions in 2019, 2020 and 2021 (*Taylor's Law*). Jennifer won the contemporary romance section in the 2020 Orange Rose Contest for *Planting Hope* and was second overall. Jennifer values competitions for the constructive, honest, not always comfortable feedback they provide.

In 2023 *Taylor's Law* placed second in the Romance Writers of New Zealand Koru Best First Book

Jennifer loves those days when words flow and the joy of writing makes the hard slog worthwhile. She's always made up stories about strangers in the street, in a café or strolling through an airport terminal; finding inspiration in snippets of conversations, news items and the sheer puzzle of human interactions.

Jennifer lives in inner-city Sydney, Australia, with the requisite number of partners (1) and animals (2). Her desk overlooks a park which nourishes her soul when she raises her head from her keyboard. She gets some of her best ideas during long yin yoga poses or walking—anywhere. While Jennifer adores historical romance, she chose to write contemporary because she thought (wrongly) it needed less research while she was holding down a full-time job.

You can find out more about Jennifer and her writing at https://jenniferrainesauthor.com or via https://www.facebook.com/jenniferrainesauthor

Or https://www.instagram.com/romanceauthorjen/

Her book(s) are available through major providers.